Pat + Trisha, Thank you for all your support! ♡ Riley



# waiting *at* hayden's

# waiting at hayden's

*Waiting at Hayden's* is the first book to be published in the new reading experience format, shopfiction™. Throughout this book you will find web addresses at the end of several chapters. Type these links into any browser to watch key scenes unfold and to shop the characters' clothes.

For more love stories by Riley Costello visit
sincerelyriley.com

# waiting *at* hayden's

*a novel*

riley costello

S+S

Sullivan & Shea
Publishing

*Waiting at Hayden's* is a work of fiction. Names, characters, places, and incidents are the products of the author's imagination or are used fictitiously. Any resemblance to actual events, locales, or persons, living or dead, is entirely coincidental.


Published in the United States by Sullivan & Shea Publishing

Costello, Riley, author.
Waiting at Hayden's: a novel / Riley Costello
Oregon: Sullivan & Shea Publishing
ISBN 978-1-7323033-0-0

**sincerelyriley.com**

Cover Design by Danielle Christopher
Typesetting by FormattingExperts.com
Author Photo by Ryan Selewicz
Videography by Define Motion
Character Photography by Olivia Ashton

This book is the first to be published
in the new reading experience format: shopfiction™.

First Edition: June 2018

*To Mom and Dad, for always believing*

# waiting *at* hayden's

# PROLOGUE

**"You'll** be there, right?" Jack asked, one last time.

Charli stood in the street outside her house with her fingers curled over the rolled-down window of his truck. She wished she were leaving first.

"Of course I'll be there," she said. "And you?"

Jack lifted her hands to his lips, kissing them both.

"No matter what."

"But if one of us isn't there," she said. "If you decide not to show . . ."

Jack's eyes pricked with tears, and he turned away from her. The road ahead was dimly lit. Just streetlights and a sliver of moon. Soon the sun would rise, alarms would go off, and people would climb out of bed, brew coffee, drive to work. It would be a regular summer day for most.

"This isn't over," he said. "I'll see you in five years at Hayden's."

Charli's bottom lip quivered. "Are we making a mistake here?"

*Maybe*, Jack thought. But what good would it do to say that?

"This is the right thing," he assured her. "This is the plan we thought was best."

Tears dribbled off Charli's chin. "Five years isn't really that long . . ." Just yesterday they were a pair of seven-year-olds, playing in a sandbox. In a blink, teenagers, cramming for tests in Jack's room. Now, twenty-two, crazy in love.

Jack kissed her forehead, then jiggled his keys to start the engine, knowing that if he didn't leave now, he never would.

“The fireside table,” Charli said with a sniffle. “I’ll see you there.”

He leaned in toward her. “If you get there first, order me six slices of the Chocolate Mint Cloud Cake.”

She laughed through her tears, knowing it would be the last time she found something funny for a while.

Jack breathed in all the moment had to offer: the crisp pre-dawn air, the smell of lavender on Charli’s skin, the banana nut muffins that Charli had baked for his long drive ahead on the seat beside him. A sob escaped from the back of his throat.

“I love you,” Charli said, wiping her eyes.

“I love you too,” Jack said and pulled away from the curb.

# one
# NOW

**Gianna** checked her phone for the hundredth time as she walked past the burly bouncer. Still, no text from Valerie.

She'd been sure her childhood best friend would text her. She'd expected something like:

*I was kidding! Obviously, I was kidding. Why on earth would I want to celebrate turning forty at a dive bar? Let's meet at Hayden's! I hope you aren't sold out of the Raspberry Gateau!*

Gianna wasn't, of course. She'd had her pastry chef, Jill, make an extra of Val's favorite cake that morning just in case she changed her mind about her party venue. She had also asked her hostess, Rosie, to reserve the back table close to the fireplace for an hour or so.

"I'm sure we'll end up here," she'd told them both, as she had hurried out the back door fifteen minutes ago to catch an Uber to the dive bar Valerie had chosen instead.

She swept the room.

It was crowded—unusually crowded for nine o'clock on a Thursday. Didn't people have jobs they had to be at bright and early tomorrow morning? Maybe not. Remote Fridays. That's what her young, hip servers said was the trend these days. Lots of their friends apparently worked remotely all the time—Instagramming, tweeting, doing other social media for companies.

It was why Gianna always saw them popping in and out of Second Story Tea Room, the tea shop wedged inside an old Victorian across the street from her restaurant. They'd work some, then smoke pot on the street corner with their remote-working friends some, then back to tweeting.

Listen to her! She sounded like an old person. She was only thirty-seven, still relatively young. She liked to smoke pot too, on occasion. She was just an "old soul." Her first-grade teacher had written this about her in her first-ever report card after Gianna spent all of one recess inside asking the teacher if she'd ever stood in front of a mirror and asked herself the questions, "Am I really here? What if none of life exists, and it's all just in our heads?"

Maybe the weather was actually responsible for the crowd that evening. For the first time in months, the sun had come out in Portland. All of her staff and her customers had been in such a good mood earlier—even Lemon Meringue Larry, the eighty-five-year-old widower who came in every afternoon for a coconut chocolate chip cookie and coffee with a mood as sour as the mouth-puckering treat. Gianna liked to match all her customers up with a dessert on her restaurant's menu. It helped her remember them.

"Oh, it's a glorious day, isn't it?" Larry had said, and Gianna had been so shocked she'd spilled his cup of coffee all over his crisp, white shirt. He hadn't cared though. The sun was shining!

She imagined all the single women who were hovering around the bar now had been sitting at home earlier that evening with their windows open when a warm breeze smelling of cherry blossoms and promise had blown in and rippled through their hair. For the first time all year they'd thought, *Wouldn't it be lovely to have a summer fling? Maybe I should go to a bar. Maybe tonight will be the night I'll meet someone who gets me and who I get, too.*

Gianna remembered indulging in those fantasies before she met Peter Clark. Those fantasies were the only reason she had ever subjected herself to this late-night, loud-music scene. Valerie, as well. They had always much preferred girls' nights in—homemade cocktails, comfy clothes, feet kicked up on the butter-yellow ottoman in the apartment they'd shared for years until Valerie and Richard got married three summers ago.

The weather wouldn't last though, just like most of the connections that were made tonight. The paper was calling for a storm tomorrow evening. Gianna had been trying all day not to read too much into the forecast.

She'd always imagined it being stormy on March 24, 2017. Every single time she'd thought of that day for the past five years, she'd pictured it being stormy—at least when she allowed herself to imagine both Charli and Jack showing up. It was because storms were romantic. It seemed much more likely they would both make The Reservation if there were rain pounding down on Hayden's roof and thunder echoing down Northwest 23rd Street. It was silly. She knew it was silly. She'd seen too many romantic comedies.

There, by the band. She spotted Val. She was sipping champagne with six other women. Champagne! A happy drink. As if this were a happy place where Valerie had happy memories. The very last time they were here, Gianna had found Valerie in the bathroom, complaining to a complete stranger as she washed her hands about how some guy had grabbed her ass while she was waiting in line for a drink and how she wished she could meet someone while sitting at home in her pajamas. Ironically, she ended up doing just that, after Gianna discovered Match.com, and they both began online dating.

How could Valerie have forgotten? Forty was a little young to have amnesia, wasn't it?

Too young to have amnesia. Too old to have a baby.

For a brief moment she heard her therapist, Linda: "Now, Gianna, let's try to avoid that type of black-and-white thinking. Every woman's life is unique. And age is just a number."

But women didn't typically get amnesia before forty. Linda would have to give her that. Or have babies after forty, as she'd pointed out in their last session. Linda had gotten sort of quiet when she said that, because it was the truth, and she couldn't argue with the truth. She preached that all the time: "No black-and-white thinking! No arguing with the truth!" Gianna sometimes walked around her house parroting these Linda-isms. It didn't really help. Maybe because she didn't really have a problem.

She caught the eye of a woman at the bar who could have been her identical twin—average height with striking dark features and trendy, stylish clothes—Gianna loved trendy, stylish clothes. She was currently wearing a new dress by one of her favorite brands, Winston White, and had paired it with flats and a bamboo clutch. The woman at the bar was speaking with a man twice her age, who Gianna imagined was feeding her lines as greasy as the gel he'd used to slick back his hair that evening.

The man whispered something in her ear, and she laughed, even though it probably wasn't funny. Gianna had been there, so many times. The lines were rarely funny. Now he was likely asking her if she wanted to share a cab back to his place.

*Don't go home with him!* Gianna wished she could somehow subliminally send the woman this message. She'd had a one-night-stand once and decided right after it was not for her. It hadn't left her brokenhearted or anything—she'd hardly known the charming doctor from New York with devilish good looks who had been in town visiting for a conference, though she did remember having such a lovely conversation with him on the balcony of the rooftop bar where they'd met. So lovely, in fact, that for a moment she'd thought, *soul mates?* Again, silly. But afterward, she had felt empty and was sort of befuddled that random hookups appealed to so many. "What is the draw," she'd asked a friend who had them all the time, "about waking up to an empty bed and a torn-open condom wrapper on your pillow?"

"Look around, Linda!" she would have said, if she were here, thinking maybe this was where they needed to have their next session. "The reason I'm anxious about not getting married is not because of some deep-rooted problem with me; it's because of the way it is today."

Linda had met her husband in the eighties at church, so she didn't get it. She said she got it, but there was no way she really got it. Gianna sometimes wished she were religious. How easy it would be to meet a nice, sweet guy at church. Or better yet, she wished she'd been dating back in the eighties when men knew what the word "chivalrous" meant. Or at least how to spell it. So many men these days couldn't spell! She once got a text message from a man she'd met online that read, *What kind of restraint do you own?* In the age of spell-check. Was he so busy texting other women he couldn't take the time to proofread his messages to her? Did he not care enough to at least try and put his best foot forward before they met? His profile said he'd gone to UCLA, so she couldn't blame his intelligence.

Then again, somehow Val and all of her friends here tonight had found men to marry. So maybe there was something wrong with her. She watched them now from the bar where she was waiting to order a cocktail. She wanted something stronger than champagne. Much stronger. They were flirting with the men surrounding their table.

Was that what this night was about?

Gianna recalled something Val had said to her just last week. "Richard's been a bit of a bore, lately." Was Val feeling like she needed to spice up her life? The comment had saddened Gianna, as she always hoped for the best for her friends' marriages—and any marriage for that matter. She was a hopeless romantic to her core. And possibly to a fault, according to Linda. But she couldn't say it surprised her. Richard had always bored her. Gianna made sure she had a coffee before going out with the two of them. "Two shots of espresso, please!" she was sure to tell Jojo, her barista at Hayden's.

She would have never married Richard. Or any of the men her best friends had settled down with, for that matter. Except for maybe

Eric, who was married to her pastry chef, Jill. Gianna found him hilarious, though Jill was always telling him he was taking it "too far." His jokes were a bit raunchy at times, but Gianna still found them amusing. Though, if she lived with him, she could see how they might get old . . .

She could hear her mother now telling her, "You're too picky!" Gianna tried to remember how her mom spent her afternoons before she used them to call Gianna up and yell at her for being "too picky." She meant well. Gianna knew she meant well. But Gianna was an only child, and Erika Hayden was desperate for grandbabies.

For years, Gianna had argued with her mom. She just hadn't met a stand-up guy. Once she met a stand-up guy, she'd marry him. But Peter was a stand-up guy. And there she sat on Linda's blue overstuffed couch every week saying, "I'm not sure if he's The One."

"Let me guess, an apple martini?" She was being checked out by a gentleman in flannel with a five o'clock shadow who might have been a nice guy. Gianna didn't think all men at bars were bad guys. She wasn't a total pessimist.

She used to drink apple martinis—sucked them down, actually, to quiet that little voice in her head that was always screaming: "I hate this scene! I hate this scene!" But she couldn't even handle apple-flavored candies anymore. She wondered if she might have a bit of apple martini PTSD. She would have to ask Linda if that was a thing.

Her phone vibrated in her purse.

"I'm sorry," she said, fumbling for it in front of the man who seemed to be hitting on her. "My boyfriend."

She stepped aside, happy to take the call. She loved when she was happy to take Peter's calls. It wasn't always the case, which was a bit of a problem.

"Please say you're in a car outside, ready to whisk me out of here," she said, covering her ear with her hand to stifle the noise.

"Actually, I'm currently cheating on you," he said. "I watched the next episode of *Lost* without you. I'm sorry! I just had to find out if Desmond kept pushing the button!"

Gianna laughed. A real laugh. Peter was genuinely funny.

She loved that the only form of cheating she'd ever have to worry about with him was that he might watch an episode of a TV series they'd been binge-watching together without her.

"Do you want to come over after?" he continued. "I know it's a Thursday, but . . ."

Gianna had implemented this rule—that they didn't spend the night together on Tuesdays or Thursdays—in the early stages of their relationship. Initially, it had been an attempt to try and maintain her independence in case things went south, but she still insisted they follow it, even now, six months into the relationship, because . . . well . . . she simply didn't have the desire to see him every day.

"Because you're independent." Linda had offered, as a possible explanation.

*Yes*, Gianna thought, as she accepted his invitation. *Maybe that was all it was.*

—

Two cocktails and two hours later, and Gianna was in an Uber, en route to Peter's condo in the Pearl District. Her ears were ringing from the bar's oh-so-loud music. Why so loud?! But at least she'd gotten a quiet Uber driver. So many liked to yap-yap-yap the whole time they drove. Gianna yapped-yapped-yapped all day. It was nice to just *be* sometimes. She relaxed her head against the headrest and thought of Val. Val seemed as if she'd had a good time.

"We must do it again soon!" she'd said, as she hugged Gianna and the rest of the partygoers out on the curb.

"Yes!" chimed in the others. "That was a ball!"

Maybe Gianna would find the scene fun, too, once she had a husband. Once there was no longer a fear in the back of her mind that she might have to one day go back out there and date again. For her, the night had done nothing other than reinforce that fear, if she and Peter ever broke up.

She thought of him now as her driver fiddled with the stereo.

"Any requests?" he asked.

"Whatever you want is fine," she said, not because she didn't have a preference, but because she didn't want to open up a line of communication. Thankfully, he settled on exactly a song she would have chosen, "Don't Stop Believing" by Journey. Soothing. Feel-good lyrics.

She imagined Peter listening to something similar on his surround-sound speakers, the lyrics echoing off his vaulted ceilings. Odds were high he was humming along as he stood over his kitchen sink peeling an orange, his nightly ritual before bed. Odds were also high he still had on his lucky gray collared shirt and navy trousers that he'd been wearing that morning. He'd had an appointment that evening with potential clients looking for a real estate agent to list their five-bedroom Willamette River waterfront home.

Gianna had no doubt he had charmed them, the way he charmed everyone, the way he'd charmed her six months ago when she showed up at the quaint Italian restaurant he'd suggested for their very first date and found him waiting at a table in the back, dressed in a suit, brown hair freshly trimmed, a corked bottle of Brunello already sitting in the center of the table.

"I saw on your Match profile that you liked Tuscan wine, so I took the liberty," he had said, gesturing to the bottle.

She'd thought, *Now this is a date.*

He pulled her into his arms as soon as she knocked and proceeded to ask about her night, as well as how Val's first IVF appointment had gone on Monday and how Val had liked the nanny she'd interviewed to help out with Luke and Bryan, the two-year-old identical twins she already had. Gianna had mentioned both events earlier that week in passing, and Peter—attentive Peter—had taken note, something she not only appreciated but found extremely attractive, as she'd dated men in the past who couldn't even remember her best friends' names, let alone what was going on in their lives.

He truly was a catch.

So, what was it, then, she wondered—for the millionth time—as she stared into his pale blue eyes while they shared a brandy nightcap on his leather couch in front of a waning fire? Why weren't her feelings for him stronger when all the boxes seemed to be checked?

She went back to what she always went back to—that maybe what she was searching for wasn't real. Maybe all women felt exactly as she did about Peter and walked down the aisle anyway. Maybe she was just an overthinker, never fully satisfied, which was advantageous when it came to her career but didn't help when it came to love.

For a brief second, her mind drifted to Charli Anderson and Jack Logan. She could still see them sitting at the fireside table they always waited for in the back of Hayden's when they used to come in. Jack's green eyes were always zeroed in on Charli like she was the only one in the room. It used to seem he got more enjoyment out of watching her savor bites of the Chocolate Mint Cloud Cake they always shared than he did eating it himself. Charli would reach over and hold his hand or bring her napkin up to her mouth to stifle a laugh from something Jack had said. They'd seemed to have what she was looking for—that indescribable factor—a true soul connection. Then again, who knew what their fate would be.

She and Peter both set their glasses in the sink and made their way down the long hallway to Peter's bedroom, where they undressed, then made love quietly in the dark.

After, Peter rose to use the bathroom, and Gianna lay there, her mind racing, her breath turning jagged. *Calm down*, she told herself.

It wasn't like she had to make any major decision about spending the rest of her life with him tonight. Or any time in the near future. For now, her only job was to keep "gathering information," as Linda had advised her in countless sessions.

She took a deep breath in and noticed then that her lips were dry—probably a combination of the sun that day and the booze she'd drunk that evening. Lip balm. She needed lip balm.

She pushed back the covers and sat up, fumbling for the light switch on the wall, then the knob on the drawer of Peter's bedside table. He had to have a stick around here somewhere. She opened it up to take a look.

And that was when she saw it. Sitting right there in plain view.

## two
# NOW

"**Today's** the day!" exclaimed Peter, as Gianna stepped into his kitchen, lured from the bedroom by the smell of coffee. She was still in her pajamas, hadn't slept a wink.

Peter, on the other hand, looked perky as could be, whistling and tapping two spoons on the counter as if they were drumsticks while he waited to flip the pancakes she could hear sizzling on the stove.

"I used to want to be a musician," he'd told her once. "Back before I understood there were realistic dreams, and then there were pipe dreams."

*The day?* Gianna froze for a brief second, wondering if he meant the day he was going to propose. But no man would announce that, she quickly realized. Not even one whose girlfriend knew that he already had a ring. And Peter had no idea that she knew he had a ring. Such a beautiful ring . . .

She'd peeked. She couldn't not peek last night after seeing the engagement ring box in the drawer of his bedside table. She was horrible with self-discipline! Peter knew this. She'd told him on one of their very first dates.

"If a cake is sitting out on the kitchen counter at Hayden's unattended, I'll have a nibble," she said. "I can't help myself!" She was lucky she wasn't seven hundred pounds. Thank God for her quick metabolism. "And on Christmas Eve, I peek at every gift that's under the tree. I hate the suspense."

She'd found his present that past Christmas—tickets to a sold-out Adele concert that she'd been dying to see. He'd caught her in the act of peeling the wrapping paper back. "You can't be mad," she'd told him. She'd given fair warning.

She could still see the diamond. It was from her favorite jewelry designer on Etsy. He must have seen her checking out this woman's ring collection on Instagram. Or maybe he'd looked at Gianna's Pinterest page. She had pinned a few of her favorite rings from this designer's line to one of her boards—not because she was trying to drop a hint that she wanted Peter to propose. So many of her friends had done that with their boyfriends. Why? She would have never wanted a man to feel pressured to propose! She'd just liked the rings, that was all. And she wanted to remember them, for when the time was right. Which was apparently right now. At least in Peter's mind.

It wasn't crazy, his thinking. Sure, they had only been together half a year. But they were both in their late thirties. And there had never been any beating around the bush about the topic of marriage.

"I saw on your Match profile that you want two kids," he'd said on their first date at Amelia's, the quaint Italian spot he'd chosen.

"Two or three," she'd said, munching on a cracker and Brie from the charcuterie board appetizer, which Peter had ordered before she arrived, in addition to the Brunello. He'd read on her profile that she was a fan of cheese plates, too.

"I think they're both going to show," Peter said now, confirming that he was not referring to His Proposal, but The Reservation.

She had told everyone about it. Well, actually she'd told her petite, college-aged, hostess, Rosie, who filled in her dishwasher, Max, who was also in college and a bit of a jokester, who shared it with her servers, who blabbed to the other waitresses who filled in Peter when he stopped in one day last week to bring her flowers out of the blue. He was great like that.

Her staff had been texting her since bright and early that morning.

*Couldn't sleep last night I was so excited!! Can't believe the day is finally here!!!* The first text came from her server, Claire, who thought Charli and Jack were a modern-day Allie and Noah from *The Notebook*, even though she'd never met them. No one on Gianna's staff had. Restaurant turnover was high. It had been five years since they'd last been in. Claire had just heard about them from Gianna and thought it was such a cute story.

*Turned your kitchen into a casino.* That text came from Max, along with a photo of him placing money in an envelope pinned to a bulletin board that said, "Neither Show." Beside it were several others: "Both Show," "Only Charli Shows," "Only Jack Shows."

Peter brought a short stack of pancakes over to the kitchen table, as well as plates and orange juice.

The very first time she slept over he'd asked what her favorite breakfast was. They were lying in bed together, twisted up in his sheets, having just had sex for the second time. *Better than last night*, she'd been thinking. *Not the best sex of my life, but nice. Definitely nice.*

"Banana pancakes," she'd told him.

"Banana pancakes it is," he'd said, popping up and running out to the corner store for the ingredients, then whipping up a batch. He'd made them for her every morning since.

"What do you think?" he asked as he returned to the stove to tidy up.

*That maybe I'm being too picky.* She almost blurted out her mom's favorite line. What more was she looking for in a man? Honestly. Floral deliveries at work! Banana pancakes! Someone who tidied up his stove and made his bed each morning with hospital corners, no less (his mom was a nurse). Men did not get better than Peter.

He must have seen her face pale.

"You worry too much, you know that?"

She did know that. But there was a lot to worry about. It might not have been productive, but it felt productive, and Gianna loved productivity.

"Just trust," he said. "I'm sure tonight will end in happily ever after."

There was no evidence to support this.

Gianna hadn't heard from Charli or Jack since she took The Reservation down. Which meant . . . nothing really, considering they'd told her they wouldn't be in touch. Each was supposed to decide on his or her own whether or not they wanted to restart the relationship and either show up for The Reservation at seven o'clock tonight (meaning yes) or not show (meaning no). *How stressful and potentially humiliating,* Gianna had thought, when they explained it to her. Then again, incredibly romantic, if they both walked through the door . . .

But five years was such a long time.

The day had felt like it would never get here to Gianna, and she had nothing on the line. For the longest time, she thought it would remain glimmering in the distance like a mirage, teasing her. Then, all of sudden, here it was.

Charli and Jack had likely each married someone else by now. Or forgotten about the date completely. Not everyone had a memory like an elephant, the way she did. And here she'd gone and gotten everyone's hopes up. Sorry, staff. Sorry, Peter.

Unless Peter was referring to their happily ever after. Was he thinking of proposing tonight? Oh, that would be just like Peter. Charli and Jack would get their happily ever after—or not. But she and Peter would get theirs, so the night would end well either way. She could see him, thinking this.

She stood up.

"Not hungry?" he asked.

"I've got to get home, get changed, get to work." *Talk to Mary Pat*, she added silently to herself. Mary Pat would know what Peter was up to. Peter confided in Mary Pat, the same way Gianna did. Her sixty-six-year-old neighbor was a good confidant. She was all about having Gianna over for front-porch chats and gin and tonics.

"Kiss, first?" he said, as she scrambled to gather up her things.

She blinked. Had she just been about to change and walk out the door without thanking him or giving him a kiss for cooking that morning?

"I don't deserve you," she said, joking, but thinking maybe there was some truth to it.

He wrapped his hands around her waist, and they swayed gently from side to side as if music were playing. She closed her eyes for a moment and saw the two of them dancing under a white canopy in her parents' backyard at their wedding. Then, years later, dancing in the evening on the front lawn of their first home, as their three kids ran amuck with the neighbors, before she and Peter rang the dinner gong—Gianna had always wanted a dinner gong—calling them home. And later, tearing up together as they danced at their kids' weddings. Some days it was so easy to picture a life with him.

Other days . . .

"I love you," he said, interrupting her thoughts.

Did he though? Did he really? Sometimes Gianna wondered if it were the idea of her he loved more than who she was at her core. Then again, he sounded sincere enough. And maybe no one got you, truly got you, in this life, anyway.

A crack of thunder sounded in the distance. Peter looked from her to the window.

"Looks like that storm the paper called for is coming, after all."

*Were Charli and Jack?* Gianna wondered.

She gave him a quick kiss and told him she loved him too, then threw on an outfit she had left at his place and hurried out the door into the blustery spring day, where everything seemed as if it was up in the air—both figuratively and literally.

Her heart rate quickened again as she hopped on the TriMet bus across the street to head home, and Linda's voice popped into her head: "When you're feeling anxious, try and find a nice, comfortable place for your thoughts to land."

Charli and Jack came to mind as she made her way to the back of the bus. Not their Reservation. But their love story. It was such a sweet love story. One she'd thought of countless times, since they'd told it to her.

She settled into an empty seat and closed her eyes.

How did it begin?

Oh yes, they were just a couple kids, she remembered. Two ambitious kids who never imagined they'd fall in love . . .

Visit sincerelyriley.com/scene-1 to see scenes from these chapters unfold and to Shop the Book™.

# three
# THEN

**The** first love of Charli's life was a frog named Leggy. She met him on a dissecting tray in her seventh-grade science lab and couldn't stop checking him out—his external nares (nostrils) his tympani (eardrums), his pharynx (throat).

When she sliced open his stomach, her lab partner, Carla Henderson, flagged over their biology teacher and asked for a hall pass to the school nurse.

Mrs. Deane sighed. "You can go when Lauren gets back," she said. "But try to tough it out. The dissection is part of your grade everyone," she reminded the class.

Lauren and five other kids didn't make it through more than twenty minutes of sixth period, but Charli couldn't get enough of Leggy's exam. She stayed in the lab long after the final bell rang inspecting the frog with the help of Mrs. Deane, who looked relieved that at least someone was not totally grossed out by the assignment.

When Charli got home that afternoon, the first thing she did after running upstairs to her bedroom, was call her best friend, Jack.

"Did you do the frog dissection today in biology?" she asked him.

"Yeah. Zoe Allen puked all over herself when she had to identify those gross, squiggly, worm-looking things in his stomach."

"The small intestines."

"Yeah. Whatever. It was disgusting!"

"I loved it," Charli confessed. She yanked up her blinds and saw Jack in his room, sitting on the wooden bench underneath his windowsill.

Jack must have felt her eyes on him because he turned toward the window. "Ew. You're weird," he said, making eye contact with her.

"No, I'm not. You're weird for thinking that. It was so cool."

Jack stuck his tongue out. "Look, I'm a frog. Ribbit Ribbit. You want to come over here and dissect me?"

"I would if I thought there was anything interesting to see in that brain of yours."

"Hey, you can't have looks and brains," Jack shot back.

"Oh, give me a break." Charli pretended to stick her finger down her throat and gag herself. She heard enough about Jack's good looks from the girls at school.

Just the day before when she was in the locker room changing for PE, she'd overheard a group of eighth-grade girls talking about him.

"He is such a hottie," said Becky Tallen, who had probably outgrown a training bra in the third grade. "I'm inviting him to my birthday party, and I'm going to make sure I get to play Seven Minutes in Heaven with him in the closet."

Jack laughed now, knowing how it irked her, and then he stood up and grabbed a baseball from the top of his dresser.

"You want to come over and play catch with me before it gets dark out?"

"Are you sure you want me to? I'm tempted to give you a black eye after that last comment."

"I trust your bad aim," Jack said, smiling.

Charli stepped closer to the window. "Is that a challenge?"

"Maybe."

"Well, in that case . . . I'll be right over."

Jack tossed the ball up in the air.

"Great. See you out front in a minute."

## waiting at hayden's

—

The first time Jack threw a baseball, he knew he was in love. He loved the "whoosh" of the ball as it sailed through the air and the "smack" when it hit his dad's glove.

"Nice power kid," his dad said, tossing the ball back.

They were out in his cul-de-sac on the first evening of the year that called for a t-shirt and shorts. It was also the first time that year that Jack could remember his dad being home from work at the law firm where he was a partner before dark.

His dad pounded his glove. "Let's see it again," he said. The two gloves and the baseball were a birthday gift from his parents last week. Jack had just turned ten.

Jack wound up a second time. Whoosh. Smack.

"What an arm you've got, kid!" his dad said.

Jack beamed.

"Hey Grace, come out and see this!" Jack's mom who was always around and willing to spend time with him, as if to make up for his dad never being home, came out of the kitchen where she'd been washing dishes, to watch. She had on the red apron Jack had gotten her for Christmas last year, and her blond hair was pulled back into a ponytail.

Jack threw another hard pitch into his dad's mitt.

"Bravo," she called, clapping her hands.

"Isn't that impressive?" his dad said. "We should've had this kid in baseball, not soccer last year."

Jack grinned with pride as his dad tossed the ball back. He was just about to throw it again when his dad's pager went off. Jack's least favorite sound in the world was that beep-beep-beep.

His dad took off his mitt and pulled the pager out his pocket. "I'm sorry," he said, frowning. "I've got to go. My assistant's paging. I'm in the middle of this big case."

Jack's shoulders sunk. He didn't care that there was a crisis. Couldn't his dad ignore it?

"Hey, maybe your mom will throw around with you."

His mom gave Jack an apologetic look. "Unfortunately, I can't right now honey." It was the first no she'd given Jack in months. "I've got to finish the dishes and bake cookies for your school's bake sale tomorrow. Your dad will play with you some more tomorrow, won't you, Paul?"

His dad walked over to Jack and handed him his glove. "Tomorrow it is then, buddy."

Standing in the street with the mitts, the ball, and his dad's empty promise, Jack felt tears start to well up in his eyes. He was about to lose it when he saw Charli walk out onto her front porch with an ice cream cone.

"Hey," he said, jogging over to her.

Charli smiled as she smoothed out her dress and took a seat on one of the porch steps. "Hi Jack."

"Do you want to play catch with me and help me break in my new glove?" he asked.

"I thought you said you wanted to break it in with your dad first."

Jack looked down at his feet. "Yeah, well . . . he had to go into work."

"Oh." Charli's tone softened.

He knew she wouldn't say, "I'm sorry," because he had told her how much he hated hearing those words. They were more common than "I love you" in his dad's vocabulary.

"Let me just go check with my parents, okay?" She disappeared into the house and returned a minute later. "I can go. I just have to be in before dark."

Jack's face brightened. "All right. Race you out to my mailbox." He took off, Charli following behind him. And as the warm breeze whizzed past them, Jack almost forgot that his dad had disappointed him. Again.

—

When it came time for Charli to start pursuing love interests outside the science lab—boys—Jack didn't even make her list of prospects. Her best girlfriend, Patti Buchannan, didn't get it.

"Come on," Patti said to her when they were maneuvering through the crowded hallways of West Hills High their third week of high school. "Don't you ever think about what it would be like to date Jack?"

"No," Charli laughed. "Jack and I are just friends."

"You're not even curious what it would be like to kiss him?" Patti pressed.

Charli felt her face flush. Actually, she had thought about that once, just last night when she and Jack were doing homework together in his bedroom. Their elbows had knocked as Jack leaned over her to grab a book, and an image flashed into her head—their lips touching, Jack's hand resting on the back of her neck. But Charli had dismissed the thought right away, thinking that it was weird.

"What girl at this high school hasn't pictured herself kissing Jack," she said to Patti. "It doesn't mean I'd ever want to date him." Besides, she thought, even if she was interested in Jack, it's not like he would ever like her in that way.

She was not Jack's type. In junior high, Jack dated girls who were older (Charli was his same age), did cheerleading (as if . . .), and couldn't seem to care less about their school work (Charli couldn't get enough of hers). And it appeared Jack's taste hadn't changed much now that they were in high school. Charli had seen him flirting with the junior captain of the cheer team by her locker just two days earlier after school got out.

"You're crazy," Patti said. "If I had a friend who looked like Jack, I'd constantly be throwing myself at him."

"That's probably why he's not friends with you."

Patti grinned, revealing her hot pink braces, which perfectly matched the pink streaks in her hair. "But still, I don't know how you resist."

They rounded the corner and spotted Jack holding court with a group of three cheerleaders outside the Spanish lab. The girls were all dressed in their baby blue and white cheerleading outfits for the football game that night and were staring at Jack with googly-eyes.

"He is soooo hot," Patti said, nudging her. "Look at him."

He *did* look good, Charli had to admit. He was swoon-worthy by anyone's standards with brown hair, green eyes, and perfectly straight, white teeth. And his confidence made him even better looking. Jack could charm anyone—even Mrs. Numan, their algebra teacher, who assigned loads of homework and was in a constant bad mood because she was going through a nasty divorce. But Jack was Charli's friend. Had been her friend since they were kids. It would be weird to think of him as something more.

"I just don't see Jack like that," she said.

"Well, some day you're going to take off your blinders and see him like the rest of us do. I'm predicting it now: you and Jack will show up together as a couple at our ten-year high school reunion."

Charli smiled. "If you were my palm reader," she said, "I'd ask for my money back."

—

On the evening of Jack's first high school baseball game, his hands were shaking as he threw some warm-up pitches to his catcher from the bullpen mound near the foul line in the outfield. There was a lot of pressure on him to perform well tonight. The bleachers were packed with students and parents who had heard the hype about Jack's talent as a baseball player from his junior high days, pre-season games, and the newspaper.

The week before, an article had been published about him titled, "Jack Logan: Jack-of-All-Trades." His coaches and friends had been referring to him as that for years because he could pitch, hit, and field so well.

He tossed the ball a few times into his broken-in mitt and then threw a fastball.

"All right, Jack!" he heard a few people from the stands call out. None of the voices was his dad's.

Jack looked up into the bleachers one last time for his old man, hoping to spot him in the black collared shirt and tan blazer he'd left the house in that morning. Maybe he'd sat down at the last minute in the empty seat next to Charli and his mom, who both religiously came to all of his games. His dad had promised he wouldn't miss his first game. "Not when my boy's the star," he'd said as Jack was eating a bowl of cereal before school at the kitchen table. But there was no sign of him.

Disappointed, Jack pulled his baseball cap down over his eyes. He didn't understand it. How could his dad prioritize his career above his only son? He got that his job was important, but was it so important that he couldn't step out of the office for a couple of hours to be here?

The ump called out to both teams that the game was about to start. Jack hailed one more hard pitch into his catcher's glove and then rolled his shoulders back and started to jog in toward the dugout.

"Psst, Jack." Charli was suddenly standing near the chain link fence flagging him toward her.

"What is it?" he asked.

"Just come here, real quick."

Jack looked over his shoulder and saw that the outfielders were still jogging in so he had a second. He went to her.

"Here." Charli slipped him a folded up piece of paper.

*Good luck*, it read.

"It's from your dad," she said.

"Nice try. That's your handwriting."

"Okay, I know, but I'm sure he's thinking that. I've seen you checking the stands for him all throughout your warm-up. I don't want you to worry. You're still going to play great without him."

Jack gave her a half-hearted smile. "I just don't understand why he's not here. He promised."

"I know. I'm sure he wishes he was here."

"Yeah, right. If he wished it, he'd find a way."

"Something big must have come up."

Jack shook his head and checked the stands one more time for him. "Remind me when I'm older to never choose my career over someone I love."

"Will do." She reached out and wrapped her pinky around his, promising. "But come on, get your head in the game. Go out there and show everyone how awesome you are. Your dad might not be here, but a ton of people are, including your number one fan." Charli flashed him a brilliant smile, and Jack stuck her note into the back pocket of his pants.

"Okay," he sighed. He ruffled up her shoulder-length brown hair. "You're pretty great, you know that?"

Why couldn't he find a girlfriend who understood him as well as Charli? She was one-of-a-kind. And was it just him or did she look kind of cute in those jean shorts and the blue and white top she had on. Jack shook his head, snapping out of it. Why was he even thinking about that? If Charli knew that that thought had just crossed his mind, she would think he was crazy!

"Go on!" she said, shooing him. "Go get 'em!"

Jack smiled and hurried to the dugout for a team huddle and then to the pitcher's mound to pitch the first shutout of his high school baseball career. The first of twenty shutouts in his high school career that his dad would miss.

# four
# THEN

"**Would** you rather . . . eat a pig you'd already dissected or . . . not be able to eat anything for a week?" Jack looked over at Charli in the passenger seat of his 1971 Chevy pickup as he was driving.

Charli grimaced. "I'd probably eat the pig," she admitted, laughing. "As disgusting as that would be! Okay, my turn. Let me think." She looked out the window, and Jack followed her gaze to the flat, green landscape, speckled with evergreen trees.

He wondered if this game, which they'd played since they were kids, was distracting her, or if she, too, was having a hard time not thinking about the fact that they were headed to Oregon State University—their new home for the next four years.

"Okay, I've got one," Charli said, turning toward him. "Would you rather . . . keep driving until we get to campus and start school on Monday or . . . pull over right now and stay in this car forever, suspended in time?"

Jack met her eyes, relieved. "You're nervous, too?"

"Of course I am! My palms are sweating!"

Jack laughed and showed her his palms were clammy also.

Charli sunk back into the worn leather seat. "At least you have the baseball team to welcome you when you get there. That's a group of built-in friends." Jack was on a full-ride baseball scholarship. It was why he'd settled on Oregon State.

"Yeah, well, you're in the Honors College and the Honors dorm," Jack reminded her. "You'll have a smart-people community."

"Yeah, I guess." Charli cracked open the window, and some fresh air blew in. "Still, it's so nerve-racking. I can't believe we're starting college."

"I know."

They drove for a few more minutes in comfortable silence, and then Charli said, "Does this mean your answer to my 'would you rather' is to keeping driving until we get to campus?"

"As tempting as the alternative is, I think we'd regret it if we didn't go."

"I guess you're right."

Jack tried to put on a brave face. "Just think—at least we have each other. Imagine how much scarier this would be if we'd decided on different schools."

"Yeah," Charli nodded vehemently. "Can you imagine the two of us in a long-distance friendship?"

Jack cracked a smile. "You'd be calling me every day."

"You'd probably call me so often I'd have to turn my phone off."

"You're right," Jack grinned. "Let's promise each other that we'll never live more than a few blocks apart."

Charli stuck out her hand to shake on it. "That's a promise I'd like nothing more than to keep."

—

"I can't believe I was nervous to start college." Charli looked up at Nick Fisher, her lanky, buzz-headed boyfriend whom she'd met her first week of school in her Biology 111 class. It was the fourth week of classes, and they were at a barn party that Jack had invited her to at one of his baseball buddy's parents' houses out in the country. Charli was slow dancing with Nick to Hunter Hayes' "Wanted" underneath the twinkling white lights that were strung up in the rafters.

"Yeah, I can't believe I was nervous either," Nick said. "Everything's so great—classes, our friends in the Honors dorm. You."

Charli smiled and rested her head on Nick's chest. It was weird having Nick as her new confidant, but that's what he'd become. She'd never had a serious boyfriend before, but it felt right to tell him everything she used to share with Jack. That came with dating someone, didn't it? She was still trying to figure all of it out.

She really liked Nick. He shared her love of science and research, which Jack supported but didn't quite understand, and he was the first guy who'd ever made her feel desirable. Jack had to get that, right?

Charli still valued her friendship with Jack, but she was growing to enjoy Nick's company more and more. And she really liked the feeling of being wrapped in his arms in a barn on this crisp November night. She was enjoying it so much that she was a little annoyed when she felt a tap on her shoulder and turned around to see that it was Jack.

"Can I steal you for a bit?" he asked.

"Now?" Charli said. "Can't I find you in a little while?" Jack used to feed her this line all the time in high school when he was chatting up a cute girl at his locker and wanted just a little more time with her before they carpooled home.

"I've barely talked to you all night," Jack said. He did have a point. Charli needed to spend some quality time with him. It had been a few weeks since they'd really caught up, and Jack had invited her to the party.

She turned to Nick. "Do you mind?" she asked, pulling lightly on the bottom of his flannel plaid shirt, thinking to herself that she really liked the way he could pull off cowboy boots and skinny jeans, and that maybe, she might even go to second base with him after they left the party.

"Not at all," Nick said. "Just hurry back."

Charli had never kissed a boy in front of Jack before, but for some reason she did then, planting one right on Nick's lips.

That kiss was the first thing Jack brought up with her when they were sitting in the rickety hayloft looking down on the party a few minutes later.

"What was that all about?" he asked.

"What do you mean?"

"I mean the kiss. The way you've been with Nick all night. And the past month. Is he a good guy? How serious is it?"

"What's with the interrogation?"

"I'm just wondering. I want to be sure that he's nice, you know. That's what friends do. Check in on each other."

"Well, he is a good guy," she said. "So, you don't need to worry about that. And I like him. We're definitely dating."

Jack nodded and took a long pull of his Budweiser.

"How are things with you and Mandy?" Charli asked. Jack had started seeing a sophomore cheerleader (big surprise) the first week of school.

"Fine," he said. Then, after another minute he added, "She reminds me a lot of Becky."

Becky Holland was the blond bombshell Jack went out with their senior year of high school from the dance team.

"Oh, so she's as smart as she is pretty?" Charli teased.

A smile tugged at Jack's cheeks. "You could say that." He went on to tell Charli a story about how there was a Van Gogh exhibit at the Portland Art Museum that they'd gone to for an introductory art class, and she had asked him on the way there if Van Gogh himself was going to be around to answer questions.

"You're kidding?" Charli deadpanned.

"Nope." He grinned.

"You may have reached a new low Jack."

"I know. What was she thinking?"

"Apparently not a whole lot."

His smile widened. "I do have to give her some credit though. She's really thoughtful. Like the other day she baked me a plate of chocolate chip cookies, and she even sat through the whole Niners football game on TV with me."

Charli rested her hand on his shoulder. "That's great, Jack. I'm really happy for you."

Jack's face turned serious. He stopped looking at Charli and dropped his gaze down on the party below them.

"What's wrong?" Charli asked.

Silence.

"Jack?"

Nothing again. Charli tried to read his mind, but she couldn't tell what he was thinking. Jack was not usually a mystery to her. Finally, he drew in a deep breath.

"Sometimes I really like Mandy, but then other times I think . . ." his voice trailed off, and he shook his head. "Never mind; it's probably stupid."

"No, you think what?" Charli encouraged him.

Jack took another long swig of his beer, finishing it off, and then set it down on one of the wooden planks.

"I think maybe I'd like to be with someone different. Someone not like anyone I've ever dated in the past."

"Wow, Jack. You could have fooled me."

"Yeah." He repositioned himself so that he was looking right into her eyes. "I want someone I can really talk to, you know?"

Charli didn't recognize the expression on his face, and she'd seen quite a few—excitement when he won the state baseball championship their sophomore year, nervousness before they took the SAT's, frustration when his dad missed his baseball games for work. She couldn't name what this one was exactly, but if she were to guess she'd say it was longing. Or desire.

"Someone who's known me for a while," he continued. "Who gets me."

Charli's heart fluttered. Jack hadn't said her name, but he might as well have.

Silence followed his confession and Charli didn't know what to say to break it. After all these years could Jack really be admitting that he wanted to be more than just friends?

Just then a couple stumbled up the ladder and into the loft, breaking the intimate spell between them. All of a sudden the ease of their relationship gave way to an awkwardness that neither of them seemed to know what to do with. They both stood up without a word and returned to the party.

—

The next day, Jack acted like that conversation had never happened. Charli couldn't get it out of her mind though.

Something changed inside of her after that night. She knew it had probably just been Jack's alcohol talking, and that he'd most likely meant nothing by what he said, but it was as if the very mention of her meaning more to him than just a friend triggered feelings of her own for him.

Whenever his name flashed across the screen on her phone, her heart raced and her palms clammed up. When they met up for lunch at Carol's Pizza Parlor that Wednesday, Charli found herself picking at her food like she might on a first date, her stomach already full—from butterflies.

"Are you all right?" Jack asked as she boxed up most of her pepperoni slice. "You've been sort of quiet the last couple of days. And you barely touched your food."

"I'm just feeling a little off," Charli replied, thinking it wasn't really a lie. She wasn't sick, but she sure didn't feel like herself.

"Do you have a fever?" Jack rested the back of his hand against her forehead.

His touch stirred something inside of her. She moved his hand, wondering why this was happening and hoping that it would stop.

"I've been up late the last couple of nights cramming for a chemistry exam. Maybe I just need some rest."

She figured that rest and a week or so away from Jack would help her feelings for him return to normal, but Jack didn't really give her a chance to put this experiment to a test. Halfway through the week, she was woken up by a rap on her dorm room window, and when she pulled open the blinds, Jack's face was on the other side.

Her heart stopped, and right away her mind started to race. *What was he doing here?* Her first thought was that something must have happened. A fight with Mandy, an injury, or worse, a family emergency. She was thinking like Jack's best friend, not the girl who had been crushing on him, as she pulled open the blinds and lifted the glass.

"Jack?" She whispered his name into the cool night quietly so she wouldn't wake her roommate, who had an eight a.m. test in the morning. He was staring out at the empty road, so she reached out and touched his shoulder. "Is everything okay?" His silence scared her. She said his name again and still there was no response. It felt like minutes had passed before he finally turned toward her. To her relief there were no signs of tears in his eyes or anger on his face, and she let out the deep breath she was holding.

He was fidgety, folding his arms over his chest and then unfolding them. Looking her in the eyes, then staring at the ground, then glancing up at the clear night sky. She tensed up again. This had to be about their moment at the party. He was acting weird like he had that night. He rubbed his hands over his face, and her chest knotted with anticipation.

"I don't know how to say this," he said.

Charli crouched down and rested her hands on the ledge of the window. Part of her wanted to jump right in and tell him what she'd been thinking about the last few days. To talk through it all with him. But the other part wanted to wait and make sure that's where this conversation was headed. What if she blurted out what was on her mind, and she'd totally misread all his signs?

Jack set his hands down right in front of hers so that the tips of their fingers touched. Her heart thudded in her chest. If this was how it felt to have him just barely touch her, she couldn't imagine what it would be like if he . . . if he actually . . . She was mid-thought, picturing Jack's lips meeting hers when his eyes drifted shut, when he leaned toward her. And then, before she fully realized what was happening, her childhood best friend, the boy who used to ride his bike around their neighborhood with her and whose house she used to sneak over to in the middle of the night to keep him company before big games when he couldn't sleep, was kissing her.

She was in shock when he pulled away.

"What was that for?" she uttered. She felt like she was floating above herself.

"I don't know." Jack dropped his head. "I wanted to. I have wanted to . . . for a while."

Charli nodded.

Jack seemed to interpret her silence as something else.

"Shit," he muttered under his breath. "I'm sorry. I should have asked before I did that. I shouldn't have assumed you were feeling the same way I was. It was stupid of me to come over like this." He stuffed his hands in his pockets, clearly embarrassed, and turned around.

Charli watched him walk a few steps out toward the road before she came to her senses.

"Wait!" she called, climbing out of her window in her pajamas and hopping down onto the cold and dewy grass. Jack kept walking with his head down, looking like he did after he lost a game or gave up a home run. "I do feel the same way," she said, realizing that she did. Any thought she'd had to the contrary was just denial. Her words reached him before she could. "I feel exactly the same way, Jack."

She crossed her arms over her chest as Jack stopped in his tracks, and then she stood there in the cold, waiting. Waiting for him to say something. Anything.

"You do?" When he turned around, he wore a look of disbelief on his face.

Charli had never seen him this unsure of himself before. Where was the confident, composed guy she always caught in the halls in high school, leaning up against a locker, making small talk and teasing girls he thought were cute?

"Yeah," she said, her heart threatening to miss its next beat.

He let out a relieved laugh. "God, you have no idea how hard this has been to keep to myself, Charli."

She swallowed hard as he approached her. "Really?"

"Yeah. Seeing you with Nick all these weeks has been awful for me. I think it took you falling for another guy for me to realize what my true feelings were." Her pulse ticked up a notch and sped up even faster when Jack reached out and lifted her hand, putting his fingers through hers.

"I know this will change things between us," he said. "But I want things to change. You're not like any girl I've ever met, Charli. You're smart, you challenge me, you're pretty, without even really trying to be and . . . I don't know . . . you're the one person I can be myself around."

It was the best thing anyone had ever said to her. She couldn't believe it. She stared into Jack's green eyes, memorizing the way he was looking at her and the feelings she had for him in that moment, thinking how she had never been so happy and how even though she had never been in love, she was pretty sure that this was what it felt like to be utterly and completely falling.

Visit sincerelyriley.com/scene-2 to watch Charli and Jack's love story unfold and to Shop the Book™.

# five
# NOW

**Gianna** paced back and forth on Mary Pat's covered front porch.

It was nearly four o'clock. Her neighbor—who could almost always be found on her front porch, rain or shine, day or night—hadn't been there when she arrived that morning.

*I'm at a hair appointment, darling*, she'd texted Gianna after Gianna sent her a string of flustered messages.

*Where are you??*

*Need you!!*

*Having a crisis!*

How a hair appointment had taken all afternoon for a woman with cropped brown hair was beyond Gianna. Mary Pat's hairdresser must have been going through a major personal crisis of her own and given her a free four-hour scalp massage in exchange for her neighbor's famous pearls of wisdom.

There. Finally! Her yellow Volkswagen was turning onto their tree-lined street, its windshield wipers batting away the rain that had been falling on and off all day.

Gianna took a long sip of her gin and tonic. She'd brought over ice and made herself a cocktail from the ingredients in the wooden bar cart by Mary Pat's front door with handles of Tanqueray, bottles of Schweppes, and limes.

"Want to come over for a G&T?" Mary Pat had called out to Gianna on Gianna's first night in her new home, three years ago.

Gianna had been hurrying to get inside with her groceries because it was thirty-five degrees out and raining. Mary Pat was in shorts and a t-shirt, sipping a cold drink. Space heaters, Gianna later learned. Her whole porch was filled with space heaters so it was actually always very cozy.

*I've moved next door to a crazy person*, Gianna remembered thinking. *Then again, maybe she thinks I'm crazy—a single woman moving into this big, impractical, five-bedroom house.*

It was Betty Grace's fault. "If you want something, act as if you already have it, and it will come!" The famous self-help guru had dispensed her prescriptions for positive living to Gianna and fifty other ambitious women who had sat in a stuffy conference room that smelled like soup from the soup kitchen across the street for four hours a day, five days straight.

Her mother had dragged her to this convention on manifesting one's dream life at her New Age church. Gianna had gone, just to appease her. She wasn't sure she bought into the whole philosophy—though she didn't *not* buy into it. She was open to any and all possibilities when it came to explanations for how life worked and what the whole point of it was.

"I would like a husband, a family, and a white and gray Cape Cod house with a great big kitchen, a wraparound front porch, and a swimming pool." Gianna's voice had sounded so loud, so scratchy, so ridiculous over the microphone when she shared her desires the first day of the conference with the ladies.

"So, go house hunting, dear!" Betty Grace had said. "And then feel the feeling of having the rest in your belly." That part was "very important," she had kept stressing.

*This is silly. So silly!* Gianna had thought, as she called up a real estate agent the following week to show her property. "I just want to check out what's on the market," she'd told her. "I'm not looking to buy yet."

But she had the money. And Valerie had just moved in with Richard, so she no longer had a roommate. The timing was right. It would be a good investment, if nothing else. And what if it did open up space in her life for a great guy and her dream family? She hadn't gotten where she was career-wise by sitting around doing nothing. Buying her dream house at least felt like a productive step on the path to falling in love and having babies. It was hard to find productive steps to take when it came to those desires, considering they depended so much on good luck and timing.

"Is Peter proposing to me?" She blurted the words out as soon as Mary Pat was out of her car.

Her neighbor's new 'do, which looked exactly like her old 'do, was being styled by the wind, so by the time she made it to her front porch, it was sticking out in a million different directions, as if she'd been electrocuted.

"Proposals are supposed to be a surprise, honey," she said.

"I hate surprises. You know I hate surprises."

Mary Pat poured herself a drink and did a silent toast to her husband, Dale, who she used to have happy hour with every single day before he lost his battle with colon cancer the year before Gianna moved in next door. She had a drink daily, to preserve the ritual, always on her front porch, just like she and Dale used to do back in Wilmington, North Carolina, where they'd lived.

She'd moved to Portland after his death to be near her daughter, Jane, who Gianna had met on various occasions when she popped over to visit with her husband and their two kids. They were such cute kids. Both girls. Six and eight. Each had Mary Pat's high cheekbones and her daughter's button nose and blond hair. Gianna sometimes just stared at them from her window, probably looking like a creepy neighbor. She was just ready to have kids. So ready, it sometimes hurt. Which was not a good thing, according to Betty Grace. Apparently, it meant she wasn't "in sync" with her desire.

"I hate to betray a man's trust, but you're driving me crazy," Mary Pat said.

"So, it's a yes?" said Gianna.

Mary Pat took a sip of her drink, then sat in one of the two rocking chairs, where Gianna sat with her a lot of evenings and played Gin Rummy, another former tradition of her and Dale's.

"He thought with The Reservation tonight it would be romantic."

Just as Gianna had suspected! She knew him well. At least she didn't have to worry about whether or not she knew him well enough to marry him. She just had to decide if she loved what she knew. Which should have been easy. Why wasn't it easy?

"I thought this was what you wanted," Mary Pat said, when Gianna went back to pacing. "That this would come as welcome news."

To be fair, Gianna understood this. She'd only been telling Mary Pat how ready she was to get married since they first met. And she'd said nothing bad about Peter, ever. Not to Mary Pat or any of her friends. The only person she'd told her anxieties to was Linda. She hadn't wanted to taint the relationship in case she ended up marrying him.

She'd had friends who confessed some of the most horrid things to her about men they eventually settled down with.

"Sometimes I see Jake and don't really want to kiss him. Is that bad?" asked Lucy Lawson, Gianna's best friend from college. *Yes,* Gianna had thought. *Terrible. Definitely not how one should feel about a prospective husband.*

"I might be in love with my co-worker, Steve!" Marcy Sanders, Gianna's gym partner, had told her as Gianna was helping her address envelopes for her four-hundred-person wedding to Brad.

Then, months later, Gianna had stood beside each of her friends and watched them exchange teary-eyed vows with those men, like they'd forgotten everything.

Gianna hadn't forgotten though. Every time she saw Lucy with Jake, she wondered: *Do you still not like kissing him?* And when she saw Marcy and Brad, she thought: *Do you still sometimes think you might have married the wrong guy?*

She didn't want her friends wondering if a spark had finally materialized for her with Peter every time they saw the two of them for the rest of her life.

But now, Linda was on vacation and couldn't be reached. And the proposal was coming this evening. She had to talk to somebody.

"You don't know your answer?" Mary Pat said.

"No, I don't know my answer!" Gianna said, continuing to pace. "I should know the answer, shouldn't I?"

"Normally you are a very decisive person," Mary Pat said.

True. Ten years ago, she'd seen the building for lease on Northwest 23rd Street where Hayden's was now and thought: *Yes. That's it!* That was the space where she wanted to open her restaurant. That corner building with floor-to-ceiling windows on that cute street filled with boutiques and white twinkle lights strung on every tree. She knew that about herself. She was capable of knowing something.

So why not this?

Maybe because marrying Peter was a forever commitment. Sure, starting a restaurant was a big commitment, too, but there was a way out if she hated it or it didn't do well. Of course, divorce was always a way out of a marriage. But she didn't want to go there. She really didn't want to go there. At least not mentally before she settled down.

Her phone rang then, startling both her and Mary Pat.

"Please don't be Peter," she mumbled as she rummaged through her purse. She pulled out the phone and checked the caller ID. It was Hayden's. Relieved, she turned in her chair and answered it. "I'll be there soon, I'm just—"

"Charli called." It was Rosie, her hostess.

"What?" Gianna jumped up, checking her silver watch, which had been a gift from Peter for Valentine's Day. It was something she had pointed out in the window of a small antique jewelry store months before and Peter had remembered. *He's a gem! I'm being too picky!*

"What did she say?" she asked Rosie.

"She asked to speak with you. I told her you'd be in shortly and would call her then. I'm sorry. I should have just given her your cell phone number. But I wasn't thinking. I just couldn't believe I had Charli on the line!" Gianna could picture Rosie all frazzled at the hostess stand, pulling at the low bun she always wore, messing it up.

"Okay, listen, I'm leaving right this second." Gianna hung up and ran over to her place to change into her black VDV wrap dress and check her makeup. Mary Pat followed. "It's Charli," Gianna said, while applying her lipstick.

"Ah, the five-year-out reservation girl. She's arrived?"

"No, but she called and asked to speak with me."

"Any word from Mr. Five Years?"

"Rosie didn't say. I mean, she would have said if Jack called, too, right? Oh my God, Mary Pat, what if only one of them shows and the other one doesn't?" She pictured Charli sitting at the fireside table they'd reserved all alone, waiting for Jack. Then Jack sitting all alone waiting for Charli. Suddenly, Gianna imagined Peter at Hayden's, waiting for her. Waiting to ask Gianna the question that she didn't want to hear because she wasn't sure of the answer and, frankly, not being sure of the answer was pretty much an answer in itself, wasn't it? Or was it? She sighed.

"You'll figure it out, hon," Mary Pat said.

"Right. I'm sure they both will show." Gianna stared at her reflection in the mirror as she pulled her long dark hair back into a ponytail. *Yes, Peter, I would love to marry you,* she mentally rehearsed. *No, Peter, I don't want to marry you.* She watched her face, seeing if one response lit it up more than another. Ugh. Wasn't working. Flipping off the bathroom light, she walked out.

"I wasn't talking about whether or not both Charli and Jack will show up for The Reservation," Mary Pat said.

"You think I'll figure out what to say to Peter?"

"Yes."

"Really?"

"I really do."

"I hope so." She pulled open her front door, and a gust of wind blew into the apartment.

"You want a ride?" asked Mary Pat.

Gianna took a deep breath in, smelling the rain, the wind, and the pine trees that were swaying in the breeze at the bottom of her stairs. "I think I'll walk. Clear my head."

"All right," Mary Pat said, handing her an umbrella. She took Gianna's other hand and gave it a good squeeze as if trying to pass along her confidence. "Call me if you need anything. I can't wait to hear the end of the story."

"You mean Charli and Jack's or mine and Peter's?"

"Both," said Mary Pat, smiling.

## six

# THEN

**Jack** got whipped by a few towels in the locker room before his team's weightlifting session started the Monday after he told Charli how he felt. His teammates wouldn't stop teasing him for turning down Mandy for Charli, calling it "a mistake he would always regret." Mandy and a few of her girlfriends weren't too happy about it either. They TPeed his truck in the freshman parking lot, leaving a cardboard sign on the dashboard that said "Cheater."

Jack didn't care. He was into Charli, and that was all that mattered to him.

In time, his baseball buddies came around to his decision. After a few months his catcher, Mike, said to him as they were tossing the ball around, "Charli's really something else, Jack. I was wrong buddy."

Even Mandy apologized for her behavior. After seeing the way he and Charli were together at a party, she came up to him, a little tipsy and confessed, "I want what you two have."

Since Jack and Charli were building on a great friendship, it was no surprise that what they had was so special. The physical stuff was new though. Initially, Jack was concerned that Charli saw him too much as a brother. He'd had feelings for her for a while, but she'd only recently started seeing him differently.

The first time he put his hand up her shirt and slid it between the crease in her jeans while they were fooling around in the back of his truck he said to her, "Are you sure this is okay?"

"Jack," she said, sitting up and scooting closer to him. "It's not like I've never been attracted to you. I just never imagined this would happen. I never let my mind go there. If I had . . . if it did . . . well . . . let's just say I'm into it."

Chemistry ended up not being a problem for them. It seemed every time they were alone together, he and Charli were making up for lost time.

"This sure beats the high fives and fist bumps I used to give you in here," Charli said to him one afternoon when they were making out in the baseball dugout. She had come to meet Jack after practice and had watched the last few minutes from behind the chain-link fence.

"I'm with you on that," Jack said, smoothing out her hair and pressing his lips to hers again. Jack had always loved the scent of the baseball dugout—that mix of Icy Hot, freshly cut grass, and dirt mixed into the air. But the smell of Charli's shampoo and her vanilla grapefruit perfume that day . . . wow. It kicked that baseball dugout scent in the ass.

Jack rounded the bases with Charli one at a time, never stealing despite his strong feelings for her. He knew that going all the way was a point of no return. There was no going back to being "just friends" after that, so he was careful about moving too fast.

But it was hard not to. After a couple months of dating, Charli told Jack that she'd gone on the pill.

"It takes a month to be most effective though. My body has to get used to it. So, maybe we could plan a night or something. Do it then?"

That was all Jack thought about in January.

Then when February came, Charli voiced some more concerns.

"What if I'm not good at it?" she asked him the night they were set to take their relationship to the next level as they were driving back to Jack's dorm from dinner. "I mean you've been with other girls, but you're my first."

Jack explained that it wasn't about being good. "Just the fact that it's you will make it way better. And besides," he said, reaching over to the passenger seat and taking her hand, "it's not like I loved any of them."

Charli perked up in her seat. "Is that a backwards way of saying you love me?"

Jack had never used the big L-word before. But there it was. Out in the open.

"Haven't I made it obvious?"

"I guess, but you've never come right out and said it."

"Well, I'm saying it now." He clenched her hand tightly, feeling relieved that he'd finally gotten it off his chest. He'd been too nervous to tell her for weeks. "Honestly," he went on, "I think I always have."

Jack ended up just talking with Charli that night. About it. About everything. It wasn't until a few weeks later that they considered doing it again.

This time it wasn't planned. It was the middle of the afternoon. They had run to Jack's dorm to escape a rainstorm they'd been caught in the middle of while they were walking back to his place from class. Charli peeled off her sweatshirt in the doorway and accidentally pulled her shirt off over her head too.

"Oops," she giggled, covering her hands over her black bra, the one with the lace and the thin straps. "Mike's not home, right?" She quickly checked down the hall for his roommate, the catcher on the baseball team.

"In the library," Jack said, his eyes on her bare, wet skin.

"Oh, good." She sounded relieved as she looked back toward him. "Do you want me to go grab a towel or something? We're soaking wet!" It seemed to take her a minute to realize that his thoughts weren't on drying off.

Jack took a step toward her and slid his hands down her arms.

"Actually, I was thinking . . . maybe now would be a good time."

She winced a little, which wasn't exactly the reaction he had been hoping for.

"You don't want to?" he said.

"It's not that. I want to. I really want to. It's just . . . well . . . I'm sick."

Sick was their code word for her time of the month. "Aw, really? Weren't you just sick like two days ago?"

"Try twenty-eight." She chuckled, although he could tell she was disappointed too. "But, hey, when I'm better, okay?"

Sure enough, the day she was "better," they got into a late night make out session in Charli's bedroom. They were supposed to be studying, but their books had been pushed to the floor, and their note cards were scattered on her duvet.

Charli's breath quickened as Jack inched his way down her body, running his lips across the hollow between her breasts, her stomach, the soft skin in between her thighs.

"Jack?" she said. His name sounded more like a moan than anything else.

"Yeah?" His voice was deep, heavy, in between her legs.

"I think I'm ready now."

Jack snapped his head up quicker than an infield pop fly.

"Geez!" Charli scooted backwards, grabbing a fist of the duvet with her hand. "I take it you are too?"

An embarrassed laugh escaped him. "Sorry. You just got me . . . well . . . excited."

"Clearly." She nodded to the bulge in his jeans.

Jack nudged her playfully. Charli smiled and then curled up beside him.

"You know," she said, "even though we've already talked about this, it's kind of weird to think that tonight's that night where there's no going back to just being those two kids ever again. I mean if this whole thing doesn't work out with us, it'd be too strange to be just friends having had sex."

"I know. But it would already be weird considering we're in love and have done other things, right?"

"I guess," she said, snuggling closer.

"And it's worth it to me to get to experience everything with you. The friendship and all the other stuff."

He lay there with her, listening to the rain patter down on the roof, a sound as familiar to him as Charli's soft, steady breathing. "I don't know about you," he said. "But I'm all in."

Charli didn't miss a beat. "I'm all in too." She sat up and looked at the bed then, the same way Jack sometimes stared at the baseball field before a game, like she was trying to imagine how it would all play out. "So," she finally said, "we just start by kissing?"

"Sure," Jack said, sitting up, "like we always do. Then we'll go from there."

"Don't you think it's kind of funny that at one point in our lives we swore we would never do this with anyone?" she said.

"You mean when we stole that sexeducation book from the library during recess in the second grade and saw all the naked pictures?"

"Yeah," she laughed. "And then remember when Mrs. Lane caught us with it and gave us the sex talk early? Just you and me in the classroom with her?"

"She was so graphic. We were seven!"

"I know! What would she think of us now?"

"I have no clue. But picturing my second-grade teacher right now doesn't really help get me in the mood."

"Come on." Charli crossed her arms over her chest. "Aren't hot teachers every guy's fantasy?"

"You're my fantasy," Jack said, and even though his tone was lighthearted, it was enough to change the feel in the room.

His heartbeat kicked its rhythm up and matched the rain's—fast, hard, thunderous. He lit the vanilla scented candle on Charli's nightstand and then flipped off the lights. She was just a silhouette when he turned back to her. Legs. Body. Lips.

"So," Charli cleared her throat. "I guess now's when we start the kissing?"

Jack swallowed hard, thinking to himself that he couldn't believe this was finally about to happen. "Yeah," he said. "Now's when we start the kissing."

Jack didn't remember much about how that first time felt for him. His focus was on Charli—listening as she told him when he needed to slow down or adjusting when he felt her nails dig hard into his back—but he did remember one moment very vividly. It was a moment when their eyes locked, and he saw all their history in a flash, just like someone might when he was on the verge of falling out of life and into death—throwing the baseball around, school bus rides, backyard campouts, swimming in the river behind their houses, kissing her outside her dorm room window for the first time—all of it. And an undeniable connection to Charli pulsed through him.

In that moment, Jack felt that *nothing* could *ever* break the two of them up. His heart belonged to Charli completely.

Visit sincerelyriley.com/scene-3 to see scenes from these chapters unfold and to Shop the Book™.

## seven
# NOW

**Gianna** kept her eyes peeled for Peter's black Mercedes as she walked the familiar two miles to work, just in case he was already on his way to Hayden's to propose to her. She certainly hoped he wasn't. She needed more time.

She thought of Charli and Jack and wondered if the opposite was true for them. Had *too much* time passed? They'd each been so sure of their feelings for one another back when they were together, but now, after five years apart, was each questioning the bond they'd once had? Were they both in a panic this very minute too?

Oh no. Up ahead.

Not a black Mercedes but a black limousine. What if Peter was inside it? He was a man of grand romantic gestures. Gianna could imagine him renting a limousine for the evening to whisk them away once she said yes.

He had no idea she might *not* say yes.

It was because of all the compliments. Gianna was always paying Peter compliments. It was hard not to. He was always doing things worth complimenting.

Like two nights ago, at dinner. They were at their favorite seafood place. Fancy joint. Right on the Willamette River. The food was even better than the sparkling water view. When the check arrived, Gianna grabbed it and paid, something she did on occasion, even though Peter always offered to pay and *could* pay. He made almost as much money as she did.

"How happy are you to be dating a guy who isn't intimidated by your success?" he'd said.

Gianna's last serious boyfriend, Fred, *had* been intimidated and used to make her feel bad about her income, something she'd never understood. It was the twenty-first century! What did it matter whose paycheck was bigger?

"You make everyone I've dated before you pale in comparison," she told him. It just sort of spilled out of her. Because it was true. None of Gianna's four serious boyfriends before Peter had come close to measuring up to him.

Kyle was her college boyfriend. She could tell he hadn't been popular in high school when they met freshman year at The University of Portland. But when he blossomed their sophomore year, his ego went through the roof. By the time they were juniors, the studious, shy guy she'd fallen for at freshman orientation had transformed into a macho meathead she was no longer attracted to.

Rich had exuded passion. They met while Gianna was getting her master's in business at Portland State. He was an art student. Everything about their relationship was intense, in a good way—their conversations, their chemistry, the sex. Oh, the sex! *So, this is what the hype is about,* she remembered thinking after their first time. She would have kept dating him . . . if she hadn't found out he was also dating someone else.

("Interesting," Linda had said, with a thoughtful nod, when Gianna relayed this story. *Which meant . . . what, exactly?* Gianna had wondered as she left that session. What had Linda been trying to say? That men she had a spark with would cheat? That men who were overtly sexual tended to want to be sexual with everyone? Was that true? Gianna was very sexual herself, and she knew she wouldn't cheat if she were in a relationship that was completely fulfilling. But maybe men and women were different in that way.)

Then there was Evan, the cute, intelligent banker, whom she met when she turned thirty. In hindsight, Gianna's eight-month relationship with him shouldn't have lasted longer than two or three dates, but they met after a long period during which Gianna seemed to be only meeting men who lacked conversational skills, maturity, financial stability, or all of the above. The fact that Evan was normal and responsible made Gianna overlook his stubborn, selfish ways until she simply couldn't anymore.

She'd then dated Fred, the financial analyst who said he was, "intimidated by her success" for two years in her mid-thirties.

Recalling these relationships made her feel nothing except relief that they were behind her.

If she and Peter ended things, however . . .

Would she turn into one of *those women?* Like Karen Willis, her friend from college? Or Stacy Reis, a friend of Val's? Both were married. Both still talked about a particular ex-boyfriend often and wistfully, in a way that made Gianna think they probably lost sleep some nights, lying there, wondering how different their lives might have been had they ended up with those impossible-to-forget-exes instead.

Gianna didn't want to live with regret, and if she broke things off with Peter, she might. What if she never did meet someone better suited for her and came to realize Peter probably had been The One, months or years later? Did that mean she should marry him?

"Yes, no, yes, no." She tried out each response to Peter's question, trying to evaluate how each answer felt as it rolled off her tongue. Ugh! It wasn't working. Picking up her pace, she crossed a busy intersection and undid the top few buttons of her trench coat.

If she didn't marry Peter, one thing was sure, he'd start seeing someone else right away.

"I'm a bit of a serial dater," he'd admitted, early on. "I don't like being alone."

This was only after they'd shared two bottles of wine at his place, of course. Peter was not a man who typically opened up unless he was loosened up, which Gianna sometimes thought might be why at times it felt like their spark was missing. It was hard to emotionally connect with someone who was always so . . . what was the word? Put-together? Poised?

Maybe it was best if she put it this way: His day-to-day behavior reminded her of the way most people acted when they were in the middle of a very important job interview. His best foot was always forward. (Which, she supposed, was better than being with someone who *never* put his best foot forward. She'd dated that type too. Fred came to mind.) Ha! Now it sounded like it was just impossible to win with her. Maybe it was.

"So, why didn't it work out?" she'd asked him that night. "You know, with any of the others?"

"Simple," he'd said. "None of them met my criteria for what I'm looking for in a life partner. You have *everything*. You are everything."

Gianna remembered thinking that that was the exact same reason she was into him.

It was *still* the reason she was into him, she realized now, picking up her pace.

"A partner meeting our set criteria is the most important thing," she heard Linda now. Linda was Team Peter. She hadn't come right out and said this, but she might as well have.

"Sparks fade," she kept stressing to Gianna in their sessions. "I'd encourage you to focus on whether or not you and your partner share values, agree on how to spend your finances, enjoy each other's company, and have similar visions for your future. You're looking to build a life with someone, not have a passionate fling."

Gianna got her point. But if meeting set criteria was all that determined whether or not two people got married, then couldn't Peter be happy with any attractive, successful woman with a sense of humor? And wouldn't she be happy with any man who had similar looks and personality traits as Peter? What made the two of them *meant for each other*? Sometimes she thought she might be more confident in their relationship if they didn't meet each other's criteria and they loved each other in spite of this. If their connection felt like it defied logic instead of was based on it.

A grassy park with a towering evergreen tree in the middle came into view, and Gianna decided she would cut through it to shave off some time. She had run through the park a couple of times and knew there was a concrete path that would let her out one block from Hayden's.

Gianna found the path and had just turned down it when something caught her eye. A long white dress was lying beside the gnarly trunk of an evergreen tree. What was that doing there? An elegant dress? Lying in a park? In the rain?

Her curiosity was piqued, but she kept walking.

"But I loved him!" A hysterical, high-pitched voice startled her. She paused and looked over toward the evergreen tree where the voice had come from. Someone on the other side of the tree snatched up the dress and then Gianna heard crying. Now there was another voice . . .

Gianna looked around to see if there was anyone else reacting to this commotion, but the streets were empty except for a few cars driving by.

Her first inclination was to walk toward the voices, but she didn't want to startle anyone. Gianna looked ahead and saw that the path curved. She could probably make out what was going on if she kept walking, so she hurried, trying to keep her heels from clamoring too loudly on the sidewalk.

As the path started to bend, the first thing she noticed was a mound of dirt right next to the tree and a shovel sitting on top of it. Maybe someone was digging up a time capsule? Or burying one? Although who did that in this kind of weather? And what about the comment Gianna had heard and the crying . . . ?

The scene grew even stranger. She saw a large woman wearing a tight black dress that looked like it had been painted on. Her breasts were popping out of the top and her giant white thighs were completely exposed—definitely not a good look for her. Gianna imagined the woman's true dress size was well into the double digits, and this dress, if she had to guess, was a size six or eight.

Next to her was another woman adorned in black. She was a stick with black, bobbed hair, and while her dress fit, it looked like something a person would find on the Fashion Police Page of *US Weekly* magazine. Gianna could just imagine the caption beneath it, something like, "Susan Boyle Wants her Frock Back." The bodice sagged off of her shoulder, and the huge billowy skirt kept getting caught in the wind and blowing up.

These two women were both staring toward the trunk of the tree. Gianna took a few more steps up the path and then saw a tall, strikingly beautiful blonde woman, holding the white dress that Gianna had seen on the ground. She was also in black, in a strapless bouffant getup that made her look like she should be heading to the ballroom instead of the park.

Gianna watched as the heavyset gal and the woman with the bob guided the attractive blonde over to the mound of dirt. *What in the world?* She pulled out her glasses from her jacket pocket to get an even better look, but just as she put them on, the beautiful blonde gal, holding the white dress, looked over her shoulder toward Gianna.

Gianna's first reaction was to look over *her* shoulder to see what Blondie was checking out, but then she realized that the woman was probably staring at her. Gianna was so used to being invisible. On the restaurant floor her black attire was like a cloak of invisibility. People carried on with their conversations when she wore it, whether she was standing there or not.

But she was *not* in Hayden's. And she was completely embarrassed that she'd been caught staring at these women. So, she pretended to get a call on her cell phone and then took off, hurrying down the path toward her restaurant.

# eight
# NOW

**Kendall** stood above the hole in the ground that her best friends, Tina and Ellie, had dug, and she sniffled as she held her wedding dress against her chest. On any other day she would have been completely embarrassed that a woman had just seen her standing in a public park in a black dress that made her feel like she was drowning in tulle, but she was too consumed with her own grief this evening to care.

"I don't know if I can part with it," she said softly, holding the dress even tighter against her. Tears spilled down her cheeks and dribbled off her chin.

"Yes, you can," Ellie said. "Tina and I will help you." Ellie bent over (her skintight dress almost ripping straight up the seam) and dropped the bottom of Kendall's wedding gown into the ground. "There. See?" she said. "It's not that bad."

Kendall stared down into the hole at the beautiful white dress, now covered in dirt, and started to lose it again.

*How could he have done this? . . . To her?* She knew it was ridiculous, to think this last part. No one was immune to being dumped. But in her twenty-eight years, it had seemed like she might be the exception.

It was because she was beautiful. Not the kind of beautiful everyone aspired to be. Kendall had always envied girls who were just the right dose of pretty. She had a friend growing up who was like this. Joanna Jones. Joanna always had girls flocking to her for beauty and lifestyle tips. Boys asked her out constantly. Even jobs seemed to fall easily into her lap later in life. (It didn't seem right that the workforce worked this way, but it did *seem* to work this way.)

Kendall was *too* beautiful. Which was like being too skinny. Or too anything, really. It was more of a hindrance than a blessing. Not that she could complain about this to anyone. No one wanted to hear a pretty woman complain about her looks! But if she could, this was what she would tell them: She'd had to be extra nice to women all her life because they automatically assumed she wasn't a nice person. (Where on earth this stereotype came from she had no idea. Were most pretty women really not nice? Or did jealousy cause people to not treat them nicely, as her mother had once suggested, and then they were rude in return?)

She'd always had to ask boys out herself.

"I thought you'd never say yes," one boyfriend admitted when she asked why he didn't approach her if he thought she was cute.

And when applying to jobs she'd had to work hard to prove she wasn't just a "dumb blonde." Once, she'd been in the running for a marketing position at a top company in Seattle and had spent weeks preparing for her interview. She researched all about the company's previous clients. She called a friend who used to work there to ask if she had any insight into potential interview questions Kendall might be asked. And even though she hated the fact that she felt she had to do this, she went shopping for a suit that wasn't too flattering, but looked "nice enough" so there would be no mistaking she was at that interview to be taken seriously for her brains, not her beauty.

She'd been thrilled when she made it through the first round of interviews, but before her second interview, as she waited outside the CEO's office to be called in, she overheard him telling a colleague that he was concerned she might just be a "pretty face."

Kendall had stood up and walked right out. All her hard work had felt like such a waste of time. She wouldn't work for someone who spoke about women like that.

But guys did not break up with girls who were too beautiful. At least in her experience. Until now.

"This was what you wanted," Ellie reminded her, wrapping her arm around Kendall's shoulders and pulling her in toward her busty chest.

"I know," Kendall sniffed. "I know."

She *did* want to bury the dress. She'd seen Tina and Ellie bury mementoes from failed relationships so many times. She'd heard them describe the relief. She'd *assumed* it would provide relief. That was why she had started this mock-funeral tradition back when they were all in high school.

Ellie had been going through her first serious heartbreak the summer of their sophomore year. "I want a box," Ellie had said. "I want to put Tyler in a box and never open it up again."

"That's exactly how I felt after Henry broke up with me last year," Tina had chimed in. They had all been at Ellie's house, watching *Sleepless in Seattle* and eating ice cream right out of the carton in her living room.

Kendall had felt so useless. She'd been happily dating Joey Manning, a junior football star, whom she later amicably broke up with at the end of his senior year right before he went off to college. At the time, she couldn't empathize with Ellie the way Tina could. And she was a doer. She didn't like to feel useless! Especially when it came to helping her friends. Tina and Ellie were such good friends. They'd fully embraced her for who she was when they met at high school orientation, and they weren't the least bit intimidated or jealous of her beauty. "Maybe a bit of your good looks will rub off on me," Ellie had once remarked playfully.

"What if we did box him up?" Kendall remembered saying.

The girls had given her puzzled looks.

"Humor me, okay?" she said.

She made Ellie gather all the mementoes from her relationship with Tyler, then drove the three of them to Goodwill and had the girls wait in the car while she rushed in and picked out the most ridiculous black dresses she could find.

"What are these for?" Tina and Ellie had asked when she returned with them.

"To wear to Tyler's funeral," she replied excitedly.

She grabbed a shovel from a hardware store next and then drove to a local park, where she dug a hole in the ground and had Ellie bury all of Tyler's stuff underneath a starlit sky.

While the funerals had obviously started as a joke, over the years, Ellie, who ended up becoming a therapist, had become convinced that they truly were the best way to deal with a broken heart, and when Kendall called her and told her what had happened, Ellie insisted that she have a funeral right away.

"So, what's the problem?" Ellie said. "Are you thinking now you'd rather return the dress than bury it? That's totally understandable. We can just bury the other small reminders of your relationship that you brought."

"No, that's not it," Kendall said. "It was only a couple hundred bucks and it's too late to return it."

She'd found it online months ago. It wasn't a wedding dress, just a stylish white dress that she had picked because she thought it would be perfect for the small ceremony. Kendall's parents couldn't afford to give her an extravagant wedding, so she and her Ex (Ellie had already reminded her twice to never speak or think of his name again. "He's dead to us!" she told her in the car ride over) had kept their guest list to fifty people and planned to host the ceremony and reception under heated tents in the spacious grassy backyard of the house her former fiancé grew up in to save money on the venue.

"What's the reason then?" Ellie asked.

Kendall blinked back tears. "It's just that I don't want to accept that it's really over. I keep hoping he's going to have a change of heart and call me to tell me he just had cold feet and that this whole thing was a mistake."

Her Ex's decision to jilt her didn't make any sense. Just a week earlier they'd looked at houses together with a real estate agent in Seattle, where the two of them lived.

That afternoon, her Ex had pinched her as they stood in the spacious kitchen of the sunny yellow house in Fremont that the two of them liked best and said, "I couldn't be happier, you know that?"

"Me either," Kendall said, wrapping her arm around him.

There had been no signs.

She believed it was called ghosting, what he'd done. She'd heard friends at work use the term when describing what happened when men they'd been happily seeing suddenly disappeared from their lives without explanations. Kendall had always thought it sounded so horrible. She couldn't believe men did such things! Now it had happened to her. The day before her wedding. Maybe this was karma for having escaped heartbreak her entire life.

She bet girlfriends from all walks of her life would see it this way—not Tina and Ellie, of course, or any of her true friends. But the former sorority sisters at UW who Kendall had seemed to upset when she dated one of the senior fraternity presidents her freshman year. And her single, female co-workers at Amazon, who had all been pining over her Ex his first day at the office, only to find out the next day that he'd asked Kendall out that morning. She'd heard several of them in the bathroom that afternoon talking about it. "Of course, he picked her. Every guy would probably want to date me too if I looked like that. Lucky bitch!"

Would they silently gloat when she changed her Facebook status from engaged to single?

Even if she never shared the details, everyone would know that Kendall had been the one who had been dumped because she'd been head-over-heels since the very beginning of the relationship. That was the only reason she agreed to go out with the man. She'd promised herself she wasn't going to date anyone the year they had met. *No boys! No distractions! A year for me. To find myself.*

She had needed to find herself. She was twenty-eight, but she had no idea what made her really tick. Or what was most exciting to her about getting up in the morning. But then, one electric moment in an elevator changed that plan. Had her Ex sensed that he was marrying a woman who didn't truly know who she was yet? Was that what this was about?

"But that's why we're out here," Ellie said, pulling her back to the task at hand. "So that you *do* accept that this is really over. Acceptance is the first step to getting over the depression this break-up is bound to put you in."

"Oh please, enough of the therapist mumbo-jumbo," Tina said, jumping into the conversation. Her black bobbed hair blew furiously in the wind. "Why don't we just call this whole thing off, and I'll go find the prick. I swear if I ever see him again I will beat his—"

"Tina!" Ellie cut her off, flashing a look of disapproval. "You know the rules. This is a memorial. We are saying goodbye. No bad feelings. Be respectful of Kendall. This was her fiancé for God's sake."

"He just stood up my best friend the day before her wedding, and you expect me to do nothing?"

"What's the point?" Ellie said, gesturing toward the ground. "He's already 'dead.' We know once a man leaves, there is no hope for a resurrection. The relationship is over, Tina. Let's help Kendall put it to rest."

"Well, I would certainly feel better if I could let him know what would happen if he ever chose to miraculously rise up from his grave." Tina pounded her fist in her hand.

"Do I need to remind you how supportive we all were at your last funeral when we buried your Ex?" Ellie countered. "Better to put Kendall's reminders of the relationship under the ground now, so she can move on." She nodded toward the hole they had dug. "Come on now, Kendall. Let's do this."

Kendall drew in a deep breath and with the help of Ellie, laid the dress to rest. Ellie patted Kendall's back when she started to cry again.

"Sweetie, it's going to be okay," Ellie said. "You will find love again. I promise. I had to bury ten men before I met Saul."

"We know," sighed Tina flippantly. "We were there."

Kendall proceeded to toss the rest of her reminders of the relationship into the hole—the pictures she had of the two of them together that she had kept in her wallet, the few ivory-and-black wedding announcements she'd brought in her suitcase, the heart-shaped Tiffany's necklace she'd received as a one-year anniversary gift—and when she was finished, Ellie picked up the shovel and started to cover all of it up.

Kendall stood beside Tina and watched. Her whole body was shaking from the cold, the shock, the events of the past six hours, and she suddenly wished she had a warm jacket on instead of this ridiculous $11.99-thrift-store dress that Ellie had picked up right before the ceremony and insisted she wear.

"Black dresses are part of the tradition," Ellie had said when Kendall protested about wearing it. The dresses they usually wore for such occasions were hanging up in their closets at the house in Seattle they all lived in together. "It'll help you heal faster if you put it on, Kendall." So, Kendall had.

When Ellie was finished covering the grave, she yanked a tissue out of her purse and brought it over to Kendall.

"All right," she said. "We're almost done. This is almost over."

*Almost over.* What an understatement. The funeral might have been almost over, but the grieving process had just begun. There would be long sleepless nights, unexpected tears when she went to places the two of them had frequented together, an almost unbearable void in her life. Not to mention the walk of shame when she went back to work. Talk about fodder for the coffee room! She couldn't think of that just yet.

Kendall cleared her throat, knowing it was her turn to speak. To close each of these mock-funerals, the heartbroken woman recited a one-line eulogy. It was the same line every time, a quote from Tennyson, but Kendall wasn't sure she could get it out.

"You can do this," Ellie encouraged her.

Kendall whimpered. "I'm not sure that I can."

"Just try," Ellie said.

Kendall blotted her eyes with the tissue and then tried to muster up the strength.

"It's better to have loved and lost," she started before choking up. Her tangled blond hair blew out of the loose bun it was in and flew in a million different directions like it was pummeling fate for what had happened, wanting to blame something, someone.

"Give it one more try," Ellie encouraged, resting her hand on the small of Kendall's back.

Kendall closed her eyes. "It's better to have loved and lost," she began again, "than to never have loved at all." The words tasted bitter, and she bent over, wanting to vomit.

"It's going to be okay," Ellie said, trying to reassure her.

Kendall knew that Ellie was right—eventually she would recover—but right now, her heart ached with what could have been.

A couple of minutes later, Tina bent down and handed Kendall the flowers that the girls had brought to put on top of the grave. Pink peonies. Just like the ones that were supposed to be the center of Kendall's wedding bouquet. Kendall laid them on top of the mound on the ground and broke down again.

She stayed there, crouched down, for what felt like forever, and then her friends helped her up to her feet.

"Come on," Ellie said. "I noticed there's a dessert restaurant right up the street. Let's go get some cake."

Kendall nodded, keeping her eyes on the grave as her friends helped her hobble to the car, knowing that her relationship was really over and wishing, more than anything, that that wasn't the case.

# nine
# NOW

**Gianna** burst through the back door of Hayden's and stepped into the kitchen. She was dying to tell *someone* what she had just seen in the park, but before she could, vases filled with blue hydrangeas reminded her of her own personal crisis. There were a couple of vases on the butcher-block prep table in the center of the room, a few others arranged on top of the cabinets where the extra china plates and crystal glasses were kept, and two perched on one of the ovens.

"Oh my God," she murmured. *Were these for her from Peter? They had to be. They were her favorite flower. Was he in the kitchen? Was he going to pop the question right this second?*

"Finally, you're here!" Her kitchen staff flocked to her and began peppering her with questions, as if they were journalists at a press conference and she was someone famous.

"We heard Charli called. Did you call her back? Do you think she's going to show?"

"Have you heard from Jack? Do you think he's going to show?"

"Peter left these flowers for you. Are they because of The Reservation?"

"He's so perfect. How is he so perfect?"

She was half-expecting photographers to appear and camera lights to start flashing, when Valerie walked into the kitchen carrying a stack of dirty plates in her hands.

"Val?" Gianna turned toward her. "What are you doing here?"

She didn't mean *here*, as in, here *in the restaurant.* Valerie had been working at Hayden's part-time for almost two years. She'd called Gianna completely hysterical a few months after she had the twins (or maybe the twins had been hysterical, Gianna couldn't remember). One of the twins was always trying to out-cry the other. "Perhaps they inherited this competitive gene from their mother," Gianna liked to tease Val. Valerie was the most competitive person Gianna knew. Growing up, she'd always done the extra credit, outsold everyone in their Girl Scout troop in cookie sales, and ran the fastest mile in PE class.

"How did I think I was cut out to be a stay-at-home mom?" she remembered Val saying. "At least when I was working at Rubicon, I was getting paid to be in a room I couldn't stand. This room's so much worse at this moment, and I'm making nothing!" (Valerie later took back this comment. "About the other day, I love the boys. You know I love the boys. I was just running on no sleep. Sometimes they drive me a bit mad when I'm running on no sleep.")

It had been the first time in months that Gianna could remember feeling grateful she wasn't in Valerie's shoes. Val's entire pregnancy had been a bit tough on Gianna. She'd been happy for her, of course. But as she'd watched as Val's belly swelled and took her shopping for the nursery and for cute onesies for the boys, she'd felt occasional sharp pangs of jealousy. No matter how much you loved a person, it was difficult to be around someone who had what you desperately wanted, even if it was just a version of it.

"You could go back to work," Gianna had said, knowing Rubicon would gladly take her back, but that Val probably wouldn't want to go back. The only thing she'd liked about her job in sales was the regular Friday afternoon happy hours and the bonuses she received from routinely outselling her quota.

"Can I work for you?" Val had asked. "Just a few days a week to get me out of the house. You only have to pay me enough that I can afford a nanny."

Gianna had gladly given her shifts. Val was a nice addition to the team. She brought in the most tips and sold more off the menu than any of her staff. Plus, it was nice to get to spend so much time together again, like they used to when they were little and when they lived together in that cozy brick house in Southeast Portland after both graduating college. And Gianna knew this arrangement wouldn't last forever. Valerie had been experimenting with making and selling greeting cards on Etsy, and business was picking up. Gianna could see her being too busy to come in soon.

What Gianna had meant was *why was Val working a shift tonight?* Valerie was not scheduled to work on Fridays. She and Richard ordered Chinese food on Friday nights and ate it in their pajamas on their living room floor in front of a fire. It was a date-night tradition that began their third week seeing each other. An unexpected wind storm had caused them to rethink their plan to go out to dinner at a Chinese restaurant where Richard had made a reservation, so they had ordered in instead.

"There was so much intimate conversation!" Val had gushed the morning after, as she and Gianna power-walked through the fallen branches from the storm. "The fire was lovely. We must have shared two bottles of wine! It felt like the rest of the world didn't exist, and it was just the two of us. We even did it on his carpet. Right there, in front of the fire."

Lately, though, these dinners seemed to have lost their romantic luster. Valerie said sometimes she and Richard didn't even light the fire. Richard often turned the TV on instead. Or she got up in the middle of the meal to feed one of the twins.

Was that what all marriages turned into after a couple of years? Interrupted date nights? Unlit fires? No passion? No romance? Was she making the whole idea of marriage a bigger deal than it was? Maybe good enough *was* enough.

"I paid Annie fifty bucks for her shift so I could be here for the big Reservation," Valerie said now.

"Seriously?" Gianna said. "Why on earth would you do that?"

She could have just gotten a table in the restaurant to spy on Charli and Jack's table. Several of her staff who weren't scheduled tonight had done this. Unless . . . she knew about the proposal, and Peter had asked for her help to pull it off. And if Valerie knew, then her mother probably knew.

Oh no, her mother!

Gianna could just imagine her mom's reaction if she were to call her and tell her she'd broken things off with Peter. There would be tears. Lots and lots of tears. Her mother seemed to view Peter as Gianna's last hope for getting married while she could still have babies. Gianna often felt that way about him too, which was a bit of a problem.

Then her mom would probably ask what she was supposed to tell her friends. For some reason, what her friends thought still mattered quite a bit to her mother. Weren't women supposed to outgrow caring about what other women thought about them? Or was that just something moms told their high school daughters to help them build up self-esteem, when really, they all still sought each other's approval as much as the next insecure teen?

"My friends ask me every week at Bunko for an update on your love life," her mom once protested when Gianna told her that she didn't appreciate being interrogated about her relationship status each time they spoke on the phone. Her mom still asked for updates on Gianna's love life all the time, so she didn't doubt that her mom's friends still grilled her.

She knew the inquiries were well-intentioned. Either people were just trying to make polite conversation like Nell and Mark Carter, two of her regulars at Hayden's, who had been married thirty years and asked her every time they came in how it was possible that someone hadn't snatched her up yet. Or people were hopeful they could find her somebody, like the Toddler and Teas. This was the name of Val's group of mom friends (who really needed to rename their friend group, Gianna thought, every time she scrolled through Valerie's Facebook). They did a whole lot more than drink tea with their toddlers—they hosted *Bachelor* viewing parties, spent warm summer afternoons boating on the Willamette River, took rainy-day trips to Powell's bookstore.

Before she met Peter, every time Gianna got together with them, they went through their phones and their Facebooks trying to brainstorm whom they could set her up with.

"What about Phil? He's the dad of one of Chloe's friends from school. No, wait, he's still going through a divorce. Maybe in a few months once it's finalized!"

"Derik's cousin was in rehab a while back, but he's out and just starting to date again. What about him?"

It was quite horrible hearing their suggestions.

Well-intentioned or not, it bothered Gianna that women's choices were always up for debate. If you were married with children but no job, people wanted to know what you did all day or when you were returning to work. And if you were like Gianna, with a career and no husband or children, people wanted to know when you were going to settle down.

Gianna loved her life! She didn't *need* a man. She just wanted one. The right one. Which might or might not be Peter.

"Are you okay?" Valerie asked. "You look pale."

"I'm fine," Gianna lied. She didn't want to share her doubts with Valerie. Like everyone else, Val was Team Peter.

After she and Peter officially became a couple and Val met him for the first time, Val took Gianna out for celebratory drinks. "Here's to kissing enough frogs," she'd said, raising her glass of champagne in the air. "You've finally found a prince!"

If she knew of Gianna's doubts, she'd start replaying all of Gianna's dating fiascos before she met Peter. Gianna could already hear her.

"Oh no, ohhh no," she'd say. "It took you *how* long to find a guy like Peter?"

"A very long time," Gianna would say.

"And you're how old?"

"Thirty-seven," Gianna would reply, humoring her.

"Right," Valerie would say. "You cannot afford to lose Peter. Don't do this to yourself."

Her server, Claire, who had seen *The Notebook* too many times, sidled up beside her now. "This is turning out to be the most romantic night," she swooned. She was also in love for the first time with a guy from her political science classes at Portland State, so everything had a rose-colored tint to it. "Oh, before I forget, Peter left this for you," she said, pulling out a note from her pocket.

"Is he here, now?" Gianna asked, trying to play it cool.

"No, he just dropped these off. Said he'd be back later."

*Flowers for my love to add to the romance tonight*, it read. *Here's to happily ever after! xo Peter.*

Happily ever after. *Did hers include him?*

"Gianna! Gianna! Come quick!" Barbara, one of her older, but most spirited servers barged into the kitchen, her red hair like a flame, igniting her entrance.

"What?" Gianna said. "Is Charli here? Or Jack?" *Or Peter?* She thought in a panic.

"No. But you have to see this." Barbara peered out through the window in the kitchen door.

"What is it?"

"Just come here!"

"Geez did somebody die?" Valerie teased.

"Well," Barbara said, "maybe."

"What?" Gianna was suddenly in full-blown panic mode. She hurried over to the door along with Valerie and almost everyone else in the kitchen—her dishwashers, her two pastry chefs, a couple of other servers.

"I know Portland's weird," Barbara said as they all peered out. "But that sure is something you don't see every day."

Following Rosie toward a table in the back of the restaurant was the group of women dressed in black that Gianna had seen in the park. The beautiful blonde was crying and leaning on her friends like they were crutches. Watching her, Gianna couldn't help but think how much she resembled her dessert, the Marjolaine—a six-layer hazelnut cake. In the same way that Blondie relied on her two friends to keep her from toppling over, the Marjolaine relied on the chocolate mousse and the hazelnut-praline crème that were piped between each layer.

"Oh my gosh, I know them!" Gianna said as everyone behind her giggled.

"You do?" Valerie turned to look at her.

"Well, I don't know them know them, but I saw them on my walk to work."

She explained the scene in the park to everyone—the crying, the white dress on the ground, the shovel on top of the mound of dirt.

Rosie showed them to a table directly across from the table reserved for Charli and Jack on the other side of the fireplace.

"Ah, lucky!" Valerie said. "You got them in your section, Gianna."

Gianna didn't usually wait on specific tables, but tonight, because of The Reservation, she'd made an exception.

"You want to trade?" Valerie asked. "I'll take the long-lost lovers' table and wait on the women in the ridiculous black outfits, and you can have the bickering married couple and awkward first date I've got."

"Not a chance," Gianna said. Not when she might get the whole story behind these ladies' actions. She watched them for a couple more seconds and then clapped her hands together. "All right everybody, back to work."

The employees behind her dispersed, and Gianna hurried out to the restaurant floor to return Charli's call.

Visit sincerelyriley.com/scene-4 to see scenes from these chapters unfold and to Shop the Book™.

## ten
# THEN

**Charli** had been so focused on mounting her pancreatic tissue slides, on selecting and peeling apart pieces of tissue, washing them with dark blue dyes and lighter pinks, and carefully placing them between two slender pieces of glass, that she didn't even hear Jack walk into the biology lab.

"I feel like a jealous boyfriend," he said, startling her. "Sometimes I think you love this place more than you love me."

Charli swiveled around on her stool. The minute she saw Jack in a suit jacket and slacks with a bouquet of roses in his hands, her heart sunk.

"Oh my gosh . . . our anniversary dinner . . ." It had been a full year since her and Jack's first kiss, and they were supposed to celebrate tonight. Jack had told her earlier he'd made a dinner reservation at McMenamins, the nicest restaurant in Corvallis, for six o'clock. She looked up at the clock on the white wall above the cabinets filled with beakers, flasks, tubes, droppers, and all sorts of laboratory equipment and saw that it was almost seven now.

"Jack, I'm so sorry. I completely lost track of time."

"That seems to happen a lot when you're in here."

"I know. I feel awful." When Charli stepped through the doors of the lab, it was like she entered another world where minutes and hours didn't exist. She'd get in a zone researching, and time stood still. "I thought I set an alarm on my phone, but it must not have gone off. Do you hate me?"

"No. Don't worry about it." He gave her a reassuring smile. "I only booked that restaurant because I thought you'd like it. Guess I should have just packed a picnic and brought it to the lab. That probably would have been more up your alley, huh?"

"If bringing food into the lab was allowed . . . then yeah," she laughed.

Jack started to walk around the room, past microscopes, test tubes, computers, Timmy the skeleton.

"What is it about this room that you love so much?" he asked.

"What is it about a baseball field that *you* love so much? This stool right here, it's like my pitcher's mound. Sitting on it day after day, understanding something so small and so complicated more intimately with each hour gives me a rush."

"It just looks kind of . . . well . . ."

"Boring?" She got that a lot.

Jack nodded.

"Trust me, it's not. Discovering something that might, in one small way or another, be used one day to save lives is such a thrill. Come over here. Let me show you."

Charli had Jack sit down on her stool and look through the ocular lens at the small slide of pancreatic islet B-cells she was analyzing.

"It's kind of like looking through a kaleidoscope," Jack commented.

"Yeah, sort of. Except I'm not just looking for pretty patterns." She explained how she was studying the tissue as part of a research project for the university to try to better understand the underlying cellular mechanisms in the pancreatic cells of a diabetic rat. "What I understand here will eventually help all of us make more sense of a much bigger issue."

"I guess I can see how that's exciting," Jack said.

Charli took a deep breath of the sterilized air. "It *is* exciting. This place is where I feel most alive. Most excited. Most inspired."

"What about when you're with me? Don't I inspire you? Don't I make you excited?"

"Obviously," she winked. "But it's an excitement and inspiration of a different sort."

"But if you had to choose, hypothetically speaking, would you rather spend the rest of your days in this lab filled with all the tools you'd need to make ground-breaking discoveries, or spend the rest of your days outside the lab with me?"

"That's an impossible 'would you rather' question."

"Come on, you wouldn't pick me?" Jack stood up and wrapped his hands around her waist, pulling her toward him.

When he started to nibble on her ear, she folded. "Now you're swaying me."

He continued to kiss her, his warm breath tickling her and eventually making her giggle.

"I'm only kidding," he finally said. "I would never make you choose between me and this room. But for tonight, can you come with me?"

She threaded her fingers through his. "Of course. Do you have another place in mind?"

"I was thinking on the way over here that it might be kind of fun to drive in to Portland for the night."

"All the way to Portland?"

"It'll only take a little over an hour at this time. We could pick something easy up for dinner on the way and then go to Hayden's for dessert."

"Ooooo, I like where your head's at." They visited Hayden's every time they went home, but it had been a while since they'd been last. She and Jack always shared a slice of the Chocolate Mint Cloud, a silky mint mouse wedged on top of a chocolate cake base, and Charli was suddenly craving it.

"Great," Jack said. "How can I help you clean up?"

Charli had him put all of her notebooks and pencils back into her book bag as she cleaned off and carefully disinfected her area, covered the microscope, and replaced her tweezers and unused slides. She was excited to spend the rest of her night with him—she really was—but she had to admit that the thought of getting back into this room tomorrow was equally exciting.

—

Jack knew his focus should have been on the pitch he was about to throw to start the game. Not only was it the first inning of the sold-out national championship versus UCLA at Rosenblatt Stadium in Omaha, but the scouts for most of the major league teams were in the stands watching Jack pitch, and he was eager to impress them. Jack had been drafted by the Philadelphia Phillies just a few weeks earlier, but he'd turned the offer down because he was only a junior and wanted to graduate from college before he went pro. He had to continue to play well to keep other scouts from other teams interested. But he couldn't get the news Charli had shared with him the night before out of his head.

As the first hitter for the Bruins tapped his bat on home plate, Jack stepped off the pitcher's mound, grabbed the rosin bag, and took a few deep breaths.

"Everything will work out," he mumbled to himself. "Charli and I will be okay."

But would they be? Really? The doubt consumed him.

Jack wished he had never made that comment about their future late last night in his hotel room after Charli snuck over. His coach had implemented a ten o'clock player curfew, but Jack needed Charli to help calm his nerves, so she'd climbed up to his balcony on the second story from the patio outside her first-floor room.

"This is just like when we were kids," Jack had said as he pulled her inside. Charli used to sneak over all the time.

"Yeah, only your window didn't have thorn bushes right beneath it," she said. Blood was trickling down Charli's leg.

"Ouch. Let's get you cleaned up." Jack draped one of her arms around his shoulder and carried her into the bathroom, setting her on the tile sink. As he cleaned the cut with a wet hand towel, Charli got him re-psyched for his game, feeding him a pep-talk like no one else could. "What would I do without you?" he said. "Thank God you're moving with me wherever I get drafted. I don't know how I could play if you weren't around."

"Yeah," Charli said softly. Too softly. Then she changed the subject. "Want to go watch TV or something?"

"And completely avoid my last comment? That is the plan, isn't it?" he asked. They'd discussed their post-college life before, plenty of times. Charli would move to the city Jack got drafted to. They'd get a place together. She would find a science-related job. He saw himself proposing a year or two after that. There was no doubt in his mind that Charli was The One. He got this feeling around her that he knew no one else could give him. Plus, she was his best friend.

"Let's just talk about it after the game, okay?" She reached for the doorknob.

"Just tell me now. Since when do you keep secrets from me?"

"Jack . . ."

"Just tell me, Charli."

She turned back toward him but avoided eye contact, staring instead at the white tile floor.

"I had a meeting with my academic advisor this morning. She just put some new ideas in my head."

"Like?"

"Like about applying to PhD programs after college. She thinks that with my grades and the research I've done that I could get into a fully funded program so that I wouldn't have to pay anything.

I was going to tell you about it later. I just didn't want to mess with your head before the game."

All of a sudden the bathroom felt stuffy, and Jack's forehead began to sweat.

"I didn't even know you wanted to get your PhD."

"It's something I've always thought about, but never seriously until this morning. I don't know, Jack, talking about it got me pretty excited. It's something I think I need to look into."

"I see. Do you mind if I step outside for a second?" He walked past her and out onto the small iron balcony. A sliver of moon stared back at him, and a warm breeze rippled through his blue cotton shirt and athletic shorts.

Jack tried to keep his head about this. If getting her PhD was what Charli wanted, he didn't want to make her feel bad for that. One of the things he loved about Charli was her independence, and he admired that she always pursued her passion. Those things made her stand out from other girls he'd dated in the past, and they made Charli, Charli. But he couldn't help feeling depressed about the news. He'd had this clear picture of their future together, and now he didn't know what was going to happen.

Charli came up behind him and rested her hand gently on his back.

"I'll apply to schools in all the cities where you think you might get drafted," she said. "This doesn't have to change anything."

But it *could* change things. Jack knew this. Charli had to too, even if she didn't want to admit it.

The roaring applause from the crowd brought Jack back into the stadium. His ears rang with the noise, and he looked up into the stands at the sea of Beaver fans dressed in orange and black, cheering like crazy. Glancing over his shoulder, he eyed each of the outfielders jogging in place and pounding their hands into their gloves. His blood started to pump more quickly, and he stepped back up to the mound, inhaling the smells of the ballpark—raked dirt, trimmed grass, nerves, sweat. God, he loved this. Being out here. In a big game. With adrenaline running through him.

But he loved Charli too. And the rush he felt when he was with her. Why did this have to be so complicated? What would happen if he had to choose between baseball and the girl he loved?

The batter, a guy who looked like he belonged more on a football field, tapped home plate two times with his bat and then stood in his ready stance waiting for Jack to throw. Jack eyed his catcher's, Mike's, mitt for his signal. *Fastball, inside.*

He wanted to say that he'd choose Charli. After growing up with his dad picking his career over him, Jack had promised himself that if his career ever came between him and someone he loved, he would always choose that person. But the choice wasn't as easy as Jack had always thought it should have been.

He swiped his cleat on the dirt to create a grip for his foot, feeling for the first time what it was like to be in his dad's shoes. Then he wound up and threw the ball with everything he had in him. Whoosh. Smack.

"Strike one!" The ump yelled, turning to his right and bringing down his arm.

The crowd erupted into applause, and a grin played across Jack's face.

Jack knew in his heart that he would always love Charli—she meant more to him than any girl ever would—but, as much as it killed him to admit it, he loved this game just as much. And truthfully, he wasn't sure that he could ever give pitching up.

—

The following December Charli stood outside her dingy two-bedroom house in Corvallis next to her mailbox and stared in disbelief at the letter from The Medical University of South Carolina that she'd just torn open. After an initial application to their oncology PhD program, a secondary application, and a flight to Charleston for an in-person interview . . . she'd gotten in. Better yet, she'd been granted a generous stipend and been allotted two thirds of her tuition in exchange for research assistantship work.

She read the letter one more time just to make sure the offer was real. It seemed too good to be true. Three other schools had offered Charli admission into their doctoral programs thus far, but this particular one was the school Charli wanted to go to the most. Not only was it in South Carolina, near the city Jack thought he might get drafted to (Myrtle Beach, where the Atlanta Brave's AA Minor League team played) but much of its research focused on cancer and the development of vaccines. With her mom's recent breast cancer diagnosis, Charli knew this was the area she wanted to specialize in.

This opportunity felt like a personal calling. She saw herself working long hours in the lab and making new friends with like-minded people in her program who would understand her nerd side and not make fun of her when she did things like compare the bacterial species of yogurt cultures in the grocery store before deciding which yogurt to buy, something Jack had teased her about just the other day. Or when she picked up a household item, such as a bottle of Lysol Disinfecting Wipes, and proceeded to state the gram reaction of each of the microbes that it could kill. That fact might have impressed a trivia team, but it had had her roommate, Elaine—who couldn't stand science—laughing at her a few weeks ago when she came home and heard Charli in the kitchen rattling those off while she scrubbed their kitchen table.

The thought of exploring Charleston, a completely new city, was exciting to her as well. During her twenty-four hour trip there for her interview, she'd been impressed by the sparkling views of the Cooper River, the rich history (and food), the horse-drawn carriages that trotted through the old, restored city blocks, and the live oak trees with Spanish moss hanging off of them like wedding veils. And with Jack only a couple hours away, he'd have the opportunity to explore it with her whenever he had time off.

Charli looked up from the letter, and the cloudy winter day took on a new vibrancy. Feeling more thrilled about her future than ever, she jumped into her car with the letter and started driving to Jack's. She couldn't wait to tell him the news.

—

Jack couldn't believe it. His coach had just called him and told him that it was looking like he was going to be drafted by the San Francisco Giants, and that he'd play on their Class-A advanced team in San Jose come summer. For the past few months he'd been under the impression that the Atlanta Braves were going to take him, and that he'd play in their Minor League system until he got called up, but the scout for the Giants had just told Jack's coach that they were going to trade two of their Minor League pitchers come summer and were now interested in bringing Jack on.

Jack had been a Giants fan his whole life. Growing up in Portland, which didn't have a professional baseball team, he'd followed the Giants since he was a kid. One of his few treasured memories with his dad was flying to San Francisco for a game when he was a freshman in high school and sitting right behind the Giants' dug-out. Though his dad must have dropped a fortune on the tickets, they'd had the best time eating garlic fries and foot-long hot dogs and seeing the players up that close.

In college, he'd also made the drive from Corvallis to San Francisco a few times with some of his teammates to watch the Giants play under the lights at AT&T Park.

Just thinking about suiting up in a Giants' uniform gave Jack chills. This was a dream come true for him. And Charli had applied to a program near San Jose, right? He was almost positive of it. He picked up his phone to call her. He couldn't wait to tell her the news.

—

Charli practically knocked down Jack's front door she pounded on it so hard.

When he answered, he had his phone to his ear. "I'm calling you," he said. "I have something exciting to tell you!"

"Me too." Charli stepped inside with her letter.

"Really? You go first."

"No, no, you!" She saw excitement all over his face and wanted to know the cause of it more than she wanted to share her own.

"You sure?" He snapped his phone shut.

"Yes. Tell me!"

"Okay," Jack said. "The scout for the San Francisco Giants just contacted Coach Blaire. He thinks they're going to draft me!"

Charli dropped the letter onto the hardwood floor, her stomach sinking. "I just got accepted into MUSC in South Carolina. I thought you were going to the Braves, and that you'd be playing in Myrtle Beach until you got called up."

"Please tell me you applied to a school in or near San Jose," Jack said.

"Yeah," Charli said breathlessly. "To Cal Berkeley. But I haven't heard back yet. And I'm not as excited about their program as I am about MUSC's."

The color drained from Jack's cheeks. "I'm not as excited at the prospect of playing for Atlanta as I am about playing for the Giants."

Charli's head started to spin. This couldn't be happening. *No, no, no, no, noooo.* She walked into the living room and took a seat on the hearth of the old stone fireplace that Jack typically kept lit.

As she stared into the blazing flames, she tried to tell herself that this wasn't the end of the world. She and Jack would work this out.

One of them would just have to give a little. And since she loved Jack too much to ask him to sacrifice his baseball career, that person would have to be her.

"I'll just throw my letter in the fire," Charli said, dangling it over the wire screen. "Forget I got in."

"No way!" Jack grabbed her arm, filling her with immediate relief. "You'd resent me forever. I couldn't ask you to do that. And besides, we don't know with absolute certainty that the Giants are going to take me yet. Look, maybe I could have Coach Blaire tell them I'm not interested."

"And resent *me* forever for following me and not your dream? I don't think so."

Jack sat down beside her. "I'm not supposed to pick my career over someone I love. And you're not supposed to let me. Remember that promise I asked you to keep me honest on?"

Of course she remembered. He'd made the request at his first high school baseball game.

"You're not your dad though," Charli assured him. "You're young, and you're supposed to go after your dream at this age."

"I am?"

"Yes, we both are."

That was what everyone said at least. Just last quarter in a creative writing class, her professor, Dr. Simonson, had spent her final lecture talking about how a person's twenties were for taking risks and for going after what he or she truly wanted. "Dream big," she'd said. "Because failing in your twenties is not so bad. Most of you don't have children yet to take care of, and your parents might still let you move home if you screw up. So, write that novel. Move to that city you've always wanted to go to. Join a band. See the world. Take a job that sounds exciting, even if it doesn't sound the most practical. If you've always wanted to be a doctor, apply to med school. If you've dreamed of being a teacher, get that credential."

Her parents too, had been enthusiastic about her pursuing her dream when she first mentioned that she was considering getting her PhD.

"We think it's great," her mom had said over the phone. "This is the time in your life to do something like this for yourself, Charli. And to live up to your full potential. Go after it, honey!"

She'd even read an article in the *Huffington Post* recently that had been titled, "Twenty Things for a Person to Do in her Twenties." Most of the bullet points were about following a dream, taking risks, and being selfish to figure out who you really were and what really mattered.

Jack hesitated. "So, what then, we do long distance?"

"That was my other thought too," Charli said. Although that didn't sit well in her gut either. Her PhD program would take five years, maybe more, to complete. That was a long time for their relationship to make it when they were almost 3,000 miles apart.

Charli saw visions of them fighting on the phone because they were both frustrated by how difficult it was to be apart. And of three-day weekends spent in crowded airports commuting across the country for a day or two together. She imagined herself rearranging her schedule and cancelling plans with new friends so that she could talk on the phone with Jack and make sure they got quality time together. And she guessed she wouldn't dedicate herself fully to her studies with a big part of her head and her heart in California.

She didn't voice her doubts to Jack, afraid they might upset him, and agreed that long-distance would be their hypothetical "if Jack gets drafted to the Giants" plan. But long after she left Jack's house she kept ruminating about it, and late that night as she was tossing and turning in bed, she convinced herself that there *had* to be a better plan. Something she just hadn't thought of yet.

—

What Charli loved most about her work in the lab was that for every problem there was a solution to be found. Earlier in the year, for example, she'd had an experiment fail over and over again, and she finally realized it was because she hadn't accounted for the humidity inside the lab. After realizing her oversight, she completely redesigned the experiment to take place under a hood where moisture could be more easily controlled, and everything quickly fell into place.

So, the day after her conversation with Jack, she retreated to the lab with the problem of their future on her brain, and she sat down at a stool. *What else could we do?* She contemplated, twirling her pencil around in between her fingers. *What haven't we thought of yet?*

It took her a week and twenty sheets of notebook paper filled with ideas, notes, and drawings before Charli had it. A different plan than long distance. A crazier plan. But something she thought might just work.

# eleven
# THEN

**Charli** was one minute into explaining her idea when Jack cut her off by holding up a finger.

"Hang on here, let me get this straight."

They were at Hayden's. Because the restaurant played into her idea, Charli had thought sharing it with Jack here would be sort of symbolic. She hadn't taken into account that the conversation might get heated—maybe even become emotional—and therefore would probably have been best to have in private.

"You're telling me you want to break up for five years and then set a date to meet up here—at Hayden's—after you've finished school to see about giving our relationship another shot? Are you out of your mind?" Jack practically yelled.

*Maybe*, Charli thought.

"I can't believe you want to break up with me!" he went on.

"No! Not break up!" Charli scooted closer to him, trying to ignore the stares from the customers dining at the surrounding tables. "Just put things with us on pause for a while," she explained.

"I can't just pause us," he said. "I'm in love with you."

She took a deep breath in, remembering that she'd had the same initial reaction when she first wrote the idea down on her notepad as she was brainstorming. She'd actually crossed it off the list with a giant X and shaken her head, saying to herself, "No. That's ridiculous. We couldn't do that." It had taken her time to warm up to it and to see all the positives. And now, after sitting with it for some time, she was convinced it was what made the most sense. Jack would get to that point too.

"Think of all the couples you know who have done long distance, Jack," she said, deciding to point out the flaws to their alternative. "Have any of them been successful at it?" Before he could even respond she brought up the example that first came to her mind. "Case in point, Patti and Justin." Patti, Charli's best friend from West Hills High spent all of high school dating a guy Justin, who she was head over heels for. Justin was equally in love with Patti, as was evidenced by the look in his eyes whenever he saw her, and the fact that he wanted to spend all his time with her. Despite that, they made it just six months at different colleges before calling it quits, with no hope of getting back together. Things got ugly between them when Justin saw pictures on Facebook of Patti with other guys at parties. She kept insisting she did nothing wrong, but Justin never believed her. "They don't even speak anymore, Jack. Do you want to risk that?"

"They were immature, Charli. Just out of high school. And I, for one, have a lot more confidence in what we have than in what Patti and Justin ever did."

"Age doesn't have anything to do with it," she said, thinking of another long-distance horror story. "The same thing happened to my cousin, Irene, who's twenty-eight, remember?" Her boyfriend, Steven, got transferred from his job in Portland to Austin, Texas, two years ago. Irene was sure that Steven was The One and that they were going to get married before he left, but at Christmas last year, after a few too many hard ciders, Irene confessed to Charli (who ended up telling Jack) that she'd actually cheated on Steven because she was so lonely. They were now both dating other people. "I don't want to end up like that, Jack. I don't want some mistake or the wear and tear of being apart to eat away at what we have, leaving nothing for us to hang on to. I think it's better to freeze what we have and then revisit it down the road."

Jack just rolled his eyes.

"Please, Jack," Charli said as she reached across the table and took his hand. "When have you ever heard someone say, 'We have the most wonderful long-distance relationship?'"

"Ryan and Tracy are making it work," Jack pointed out, bringing up his high school buddy and girlfriend who were still together. Charli had thought of them too as a positive example a while ago, but then she realized they were hardly in a long-distance relationship.

"They see each other every other weekend," she reminded him. Tracy was at USF in San Francisco, and Ryan went to school at Santa Clara University which was only about an hour away. "We'd be seeing each other maybe once or twice a year."

"We could see each other more than that," Jack said.

"Do you know how expensive plane tickets are from California to Charleston? They're like five hundred dollars. I'm not going to be making much money, Jack. And you won't be making much either to start out." Jack's contract wasn't for much. Just enough to live on.

"I'm sure I could borrow money from my dad."

"And be indebted to him in some way? Like you'd really want that?"

"Hey, I'm trying here."

"So am I! That's why I came up with this idea. This pact will allow us to each go out and fully embrace our new lives in our new cities. And then, if both of us still feel like being together is what we want after we've accomplished our dreams, we'll have a date to come back to each other on, with only good memories of our relationship to return to."

Jack shook his head, letting Charli know that she still hadn't sold him on her plan. She tried a different angle.

"We both have so much growing up to do as individuals, Jack. Do you feel that at all? I want to be with you later on—we have a forever kind of love—we've always said that. But I also want to become the best version of myself, which means going to MUSC and really being present while I'm there. If I don't, I'll lose you to regret. And if we do long distance I'm really concerned about losing you to anger and frustration."

She reached over for her water and took a sip as she searched Jack's face to see if her words had resonated, but he gave no indication. He started searching the room as if on the lookout for their waiter, to order a drink, or for Gianna, who had popped over earlier to say hi. Maybe he wanted her to weigh in on this. There was no doubt she would side with Jack and tell Charli her plan was nuts. She was always commenting what a cute couple she thought they were. And recently, she'd shared how envious she was that they'd found each other so early in life. She was thirty-two and hadn't met anyone even close to The One—which was shocking to Charli, given what a catch she thought Gianna was.

"Jack," she said, desperate to keep him checked into the conversation. "You have to see some of the benefits of what I'm talking about doing."

He didn't answer her.

"Jack?"

"Okay, fine!" he said, letting his hands fall down to his sides. "I get the benefits! I do. But Charli, what you're asking sounds impossible to me. You're not just my girlfriend. You're my best friend. You're my cheerleader. You're my *Law and Order* watching buddy. You're the keeper of my secrets. You're my late-night pillow-chat companion. You're the person who always makes me laugh. You're my backseat driver. You're my beer pong partner. You're the only person I never get sick of. You're my favorite buddy to spend an afternoon on the couch doing nothing with. You're my rock when

I'm struggling with my relationship with my dad. You're the first person I want to see when I wake up. And you're the last person I want to talk to before I drift off. You. Are. My. World. Do you realize how much you're asking of me, to give you up?"

"I'll take you if she won't," whispered a young brunette gal at the table nearby, who had obviously heard Jack's speech and was staring at him, looking love-struck.

Despite the tension, Charli chuckled as she took her napkin out of her lap and blotted her eyes, which had teared up listening to Jack. "I'm not your whole world though, Jack. I'm just half of it, remember? That's why we're in this predicament."

Jack folded his arms over his chest. Maybe because he saw her point. Maybe because he still thought she was crazy.

"I know that this is going to be hard." She realized that she must look so calm and collected to Jack as she laid out this proposal for their future, which had him spinning. But what he hadn't seen were all the sleepless nights she'd spent wrestling with the idea, just like he was doing now. "It'll be insanely hard. You mean just as much to me as I do to you. But it's the only option I see that will give us a chance of a happily ever after down the road. And God," she stressed, pounding her fist down on the table and making their silverware jump, "I want a happily ever after with you more than anything, Jack."

He rested his head in his hands and Charli softened her tone. "You know that saying, 'if you love someone, let her go?'" She'd seen a rustic sign with that quote from the Lebanese American writer, Kahlil Gibran, in the window of a used bookstore in Corvallis right before she came up with the pact. Although it hadn't immediately triggered the idea, looking back, she figured that it was what had planted the seed. "I think you and I are approaching a point in our lives when we need to do that for each other. Let each other go and trust that we'll both come back to one another later on."

Resting her hand on his back, she whispered over the chit-chat at the tables around them and the crackle of the fire behind the glass screen. "If I thought there was a better option—one where we didn't have to split up at all and could still be happy and accomplish everything we both want—then I wouldn't be suggesting this. I just see it as the option that makes the most logical sense." Following logic had never steered Charli wrong—not in the lab or outside of it—and she didn't see the point of switching gears and abandoning it at this critical juncture.

Jack kept his head in his hands, and Charli started to run her hand back and forth over the folds of his sweater, giving him time to think. And hopefully to come around like she had to the idea after some reflection.

She stared out the icy window and watched as a group of thirty-something women sipping from red Starbucks cups and pushing strollers with swaddled babies, walked by. After them came a couple with dreadlocks, holding hands, giving the illusion that their relationship was perfect. And then an older couple emerged, both with canes in their hands and hair as white as . . . snow.

"Jack," she said, tapping him urgently. "Look outside."

In the light from the lamppost, Charli saw the first few flakes of the year glisten and sail onto the dark pavement. She wasn't the only one to notice the flurries. From the other tables she heard "ooo's" and "ahs" and lots of, "It's snowing!"

She tapped Jack again, and this time he poked his head up and looked out. The flurries were swirling in the wind, zig-zagging and looping in circles. Charli stared at them with childlike delight.

"I'm afraid," Jack admitted, keeping his eyes out the window. "That's why I'm so opposed to this. I don't want to lose you, Charli."

"You won't lose me," she assured him. She set her chin on his shoulder and watched as the sidewalk slowly started to turn white. The snow was sticking. "Think of it like a boomerang," she said.

"We'll throw our relationship out, and it will come back to us. What we have is strong enough."

Jack reached for her hand and slipped his calloused fingers through hers. "How sure of that are you?"

"As sure as I can be about something that hasn't happened yet."

Jack seemed to consider this for a moment. "You really want to do this?"

No, she really didn't want to do this. What she wanted was for her and Jack to both be able to live out their dreams in the same state. But if that wasn't an option . . . "I really want the promise of a someday with you. So yeah, if you get drafted to the Giants or to a team that's far from Charleston, I want to do this."

"If I agree to it," he said, "it's only because I love you."

"I'm only suggesting it for the same reason," she told him.

Jack turned away from the window, and Charli gave him a minute, watching as he picked up his fork and dipped it into their forgotten slice of cake. He took a bite and chewed slowly, meditatively, his eyes trained on his plate. "A boomerang, huh?"

"Yeah," Charli said.

There were three things in his eyes when they met hers. Reluctance. Submission. Love. "Okay," he said.

## twelve
# THEN

**Something** was off between Charli and Jack. Gianna had noticed this earlier that evening when she stopped by their table to say hello, and it was even more apparent now, as she spied on them from the window in the kitchen door.

She knew she shouldn't be staring. She had better things to do, for starters. It had just begun to snow, so she should have been looking into road conditions and thinking about closing early. Charli and Jack also appeared to be having a very private conversation. Though they had chosen to have this private conversation in a very public place so wasn't it at least partly their fault if people eavesdropped? (She was using this logic to justify what she knew was not socially acceptable behavior.)

Gianna had been thrilled when she first saw the couple walk through the door that night. She could usually always count on them to boost her spirits about love and her spirits had needed some serious boosting after the date she'd gone on the night before. (So terrible!) She'd been so hopeful about it too, which made the disappointment all that worse.

"You and Ron will be a perfect match!" Suzie Miller had assured her. Suzie was one of Gianna's most beloved customers. She came in every Friday afternoon for a slice of the Triple Chocolate Oblivion and enjoyed it while reading a romance novel.

The romance novels were what had initially sparked their conversations about love. Suzie had found love twenty-seven years ago with her late-husband, Noah, and in his absence preferred to read about love instead of looking for it again with someone else. And Gianna kept her filled in on her romantic escapades. (Recently all disasters.)

Then, one Friday two weeks ago, Suzie informed Gianna that her attractive, responsible, delightful son, Ron, was newly single and would love to take her out. "He'll take you somewhere nice and pick up the tab—don't you worry," she said. Gianna had shared with her how men these days often wanted to go Dutch on first dates. "Ron has manners," Suzie told her. "And a *great* job."

During the date, Gianna heard all about his great job (Vice President for E-Commerce at Columbia Sportswear). And his college water polo glory days (undefeated in regular season both his junior and senior years at Cal Berkeley). And his obsession with sailing. "Are you interested in sailing?" he had asked. It was the first question he had directed at her all evening. "Because I couldn't date someone who wasn't interested in sailing." (Gianna was interested. Though she was pretty sure she'd jump off a boat if she ended up trapped on one with this guy.) She even knew his blood pressure! She still wasn't sure why that came up in the conversation. Maybe because he'd ordered a steak? She'd stopped listening at that point and had begun to practice mindful eating because the scallops and lobster risotto she'd ordered had been quite delicious, and she knew she would never eat this meal again—at least not here. She couldn't come back without remembering this awful date. It was a shame how many lovely restaurants had been ruined for Gianna by horrible dates.

But the worst part about the whole thing was that she might lose Suzie as a customer. Surely Suzie would want to know why Gianna wasn't interested in Ron. And Gianna could only sugarcoat, "Your son is entirely self-absorbed!" so much.

*Note to self: never let a customer set me up on a blind date again.*

A touching moment between Charli and Jack had been just what Gianna needed. Only it seemed there was nothing touching happening between them tonight. They were arguing. And they never argued.

Now their waiter, Mel, was leaving their table and walking toward Gianna. Maybe she would have the inside scoop.

"Get this," Mel said. Mel was studying to be an actress and spoke with dramatic effect even when there was nothing dramatic about a situation, though this time, Gianna thought her tone might be warranted. "Charli and Jack want to talk to you about making a reservation for a date in *five* years."

"Why on earth would they want to do that?" Gianna asked. Who knew if she would even be in business in five years. It certainly seemed she would, given how well things were going, but there was no way of knowing for sure in her line of work.

"That's all they told me," Mel said with a shrug of her shoulders, leaving Gianna no choice but to go find out for herself.

"You know," she said, pulling up a chair when she got to their table. "I just had a customer in here telling his buddies about a trip to Belize he's planning on taking in ten years. Maybe you three should chat."

They each gave her a faint smile. "Look, we know it's an unusual request," Charli said. "But we can explain."

"Please," Gianna said. "You've got me very curious." She listened intently as Charli filled her in on the pact she and Jack were thinking of making. The whole time she couldn't help but think how crazy it was. All her life she'd been looking for true love. Charli and Jack had found it in each other and were considering letting it go and running the risk of losing it forever. Did they not realize how lucky they were? Although maybe they were thinking the same thing about her. Though she didn't have a guy, she did have her dream job. If she had to make a choice between this job and her dream guy, she guessed she could understand how that would complicate things.

"We aren't sure if it will come to this," Charli finished up saying. "We just want to check if it would be an option to reserve our favorite table that far in advance."

"You know you can count on me to help you out," Gianna said. "Assuming I'm still in business, of course I will hold your table for you. I really hope to see you both there."

# thirteen
# THEN

"So, you mean to tell me that I actually agreed to this ridiculous plan to break up for five years six months ago?" Jack tried to make a joke and break the tension between him and Charli as they sat on the dock behind his parents' house, dangling their bare feet into the cool dark water the night before Jack was supposed to take off for San Jose.

The Giants had drafted him two weeks earlier. Jack got a call from their general manager while he was watching the draft on TV with Charli at his house in Corvallis. After verbally accepting their offer, he hung up and turned to her, his heart pounding.

"I'm going to the Giants," he said.

Her eyes glistened. "Oh Jack, I'm so . . . happy for you." When she drew him into a hug, they both lost it and cried mixed tears of happiness for their careers and sadness that it meant the hypothetical pact Charli had come up with were this to happen was no longer hypothetical.

They graduated the following week and then moved all their stuff out of Corvallis and back home, where they'd been since, trying to enjoy their last few days together.

Charli kicked up some water. "Yeah. Why'd you agree to it? Now here I am with cold feet."

Jack didn't want to have to mentally adjust to a different plan, so he nudged her and said, "Pull your toes out of the river then."

Although he'd left Hayden's only partly sold on Charli's idea that night she suggested it, when he got home, he'd jostled his mom awake. In their kitchen over coffee, he told her Charli's plan, and when he finished, his mom looked at him through the steam rising out of her mug and said, "Actually, Jack, I think that's kind of smart."

"You do?" he replied.

"Yeah," she said. "I think it might work for you two. Timing is everything in relationships, and you two unfortunately met too early in your lives. This plan—to reintroduce yourselves to each other at a point in your lives when the timing is better—kind of sounds perfect given your situation."

Something about hearing his mom say that made Jack feel better about the pact. And over the months, the more he thought about it, the more it made sense to him.

"You're right, we can't second-guess this," Charli said, catching his drift. She stood up and walked over to the old ragged rope swing hanging from the willow tree beside the dock. Pulling on it she said, "Remember when—"

"Yeah," Jack cut in, knowing she was going to take him back to that day when they were ten or eleven, and she fell off the swing too close to the dock and split her chin open on it. "You were crying so hard, and blood was everywhere."

"I never thanked you for carrying me all the way up to my house."

"Or for watching the doctor sew in all those gross stitches," Jack added.

"You didn't *have* to watch."

"Like you would have let go of my hand. God, I thought the doctor was going to have to amputate my fingers next."

"Hey, you try having a needle threaded through your skin," she said playfully.

It struck Jack how strange it was going to be to not make memories together for the next five years. Charli was in most of the ones he could remember.

She must have been thinking the same thing because in the light from the full moon hanging above them, he saw a tear roll down her cheek.

"So before I break down here, let's talk about rules," she said.

"Right." That was why they were out on the dock. To discuss the rules of the pact. They probably shouldn't have saved this for their last night together, but every other time they'd tried to discuss it, one of them hadn't been in the mood.

Jack leaned back on his hands and stared up at Charli's face in the milky light. "Let me guess . . . you wrote down a whole list of rules you think we should have."

"You know me too well." She reached into the back pocket of her faded jean shorts and pulled out a folded up sheet of paper. "Voila."

Jack chuckled. "Always prepared."

"And I'm guessing you *don't* have a list."

"I figured it was pointless, just like making study guides for our chemistry tests freshman year of high school when I *knew* you'd make them, and they'd be way better than what I could have come up with."

"You're lucky I was nice enough to make you copies of those," Charli said.

"And . . . did you make copies of this as well?" Jack said half-joking.

"It just so happens that I did." She pulled out a second folded sheet from her pocket for him. "I was going to give it to you afterwards to hang onto, but I guess you can have it now." He took the paper from her, unfolded it, and squinted his eyes at it in the low light. "Rules of the Pact" was printed at the top, and it was numbered in outline form. *Typical Charli.*

"Number one," Jack read out loud. "Delete each other from Facebook."

Charli peered down at him over the top of her copy. "That only leads to jealousy and nostalgia, don't you think?"

"Yeah," Jack said. "If you hadn't had that on here, I would have added it. Let's take care of that right now." He pulled up Facebook on his phone, searched for Charli, and clicked the defriend button right next to her profile picture of the two of them all dressed up for Charli's last birthday. "We are officially not friends," he announced sadly holding his phone up, so she could see.

Charli frowned. "Weird," she said.

"Yeah," he agreed.

They stared at each other in silence for a second, the reality of what they were doing really setting in. Jack knew if he looked at her for much longer, one of them would start to lose it, and they wouldn't get through the rest, so he lowered his eyes again.

"Rule number two," he read. "No texting, calling, or emailing. We'll stay in touch by writing letters. Letters?" Jack looked up at her. "What are we, in the 1920s?"

"I know it's a little old-fashioned, but think: if we call, email, or text, then we'll probably be in touch *all the time*, and it will hardly feel like we're broken up. It would basically put us in a long-distance relationship, and we've already gone over all the problems with those. Letters are safe. They'll allow us to keep each other informed about how we're doing with our dreams, but they won't be too much. And they won't give away other details about our lives that our voices might, like, for example, if one of us starts dating someone else."

"Wait," Jack said. "So, you mean we're allowed to date other people?"

"Sorry, I'm getting ahead of myself. Do you want to read the next rule?"

Jack looked down and saw that his paper was shaking. He tried to steady his hands as he read, "Dating other people is okay. But no kissing and telling. If either one of us starts seeing someone else, leave that out of the letters so that we don't crush each other."

Charli took a seat back beside him. "It's not like I can imagine dating anyone now, Jack. But five years is a long time. I don't expect either one of us to shut down romantically."

Jack inched his hand over to hers so that their pinky fingers were touching. "I don't think I could ever meet someone as perfect for me as you."

"I hope not," she said with a nervous laugh. "And I don't think I'll meet someone as perfect for *me* as *you* either. But I'm just saying we're both going to new places, and we're going to meet new people. If you *do* want to go on a date with someone or even kiss a girl drunkenly at a bar, I won't hate you for it, but I don't want you to tell me about it."

"I guess part of being broken up is having that freedom," Jack said, realizing the rule probably made sense. He was most likely going to be put in a lot of situations by his baseball teammates where he'd be given a hard time if he didn't flirt with other girls or make out with a stranger, especially if he told them he was single.

"Exactly," Charli said. "We just have to trust in what we have, and if we're meant to be, we'll have our date at Hayden's to come back to each other."

Jack thought of that day five years out. "Damn, when I see you again at that restaurant . . . I'm going to kiss you so hard."

Charli giggled. "Can you imagine? It will be like a scene from a movie if we both show up."

*If we both show up.*

The words hung in the air between them.

"Sorry," Charli said, shaking her head. "I mean *when* we both show up."

"No, technically it is *if*," Jack said. "Right? I mean, over the course of five years one of us could decide that we don't want to get back together."

"I guess," Charli said sadly.

"And what do we do then?" Jack asked. "Do you have a rule about that?"

"Actually, no." She sounded surprised with herself. "What do you think we should do?"

Jack considered this. "Part of me feels like it would be awful to show up and get stood up. But I also don't want us influencing each other's decisions. I don't want you to feel like you *need* to show up if you don't really want to, because I told you *I* was planning on it, for example. Or, say I thought a month before the reunion that I wasn't going to go back for you, and so I wrote you that. But then the day got closer, and I changed my mind. At that point you'd already cancelled your flight and grieved about me, so I would have ruined everything."

"Sounds like you're leading more toward keeping it a mystery then?" Charli pulled her knees up to her chest.

"Yeah, I guess."

"Well, it'll be incredibly romantic if we both show up, and incredibly tragic if only one of us does."

"I'm pulling for it being romantic," Jack said, leaning into her.

"Me too." Charli smiled, and they both looked back down at the sheet. "Okay, the last rule is no seeing each other at all."

"I figured given the other rules that that was going to be the case," Jack said.

"It'll be easy to implement considering my parents' move." Charli's dad had gotten transferred to Chicago for work. Her parents would be gone before the holidays this year. "And I just feel like if we met up at all during the split, it'd be too hard to let go again. It'd be like we were breaking up all over."

"Yeah," Jack said. "That's something I only want to go through once." *And not even,* he thought.

"So, you're okay with that?"

"As okay as I am with all the other rules. I'm not crazy about any of them, but I know that they're all in our best interest to pull this thing off."

Charli nodded. "Exactly." Then, looking out over the river she said, "So, there's just one more thing we have to do."

"What's that?" Jack asked.

"Pick a date and a time for our reunion."

"Right." The most important part. They had told Gianna they would call and let her know. "Do they even make calendars that go out five years?"

"I'm sure I can find an infinity calendar on the Internet." Charli took out her phone and started to search. "If all goes according to plan, I should be done in June 2017. My financial aid is for five years, so I will make it my mission to finish in that time frame. But since June's your baseball season, maybe we should meet in March of that year, in between winter league and your regular season."

"I'll be in spring training," Jack said. "But I'll find a way to be there."

She continued to look at her phone. "Okay, found a calendar. How about March 24? A Friday? At say, 7 o'clock?"

"Friday, March 24 at seven," Jack said, thinking to himself that it couldn't come soon enough. "Okay."

"We should write this down so that we don't forget," Charli said.

"Yeah, should we put it on our rule sheets?"

Charli seemed to consider that for a second and then shook her head. "I have a better idea." Crossing the dock, she went over and got her bag. She brought it over to where Jack was and pulled out a to-go box from Hayden's. "I got a slice of our favorite cake for our last night," she said. "I thought it would be symbolic, or something. Although now I don't really have much of an appetite." She set it down between them. "What if I write the date and time on the receipt for me, as my reminder? And for you, I'll inscribe the information on the inside of the to-go box lid?"

It seemed fitting to put the date and time on something from Hayden's. "All right."

Charli took out a pen and the receipt from her purse and wrote down the information there first, then she opened up the to-go box and did the same. "Put this somewhere safe," she told him.

"I'll take it with me," he said. "Keep it in my room next to a picture of you or something."

"Okay," Charli nodded. "I'll do the same." She finished up and then capped the pen and stuck it back in her bag. "You know, Jack, I was wrong a few minutes ago."

"About what? You're never wrong about things."

She smiled softly. "I said that picking a date was the last thing we had to do . . . it wasn't."

"Oh?"

Her eyes were suddenly glossy. "Saying goodbye actually is."

"Charli . . ." his voice broke. "Come here." He had her sit between his legs, facing the water, and he wrapped his arms around her. Holding her tight, he closed his eyes and listened to the warm wind rustling through the trees and the river water rushing downstream. When he was on the baseball field, there were certain moments that he wanted to slow down and live in longer, like right after he threw a strikeout pitch with a bases-loaded count, and the crowd jumped to their feet to applaud him. This was one of those moments off the field. He wanted to keep Charli in his arms for as long as he could and never let her go.

"Jack," Charli whispered.

"Hmm?" He leaned his face down close to hers so that their cheeks brushed.

"Will you make love to me?"

"Here? Right now?"

"Here. Right now." She turned in his arms and latched onto the bottom of his shirt, clenching it into a ball. "And make it count. In case, you know . . . this is it."

Her words made him shudder. "Charli, this won't be it," he said. He cupped her chin in his hand, tilted it up, and looked her square in the eyes. "This *can't* be it." With tenderness, he kissed her forehead and then trailed his lips down to hers and eased his tongue into her mouth.

Charli pressed her forehead against his. "I'm scared of losing you," she said. "I mean, I know this was my idea, but still . . . I'm really afraid."

"I know you are," Jack said. "I am too. We just have to remember that this is us. And this is *our* love we're putting through this hoop."

A few tears fell down her cheeks, and Jack reached up and wiped them off with his thumb, hating how much this hurt.

"I miss you so much already," she breathed.

"Me too," he said heavily.

She made eye contact with him for a couple of seconds and then glanced down at his lips.

Jack kissed her. Softly, at first, and then more urgently. Though he didn't think this was it, though he didn't want it to be, what if it was?

She kissed him back with the same sense of urgency, as if she were thinking the same thing, and then she crawled onto his lap and wrapped her legs around his waist.

A wave of desire coursed through him, and he reached for the bottom of her shirt and yanked it off over her head. For a brief moment, he took in the sight of her—the twinkle in her eyes, her angelic skin glowing in the moonlight, her nipples poking out of the sheer fabric of her bra, her hair blowing back behind her in the warm breeze—and he thought to himself that he'd never seen anyone so beautiful. She was his wildest dream right there in front of him . . . for one more night.

Charli broke his trance by moving her hand down and resting it on the spot where his pants were mounting. A shiver of pleasure ran down his spine. With her other hand, Charli lifted his shirt off and then dropped it on top of her own and leaned in to kiss his neck.

Jack remembered that this was her bra that unhooked from the front, and he unclasped it with his eyes closed and felt her fall into his hands. Her breasts—soft, full, familiar—still drove him crazy no matter how many times he touched them. He tipped his head down and drew cold wet circles with his tongue around their soft skin, making her whimper and making him grow harder at the sound of it.

"Jack," he heard her say, faintly, breathlessly.

He looked up, meeting her eyes, and knew in an instant that she was as desperate for him as he was for her. He laid her down on the dock, working to undo the hard buttons on her shorts and then sliding off his jeans. Then he moved over her, hovering there for a moment, taking in the electricity between them, the intense high he was feeling, the unreal sensation of being *this* alive. And when he couldn't take it any longer, he pushed himself inside her.

Jack had made love to Charli hundreds of times over the four years they'd been together. They'd had make-up sex. Just-woke-up sex. Too-many-drinks sex. Holiday sex. Out-in-the-open sex. Back-of-his-truck sex. Rainy-afternoon sex. I-won-a-baseball-game sex. I-love-you-sex. But tonight was different. This was earth-shattering sex. This was can't-live-without-you sex. This was sex that said, "I'll wait for you. I'll come back. What we have is strong enough."

Visit sincerelyriley.com/scene-5 to see this scene unfold and to Shop the Book™.

# fourteen
# NOW

**As** Gianna wove through the crowded dining room toward the hostess stand to return Charli's call, she thought about the pact Charli and Jack had made and about how strong their love had to have been for them to think they both might show up for this date five years down the road. And for Charli—at least—to have remembered it and called.

*Would I have shown up?* Gianna wondered. *Would I have even remembered, if Peter and I had made a pact like theirs?* She didn't know, and that frightened her.

"I feel as if I'm actually *in* a romantic comedy," Rosie said when Gianna joined her up front. "I thought I would like this feeling, but it's actually quite stressful!"

"Is there anything that doesn't stress you out?" Gianna teased. Rosie often looked like she might faint when there were more than two people waiting for a table, and the other week, she'd admitted to everyone on Gianna's staff that she found going to the gas station to be a stressful experience! (Apparently, she couldn't figure out how to re-park her car when she pulled up on the wrong side of the pump and ended up driving in circles while the attendants just laughed. "Oh, Rosie!" Gianna had said, when she explained what had happened, and they'd all shared a laugh at her expense.)

Gianna thought Rosie's next job should be somewhere a bit less high-volume. Like a tiny mom-and-pop bookshop. But she would miss Rosie if she ever left, the way she missed everyone on her staff who left. They were like her family.

She *had* started a family. She liked to remind herself of this on days she felt bad about not yet being married or having children. It might not have looked like the family she'd always envisioned herself having, but maybe it was even better. Was her vision of how her life *should be* the real problem here?

"Any more word from Charli?" she asked.

"No."

"And still no word from Jack?"

"No. Do you think that's bad?" Rosie's question hung in the air as the door flung open and two bundled-up, middle-aged women that Gianna had never seen before stepped in from out of the cold. No Charli. No Jack. No Peter.

"I don't know," she answered honestly.

"Maybe when you call Charli back, you'll find out," Rosie said. She handed over Charli's number before she greeted the women with a friendly customer-service smile that neither seemed to notice. They were too busy ogling over the three-tiered glass dessert case to Rosie's left, which featured all the desserts on the menu, as if it were the Mona Lisa exhibit at the Louvre. Butterflies instantly filled Gianna's stomach the way they did every time someone complimented her restaurant or seemed to take delight in the experience of dining there.

How would Linda explain that?

"Butterflies fade." That was what she always said. But here Gianna was, ten years after opening her restaurant, *still* feeling them. Which meant . . . that she *was* capable of feeling butterflies for the rest of her life when she truly loved something or someone. If that was the case, wasn't it of the utmost importance that she marry someone who gave her butterflies?

She dialed the number Rosie had written down.

"Hello." A woman answered.

"Charli?" Gianna's breath caught. Had she really just gotten her on the line?

"This is Charli. Sorry I missed your call, but if you leave a message . . ."

Gianna sighed. What if the last time Charli called had been Gianna's only opportunity to talk to her? She apologized for missing her call earlier and told Charli to call back at her convenience. She thought about adding that she hoped to see her soon but decided against it at the last minute. Regardless of whether or not Charli was planning on showing up tonight, Gianna bet she was feeling pressure, and Gianna didn't want to add to it.

"No luck?" Rosie asked, just as Gianna hung up.

"Voicemail," Gianna said.

"I can keep trying her, if you'd like?" Rosie offered.

"No," said Gianna. "I don't think we try her again. I don't think we do anything. We just wait."

—

Gianna was good at waiting. Maybe too good. Look at her—thirty-seven and *still* waiting for the right man to come along and sweep her off her feet. Maybe if she were a little more impatient, she might have looked a little harder or decided to just move on with her life and be content with her professional success. Waiting had paid off there.

She'd spent ten years in the restaurant industry earning her stripes before opening Hayden's. Her first job in high school had been at a small diner owned by Patrick Hannigan, a sweet, soft-spoken man, much like her own father, who taught her the ropes of the business. Then in college she worked for Ron and Patricia Harden, a husband-and-wife culinary team whose love for delighting people with good, beautifully presented food made her fall in love with the lifestyle of a restaurant owner.

"My kitchen is like my home," Ron had said. "And I love always having my door open, hoping that the experience I provide converts strangers into loyal customers."

Since opening Hayden's, Gianna had seen a lot of strangers walk through her doors, but she had to admit none were as peculiar as this funeral party.

She found herself eavesdropping even more than normal as she poured ice water into the cup of the beautiful crying blonde—the woman who had reminded her of her hazelnut cake, the Marjolaine, earlier.

As she introduced herself, she heard Marjolaine's friends saying things to her like, "Everything's going to be okay, Kendall." And, "You'll get through this."

*Get through what?* Gianna wondered as she rattled off a few of her dessert recommendations—a seasonal blueberry tart, a cappuccino brownie with creamy espresso mousse called the Café au Chocolat, and an English Toffee Cheesecake.

During Gianna's monologue, the heavy-set gal reached across the table for Kendall's hand and told her again that she was going to be fine. *Café Cassata,* Gianna thought when she saw the gesture. This woman was definitely a reincarnation of her espresso sponge cake called Café Cassata. She was clearly on a mission to soak Kendall's pain up, the same way the Café Cassata sponge cake soaked up the kahlua and espresso, making for rich flavorful layers that made every bite worth savoring.

"So, does anything sound good?" Gianna asked once she'd finished. "Or do you ladies need another minute?"

"Kendall, what would you like?" Café Cassata asked, patting Kendall's hand. "Get anything you want. Order two slices if it'll make you feel better."

Kendall's shoulders sunk. "I don't think two hundred slices would make me feel better, Ellie," she said.

Ellie looked to the woman in the Susan Boyle frock seated next to her for help. This lady was a dead ringer for Gianna's Midnight Lava Cake. Anger appeared to be oozing out of her just like dark chocolate oozed out of Gianna's rich, chocolaty creation that was served with a scoop of vanilla ice cream.

"Maybe instead of ordering dessert," the Lava Cake Lady said, "we should be tracking your Ex down and giving him his just desserts."

"Oh Tina, cut it out," Ellie said. "Seriously. There's no need to go down that road again." She yanked her silverware out from her cloth napkin and smoothed it down on her lap. "He's dead for Christ's sake!"

"What?" Gianna didn't mean to speak out loud, but she must have because all of the women looked up at her. She didn't usually involve herself in customers' conversations unless they directly pulled her into them, but these women had been so intriguing that she'd slipped. "I'm so sorry. I shouldn't have been listening. And I'm sorry for the um . . . for your loss." Had these women been burying reminders of this guy in the park when she'd seen them? But if they hated him, why would they have held a memorial?

Kendall, the crying blonde, looked up at her. "Hey, weren't you in the park earlier? Didn't I see you?"

She nodded, guiltily. "That was me."

All of the women exchanged embarrassed glances. "Okay, look, no one actually died," Ellie said, clarifying. "I was being metaphorical. We have this ritual when one of us goes through a breakup. We hold a mock funeral and bury all the reminders of an ex so that we can mourn and move on."

So that's what they'd been doing out there! Her kitchen staff was going to get a kick out of this . . .

"A breakup is such a loss, you know?" Ellie continued. "You go from spending every day with the love of your life to never speaking to him again. He really does drop off the face of the earth. At least in your world."

Okay, that was either the craziest thing Gianna had ever heard. Or the smartest . . .

"I have to say, you ladies may be onto something."

Ellie smiled. "We came up with this idea years ago as sort of a joke, but now I'm a therapist in Seattle, and it makes complete sense to me from a psychological standpoint. Clients who come in for my help after a death in their family are in and out of my office in a couple of months. But clients who come in after a breakup . . . some of them are in there forever, because they don't accept that it's really over. They hold onto this unrealistic belief that their ex might come back."

Gianna immediately looked over at the table reserved for Charli and Jack. What would these women think of their pact? They'd probably think it was the unhealthiest decision in the world. Maybe it was.

"We try to prevent that mentality in our group," Ellie went on. "When it's over, it's over, no looking back."

Gianna shifted from one foot to the other, processing this. "So, what was the breakup this time?" She realized it was nosy, but the women had already shared so much. Would it really hurt them to finish the rest of the story?

Ellie and Tina looked across the table at Kendall. Clearly, from what Gianna had seen, she was the heartbroken one.

"My fiancé stood me up the day before my wedding," she said. "He just left. Without an explanation. I was at his house helping set up for the wedding." Kendall closed her eyes for a moment, and Gianna imagined her mentally going back to that moment, reliving it again. "He found me out on at the gazebo where I was stringing up lights to make our altar, and he said, 'Kendall, I can't do this.' That was it. Like he was cancelling dinner plans! And then he left and drove away." She shook her head like she still couldn't believe it. "I should be getting ready for my rehearsal dinner right now, not sitting here."

Ellie reached across the table for Kendall's hand again, and in that moment, Gianna felt a rush of gratitude pass through her for Peter. He would never jilt her like that. Not in a million years. Wasn't that worth something? Maybe even everything?

Perhaps Peter was just the kind of guy she should be with. And maybe these women had come into her restaurant so that she would realize this . . .

"Obviously you know that dessert is the best cure for a broken heart?" Gianna said to Kendall.

"Yes, I have heard that." Kendall dabbed her eyes with her cloth napkin. "And you know what, I think I'm ready to order."

"Oh, good," Ellie said enthusiastically as though Kendall had just had a major breakthrough.

"Yes, that's great," Gianna smiled, feeling good about her answer to Peter's proposal for the first time all night. "So, ladies," she said, "what'll it be?"

# fifteen
# THEN

**"Okay**, don't make fun of me," said Rebecca Green, Charli's new freckle-faced friend from Dayton, Ohio, who was in her PhD program. "But I see this stick on the ground right here, and I think, multipolar neuron."

Charli looked at the stick, which had multiple branches jutting out from it, and laughed because it was *so* something she would have said.

"Don't you just love being back in school mode?" Charli asked.

"I don't know how *not* to be in school mode," Rebecca laughed.

They were having lunch in between classes on a bench at the pond-sized lake down the street from their campus. It had become their routine in the few weeks since they'd started their program—a program that Charli absolutely loved.

She had known she made the right choice in schools since day one at the Welcome Reception out on the university lawn. She'd listened to past alumni talk about all the research they had done during their PhD years at MUSC and what they were currently working on in the field.

Charli had been so stimulated by the discussion that she'd barely been able to sleep that night. She'd stayed up late in the one-bedroom colonial flat she lived in on Council Street, just a few blocks from campus, and wrote down ideas for possible research topics of her own in an Idea Notebook that an alum had given her and instructed her to use diligently.

And then she'd met Rebecca the first day of class, and they'd clicked instantly.

Intellectually, this was her paradise. But, emotionally . . . she missed Jack every day.

They'd started writing letters the week he left, and she'd read each one he sent so many times that the white-lined paper he wrote them on was wearing at the creases from her continuously folding and unfolding of them. She had just sent him a letter giving him her Charleston address, telling him how much she liked her classes and letting him know a little about Rebecca, and she was checking her mailbox daily for his response.

It was just so weird not talking to him whenever she wanted. She constantly had to resist the urge to call him after something exciting happened, because that had been her habit for so many years.

"You thinking of your guy from home again?" Rebecca guessed.

Charli had told her about Jack the second day she met her, after Rebecca had caught her sketching a picture of him in her notebook during their lecture on protein synthesis.

"Am I that obvious?"

"You just get this faraway look in your eyes when you think about him."

Charli sighed. "I've been feeling kind of guilty lately. Like I chose all this over him."

"Aw, come on, you didn't *choose* this." Rebecca peeled the crust off her turkey sandwich. "This chose us. This is what we're supposed to do, you know? If you're anything like me, you have a creative, curious side of you that demands you pay it attention."

*This girl really got her.* "Yeah, but I also have a side of me that's really into Jack." She pulled her hair up off her neck and tied it up, sweating from the topic of conversation and the southern humidity that she still hadn't adjusted to yet. "Did you leave anyone special behind in Ohio, Rebecca?"

"Yeah," Rebecca said. "Henry."

So, she could relate. "What was he like?"

"Well, for starters, he was fat."

"Fat?" Charli wrinkled her brows.

"Yes, very, very fat. Furry too. And a great cuddler. Unfortunately, my landlord doesn't allow cats."

Charli cracked a smile. "Very funny."

Grinning, Rebecca continued. "No, I've never had a great love. A couple of boyfriends here and there, but nothing serious."

"Well, I'm still trying to decide if it's a blessing or a curse to fall in love when you're young," Charli told her. "So, since I haven't figured it out yet, feel free to consider yourself blessed."

"Okay," Rebecca chuckled.

They both looked out over the blue-green water and at the walkers who were trekking around the lake on the concrete path, enjoying the sunshine. For a minute they ate quietly and then, breaking the silence, Rebecca said, "Christopher's certainly upset that you're hung up on someone else."

"Christopher?" Charli squinted at her.

"The curly, dark-haired boy with the Johnny Depp retro specs from our program."

"Oh, right." Charli had chatted with him a few times.

"We're in the same apartment complex," Rebecca said, "so we've gotten to know each other pretty well, and the last few nights all he's been talking about is how cute he thinks you are."

Charli blushed, even though she wasn't interested. It had been a long time since she'd heard any guy other than Jack pay her a compliment. She quickly recovered as she dug into her strawberry, spinach, and feta salad.

"Well, tell him he better set his sights on someone else. Jack holds a special place in my heart. I don't think I'll ever get over him. I'm hoping that down the road things will work out with us. When this is all over."

"When this is all over?" Rebecca looked at her, amused. "You do remember this is a *five-year* program you committed to, don't you?"

Charli smiled faintly. "I get it's a long time." She hadn't yet told Rebecca about the pact she and Jack made and wasn't sure she should share the details. The only people who knew about it were her parents, Jack's mom, and Gianna from Hayden's. She figured that to anyone who hadn't known her and Jack together, the idea of their five-year-out reunion would seem ridiculous, but at the same time Charli wanted someone in her life out here to know in case she ever wanted to talk about it.

After debating it for a moment, she made Rebecca swear not to tell anyone and then filled her in.

Rebecca whistled when she finished. "That's some plan. You two must have really had something great."

"We did," Charli told her forking a strawberry. "We were a perfectly bonded pair, like adenine and thymine."

Rebecca smiled at her reference to the nucleotides that joined together to form hydrogen bonds in DNA. "Just keep your mind open," she said. "That's all I want to tell you. You never know what could happen down the road."

Charli did know though. The same way she knew science was her professional calling. She and Jack were meant to be. And no other guy or amount of time could change that.

—

Jack lay on top of the faded floral-printed comforter in the musty motel room he was sharing with his away-game roommate, Bobby, another new draft pick. Wide awake at two o'clock in the morning, he held his phone up to the latest letter that he had brought with him from Charli so he could read it again in the light from the glowing screen.

*It's like being in my own little piece of heaven.*

Jack smiled as he thought of Charli enjoying her book-worm life in Charleston. He scanned down the page a little further and then read another sentence that kept catching his attention.

*Imagine only having to read your favorite chapters of your favorite textbooks in college—that's how much I'm enjoying what I'm studying.*

Jack rolled onto his side, set his phone down, and held the crinkled letter against his chest. *Now that,* he thought, *is how a person who's following her dream is supposed to feel.*

Jack had been trying to keep his spirits up since he got to California, but Charli's letter made him realize how much he wasn't really loving his Minor League life.

He would definitely not describe it as a "piece of heaven." His days were long and exhausting. They usually started around one o'clock in the afternoon with a pre-game warm-up that included batting and pitching practice and ended around midnight after a post-game lift. Jack had a couple of friends, but the guy he was closest to, Ian, had just gotten released, and another dude he'd bonded with, Kimmel, had been bumped down a league mid-season. He was trying to get along with the other guys, but it was hard considering the ringleader of the team was a twenty-eight-year-old hothead who played Jack's same position and who couldn't stand Jack because he saw him as a threat to his chances of getting called up. The traveling was wearing on Jack as well. He wasn't sure how many more hot, bumpy bus rides he could take or how many more Subway sandwiches he could eat. To be honest, he was grateful that the season was going to be over after they finished their three-game series in Visalia.

Jack picked his phone back up and shined the light on Charli's letter again.

He read over some other parts.

*I wish you could meet Rebecca. She's exactly like me in every way except physically. Her face has so many freckles it reminds me of a connect-the-dot game. We do everything together.* Go *to class, study in our state-of-the-art library, grab lunch near campus.*

He scrolled a few more paragraphs down.

*On Saturday my classmates and I took a break from studying and went to the beach. Even though it's October, the weather is still so beautiful here, and the water was warm when I splashed through it. We played a competitive game of beach volleyball as the sun was going down. You would have loved it.*

Jack rolled onto his back again.

Reading through those passages, he couldn't help but fantasize about moving out to Charleston and being with Charli. He hated missing out on her life, and it hurt knowing that she was building an entire new world without him.

It wouldn't have bothered him so much, he didn't think, if he felt like he was missing out on time with her for something that felt fulfilling. But that just wasn't the case. Sure, there were moments when the game still gave him the same high that it did in high school and college, like when he released a ball that felt just right as it rolled off his fingertips. Or when his coach gave him a pat on the back after a well-pitched inning. Or when he got a whiff of the grass as he was jogging out to the mound. But most of the time, Jack felt like he was just going through the motions out there, passively making it from one game to the next.

He'd mentioned some of these feelings to his mom when he talked to her on the phone, but he hadn't said anything to Charli yet. Mostly because he figured that his feelings for baseball would kick back in again. They had to, right? How could they just turn off completely?

Feeling antsy, he stood up and slipped some shoes on. Luckily, Bobby was a sound sleeper, like most of the guys were. Practices, games, and the on-the-go schedule managed to keep most of them sleep-deprived, so when they had the opportunity to rest, they made the most of it. For Jack, those quiet moments gave him time to think, and when he let himself, like tonight, get carried away, he knew better than to toss and turn in hopes of getting some shut-eye. It was best to admit defeat and try to clear his head. Grabbing his room key from his wallet on the bedside table, he quietly walked over to the door and opened it, stepping outside into the hallway.

Although it was late, he felt the need to go outside. He took the stairs down to the empty, quiet lobby, nodded at the sleepy front desk receptionist who was reading *A Farewell to Arms*, a romance he remembered Charli finishing in tears, and left the motel, turning right toward the Rawhide's stadium, which was only a couple of blocks away.

As he walked, he found himself thinking back to that day Charli helped him break in his first glove after his dad said he didn't have time to.

"You're really good," she'd told him after his first few tosses. Jack's ego had appreciated the stroking, especially from Charli, whose opinion always meant more to him than anyone else's.

He smiled at the memory and then thought of another—his first Little League game. Charli had gone with him beforehand down to the 7-Eleven near the field to buy a pack of sunflower seeds. He'd poured them each a handful, and they worked to crack the shells open in their mouths as they walked. While he'd quickly gotten the knack for splitting open the salty shells in his mouth, Charli had had a harder time.

"I can't do it," she had said, spitting out a mouthful of shells and seeds onto the sidewalk. She took another handful from Jack and proceeded to open them with her fingernails, claiming that method was easier and stating that was how she was going to eat them from then on.

He chuckled to himself because she *still* did eat them that way, and then he let his thoughts drift to all those times Charli had gone to the batting cages with him in high school. She always sat on a crate outside the cage, doing schoolwork while he hit ball after ball. When he turned the pitching speed up close to ninety miles per hour, she always stood and walked over to the wire fence, curling her fingers around it and watching in amazement as Jack hit the tough pitches.

"Aren't you afraid of getting hurt?" she asked him one time.

"That's part of the thrill," he'd said, swinging the bat and cracking one hard into the net.

Now that Jack thought about it, Charli was in every baseball memory he could recall. She had been in the stands for every single game of his until he got drafted as well. He had always been able to count on seeing her in the crowd, whistling, cheering, and holding up encouraging signs.

All of that meant so much to him, and he suddenly couldn't help but wonder . . . had he ever really *truly* loved baseball in its pure form? Or was it Charli he had always loved purely? And baseball had just been fun *because* of her?

He gave that some serious consideration as he arrived at the field. Pulling open the gate, he jogged out to the mound through the wet grass, which must have been watered earlier that evening. In the darkness he stood on the mound, put his hands in his pockets, and closed his eyes, listening to the wind like he usually listened to applause.

The pitcher's mound was his focus spot. To survive up there, he had learned to tune everything out—the screaming fans, the play-by-play announcer, the jeering dugout—and just concentrate on his catcher's signals and the strike zone. Tonight, there wasn't much to screen out except the voice that kept telling him he "should" keep chasing the dream, even though nothing about it felt right anymore. Instead, he focused on the signals that he "should not"—Charli's elation, by comparison his emptiness, and the strong gut feeling that he wasn't happy.

Opening his eyes, he looked around at the dark field and up at the empty bleachers. Never, in a million years, could he have predicted that he would be standing out on the mound, at the end of his first professional baseball season thinking that maybe he'd picked the wrong dream to follow.

# sixteen
# NOW

It was six forty-five, and there was still no sign of Charli or Jack.

Gianna was checking the door fairly often for them and for Peter. Although the idea of getting engaged was sitting better with her now, like a calorie-packed, sick-to-her-stomach slice of cake that was finally starting to digest, she still couldn't believe Peter was planning to ask her to marry him tonight with everything that was already going on—Charli and Jack's potential reunion, the funeral party's crisis, the wine glass that all of a sudden smashed onto the floor behind her . . .

Gianna turned on the heel of her shoe toward the crash.

Her servers didn't drop glasses or plates often, but occasionally someone would stack too many plates at once, or a customer would push out her chair at the same moment that one of her servers was walking by, and an accident would happen. It was part of the business.

But this time, it wasn't the fault of any of her staff. It appeared that a customer in Gianna's section had shattered her own wine glass—a customer who was now crying hysterically.

When Gianna had waited on this woman earlier, she had nicknamed her and her date St. Georgen after her German chocolate cake because they'd appeared to complement each other perfectly, just like the coconut-pecan filling and the chocolate buttermilk cake did in this sugary-sweet concoction. Physically, Gianna had thought they went well together—they both had brown hair and were rocking the Portland hipster look—a fashion trend Gianna appreciated but couldn't personally pull off.

The woman was wearing a fedora, with a graphic tee and striped pants, and her date had on a collared shirt with fitted jeans and a bowtie. They also seemed to have an intense emotional connection. Although they had been seated across the table from each other, the woman had picked up her chair right after she sat down and moved it next to her date's, so she could hold his hand.

But now they reminded Gianna of her Lemon Tart because their date had gone as sour as the filling in this pucker-inducing lemon treat. The woman, who was still crying, got out of her chair and picked up her purse. She reached into it for some cash, threw it on the table, and then rushed out the door in the back of the restaurant. The man remained seated throughout the whole ordeal and turned as ghostly white as his shirt.

It wasn't hard to guess what had happened. The man had obviously messed up somehow. He'd either told his date he'd cheated on her, or confessed that he was in love with someone else.

"Why are men such pigs?" Gianna heard Tina from the funeral party say. "How are Kendall and I ever going to find good ones?"

Again, Gianna felt a rush of gratitude for Peter. Tina was right—it *was* hard to find a good guy. And Gianna had a *great* one. If she said no to Peter, she'd have to go back out into the horrible dating world, where there were guys like Kendall's ex and this man in front of her.

"Jackass," she heard Kendall mutter.

She took the words right out of Gianna's mouth. Gianna wanted to sock the guy in the head, not go pick up the glass at the foot of his table.

Valerie appeared on the scene then, bearing one plate of cake in hand. "What in the world is going on with your section tonight?" she asked under her breath.

"It's a madhouse, right?"

They both looked down at the mess.

"I've got to clean this up before somebody steps on the glass," Gianna said.

"Why don't you let me do that?" Valerie said. "*You*, Miss, have a visitor waiting in the kitchen."

Gianna turned toward Valerie, her heartbeat picking up. "You mean . . . ?"

"Yep!" Valerie squealed, grabbing Gianna's arm with her free hand and squeezing it tight. "Peter just showed up. And I think he has an important question to ask you!"

Gianna gulped. *Ohmygod.* This was it. She needed an answer for him. Right now.

## seventeen

# THEN

"**Can** I walk you home, Charli?" Christopher asked.

It was midnight, and Charli, Christopher, and Rebecca had just finished up a study session at the library and were standing outside on the concrete steps under the bright security light.

"I'll walk her home," Rebecca said, coming to Charli's rescue.

Charli mouthed a silent, "Thank you," as she adjusted her heavy backpack.

Irritated, Christopher cracked his knuckles. "Well, if you walk her home, then who will walk *you* home?" he asked.

"We'll both walk her home then," Rebecca answered, rolling her eyes. Rebecca had told Christopher a number of times that Charli was hung up on someone from home and wasn't interested in a relationship, but he still tried to get one-on-one time with her whenever he could.

There were times Charli *did* hang out with him alone. Because she liked to. She *liked* Christopher. When it was just the two of them, they had the most intense conversations about the kind of stuff that kept her awake at night. Last Friday, for instance, when they went to Big John's Tavern, a dive bar downtown, for a couple of beers, they'd talked about how amazing it was to think that all human beings formed themselves from a single cell and how miraculous it was that they all could breathe, circulate their blood, and digest their food without even thinking about it. Wow!

She would have been fine kissing Christopher a couple of times. Or going out on a date with him. But she wasn't ready to get seriously involved with anyone. In order for her arrangement with Jack to work, she'd decided she really needed to listen to her heart. Moving on at this point didn't feel right.

"Well, maybe on Friday we can grab another drink," Christopher said, clearly trying to play it cool as they started walking.

"Maybe," Charli said, staring down at her feet. She'd decide later if she would actually go.

Rebecca fell into step beside her and whispered in her ear. "Do I need to say we have dinner plans?"

Charli smiled. "I'll let you know."

"What are you two talking about?" Christopher asked.

"Nothing," they both said in unison and kept walking.

—

November 11, 2012

*Dear Charli,*

*I know this may come as a surprise to you, but I've been wavering on my feelings about baseball ever since I got to San Jose. I know . . . crazy, right? I just started up winter league in Arizona and am hoping that a change of scenery and a new group of guys might change how I've been feeling. But . . . if it doesn't, how would you feel about me retiring from baseball and moving out to Charleston to be with you? It's something I've been considering a lot lately, so please, write me back to let me know your thoughts. Hope school's still going well for you. I don't doubt it is. Miss you.*

*Jack*

—

November 30, 2012

*Dear Jack,*

*Who are you and what have you done with my best friend? You've fallen out of love with baseball? You might give it up? This sounds like crazy talk. You want my honest opinion? You have too much of a history with the game to not see it through another full season with the Giants. You owe it to yourself and to baseball to keep at it. If you don't give it more time and you do quit and move out here, one day you will come to resent me. I can't live with that. For yourself and for our relationship, please see this through a little longer . . .*

*All's well here in Charleston. Finals are approaching, so I'm busy studying but loving every minute of it. I know that makes me a total nerd, but at least you now know I haven't changed much.*

*Keep me posted on everything. Miss you too.*

*Charli*

—

December 15, 2012

*Dear Charli,*

*I figured that was how you'd respond. Maybe you're right. I'll try to hang in here. I guess it has to get better, right? That's what I keep thinking . . .*

*Winter league is well underway. My team is 8-3, so we're winning quite a few games, and I'm pitching great. Just threw a personal record fastball—ninety-two miles per hour. I'll admit that felt like quite the accomplishment, although it did leave me with a sore arm for the next week.*

*I miss seeing you in the stands when I play. It makes the game feel so . . . different. I don't know how else to explain it.*

*Keep doing your thing out there. Thinking of you often.*

*Jack*

# eighteen
# THEN

**There** were a lot of things Jack expected to see when he looked up in the stands during a game—cheering fans, foam fingers, men in uniformed jackets peddling cotton candy and Cracker Jacks, beer cups touching people's lips, baseball caps, empty sections of hard metal seats.

What he never expected to see were two fans from opposite teams slapping hands, a herd of elephants, Santa Claus, or his dad. So, when he caught a glimpse of a guy in a pin-striped suit sitting in the seventh row during a home game at San Jose Municipal Stadium the following August, he had to do a couple of double takes before realizing it really was his old man.

*What was he doing here?*

Jack immediately feared that something was wrong. His dad had never been out to a game since Jack had been with the Giants. And the few college games he'd been to he'd only come because Jack's mom had (obviously) dragged him. Every time Jack had looked up into the stands, he'd found his dad with his back turned to the game and his phone pressed up against his ear.

*Was something wrong with his mom?* Jack wondered. *Had his dad's dad, Jack's only living grandparent, passed away? Had their house burned down?*

Anxiously, Jack tapped his feet on the cement dugout floor during each of his team's at-bats and glanced up at his dad in between pitches whenever he was on the mound throwing. When the game finally came to an end and his teammates went to the clubhouse gym to lift, Jack bounded up the bleachers.

"What's wrong?" he asked his dad immediately. Although the night was warm, Jack was shivering from the fear of what his dad was going to hit him with.

"Something has to be wrong for me to see my boy play?" his dad said lightheartedly as he rose to his feet.

"Cut the crap, Dad."

His dad opened his mouth like he was about to come back at Jack with a defensive comment but then closed it, confirming Jack's suspicion that something was definitely wrong. His dad stared down at his loafers. *What kind of a man showed up to a baseball game in a fancy outfit like that anyway?*

"What is it, Dad?"

His dad folded his arms over his chest. Then he sighed deeply as he said, "Your mom asked me for a divorce."

Jack wasn't surprised by this. Over the past six years or so, his mom had voiced to Jack a number of times how much his dad's absentee lifestyle bothered her. When Jack was growing up, she'd always acted like she didn't mind it. She'd defended him to Jack, saying things like, "The way your dad supports us is by being at his job and making money to provide for this family. Work is his way of showing his love." Jack didn't know if she ever really believed that, or if she just said those things to try and make Jack feel better. But once he got to high school, she quit coming to his dad's defense. Sometimes she bashed him in front of Jack when they were at the dinner table, just the two of them, eating one of her home-cooked meals while his dad's plate sat there getting cold. Other times, Jack heard her crying softly in her bedroom after his dad didn't show up to take her to a movie like he said he would, or to a play downtown she'd been dying to see.

"She said she couldn't do it anymore," his dad continued, raking his fingers through his hair. "She told me she doesn't want to grow old alone."

Jack grabbed the brim of his baseball cap and pulled on it. What was his dad expecting? Pity? Jack couldn't give that to him. He sat down on the bleachers, and his dad took a seat beside him.

They both looked out over the field at the sprinklers as they kicked on. Then, before giving an awkward silence time to set in, his dad changed the subject.

"So, I was sitting at my office last night going through a bunch of things, and I found a picture tucked away in a drawer of you in your green Mighty Warriors Little League uniform. I think I saw you play one time that season."

"Yeah. You did," Jack said, thinking back. "It was a Tuesday evening game, and it got rained out halfway through. You saw me hit a double, bringing one guy in, and pitch three innings where I struck out seven people."

His dad looked at him incredulously.

"I remember every detail of every game you were at, Dad. But more than that, I remember the disappointment I felt every game where you didn't show up."

In his entire life Jack had never seen his dad cry. Not when his grandma passed away when Jack was seven. Or when their golden retriever, Rusty, got hit by a car. Or when he lost a big trial that he had spent years preparing for. But now, out here underneath the florescent stadium lights, he saw a single tear roll down his old man's cheek.

"I know I messed up, Jack," he said. "I get it now—now that it's too late. I chose the less important thing in life for too many years. And now . . . well . . . I have incredible success, a solid income, nice things, but no one to share any of it with."

Immediately Charli popped into Jack's head. And the decision he'd been belaboring for the past eight months or so. Jack had been looking for a sign that he should call his baseball career quits, and here his dad was, sitting right next to him, telling him that the most important things in life were the people in it. And if he were to get a do-over, he'd choose his family over his career.

Jack couldn't believe that his dad was the one shedding light on his decision. It was a definite curveball, and the irony of it wasn't lost on him. It was as though his life script read, "Dad enters left" right at this critical point, and Jack had to believe there was a reason for that.

"I'm here because I want to be at your games. I want to be able to talk to you on the phone. I want to be a presence unlike I was before."

Jack had heard similar things come out of his dad's mouth in the past and wasn't sure he believed that he'd changed. But strangely he felt kind of grateful to him. His dad had made a mistake. Jack didn't have to make the same one.

Of course, his dad had no clue that he had just given Jack the insight he desperately needed. He was just there trying to make amends. But still, that was worth something. Maybe not complete forgiveness, but a hug at least.

Surprising the both of them, Jack pulled his dad into his arms. It had been years since the two of them had embraced, and at first, the gesture felt awkward, stiff. But then both of them relaxed and eventually his dad put his arm around Jack's back and patted it a few times.

Jack told his dad that he would keep him posted about his schedule. He didn't want to share the details of how uncertain his baseball future looked at that very moment. It was one thing to embrace his dad; it was another to bare his soul to him. For now, he was keeping those thoughts private, but it was clear what he wanted to do.

After his dad left, he would go right to Coach Berry's office in the clubhouse and tell him that he was done with baseball. Then he planned to pack his bags, drive home, and spend a few days with his mom to make sure she was okay. And later, he was going to fly out to Charleston, surprise Charli, and ask her to marry him.

Was it crazy? Sure. Impulsive? A little. But Jack knew it was the right thing. He didn't want to end up where his dad was years down the road—on top of his career but without the love of his life.

Charli was too important to him. And the thought of being with her was way more exciting to him than shacking up in dingy motel rooms with a bunch of guys all chasing the same dream, which all of them realized only a very few had a slight shot at.

It wasn't like he had to give up baseball for good. He could get a job coaching at a high school or as an assistant coach at a college. He could even start up some baseball camps out there. Those baseball equations included Charli and sounded much better to him than where he was now.

When he and his dad finally stood up and started to head down the bleachers, Jack found himself smiling. He playfully knocked his dad with his shoulder, and his dad, in turn, ruffled Jack's hair.

"What do you say we grab a bite to eat?" his dad asked.

Jack nodded. "I just have to take care of something first."

—

"What are you doing home?" The shocked expression on Jack's mom's face was priceless when she opened the door for him and saw him standing there with his packed suitcases and his truck parked in the driveway. It was the same look Jack hoped to see on Charli's face when he surprised her next week in Charleston. "Don't you have a game tonight?"

"I quit," Jack said, stepping inside, glad to be home, glad to be one stop closer to being with Charli again.

"You, what?" His mom gasped. "Are you okay?" She put her hands on his shoulders and checked his face for signs of regret frantically, like the mother of a toddler looking her little guy over for scrapes after a big fall.

"Never been better," he said and smiled to assure her that he was fine. He lugged his suitcases into the house behind him and closed the door on the hot August afternoon.

Tentatively his mom reached out and rested her hand on his shoulder. "This isn't because of your father and me, is it?"

"Actually," he said, prepared to fully open up to her unlike he had to his dad. "This *is* sort of about that."

"Oh no." Her face crumbled.

"Don't worry," he told her. "Honestly, this is a good thing."

He followed her into the kitchen where she immediately started to boil a pot of water and to pull out the ingredients for his favorite meal—spaghetti and meatballs. Cooking had always been her go-to when she was stressed. When he talked with her on the phone after his dad came out to San Jose and broke the news of their divorce, she joked that if he'd been around more, he would have known the divorce papers were coming because their kitchen had been full of gourmet meals that week—braised lamb, pork chops with garlic mashed potatoes, her famous jambalaya.

Jack hopped up onto the granite countertop. "Hearing Dad talk about not spending more time with you and me—it really put things in perspective. You know I haven't been crazy about baseball in a while, but what I *am* still crazy about is Charli." He cleared his throat preparing himself for his even bigger reveal. "Which is why I've decided to fly out to Charleston, surprise her, and ask her to marry me. I leave next week. I just bought my plane ticket."

"What?" His mom dropped the box of opened spaghetti noodles, which hit the floor and proceeded to roll everywhere.

"Shoot!" She dropped to her knees to pick them up.

"You don't like my idea?" Jack had thought she would completely embrace it. He had been so excited to tell her about it his whole car ride home. He'd even been hoping she'd give him his grandmother's antique diamond wedding ring to use to propose to Charli. Years ago, before he and Charli were even dating, Charli had found it in his mom's old wooden jewelry box stored in the attic on top of a distressed pine console table. She'd tried it on for fun, loved the look of it, and the fit had been perfect.

"You're just . . . hitting me with a lot here, Jack."

"Really? How can you say that?" He jumped off the counter and squatted down to help gather up the noodles. "You've been on the other end of my phone calls since I left for San Jose, Mom. And your advice the whole time has been to follow my heart. Didn't you kind of anticipate that that advice might lead me to do this?"

"To quit maybe. But I did not anticipate that it would prompt you to surprise Charli with a proposal. Are you sure that's the best idea?"

"I've lived with the fear of losing her for over a year," he said. "I can't do it anymore. I want to start a life together."

His mom held out the box for him to stuff the noodles he'd gathered back in. "But do you have any idea where her head's at with you? What if she's not ready to get engaged?"

"The reason we made the pact was so that we might have a shot at a future together. Now that I've quit baseball and can move where she is, I'm sure she'll want to start a future with me sooner rather than later."

"Maybe," his mom said. "But maybe not. What if she's seeing someone else? Have you thought of that?"

"Well, she definitely doesn't sound like she's seeing anyone else from the tone of her letters." She still wrote things at the end of them like, *Miss you*. And, *Wish I could see you soon.* She wouldn't have included stuff like that if she was involved with another guy, would she have?

"I'd feel a lot better about you going down there if you gave her a heads up. What's the harm in that? You could even keep the proposal a surprise. But at least tell her you're coming to Charleston."

Jack could feel himself starting to lose his temper. "I don't want to give her time to weigh in with her voice of reason. You know how she can be."

If he called, Charli would be furious he quit baseball, encourage him to reconsider, and oppose his coming out there. But if he showed up and let her see how happy he was to have quit, he knew she wouldn't protest.

His mom set the spaghetti down on the counter and held Jack's hands while she looked him in the eyes. "Don't get mad at me. I just don't want to see you get hurt."

"I appreciate your concern," he said, trying to keep his voice even. "But this is what I really want."

"Will you just sit with all this for a couple of weeks, and then if you still feel like going out there and proposing is the right thing, you can do it?"

"I've already sat with it, Mom. And the longer I wait, the more time Charli *does* have to maybe meet someone else." He turned away from her and looked over at the framed picture of him and Charli that was tacked up on the refrigerator door. The picture was actually two similar shots mounted side by side. In one they were seven years old, standing in a high pile of leaves that they'd raked up in Charli's backyard and thrown up in handfuls into the crisp autumn air. The second picture was taken in a leaf pile too, but just a few years ago by one of their photographer friends on a sunny fall day on the Oregon State campus. Charli had her arms draped around Jack's neck, and they were both sitting in the leaves, smiling at the camera. He wanted to be as happy as he was in both of those photos again. And he didn't want to have to wait.

Stubbornly he said, "I'm going to go and propose either way, but I'd enjoy it more knowing you were behind me."

For a second, the only sound in the kitchen was the water boiling on the stove. And then Jack heard his mom leave the room.

*So much for being behind him.* Really? That was how she was going to respond? Why was she being so negative about this? And worrying so much? Couldn't she just be happy for him?

A moment later he heard her reenter.

"Maybe I'll just go ask Dad for his approval," he said, even though he knew it was insensitive. His dad's approval really meant nothing to him.

He heard his mom draw in a deep breath. "If this is what you really want and how you really want to do it . . . then I want you to have this ring."

Jack spun around and saw her standing by the stove, holding his grandmother's ring in her fingers.

"Mom—" he started, apologetically.

"You *do* have my support and my blessing, Jack."

"You don't know how much that means to me." He went to her, took the ring, and examined it, picturing the way it would sparkle on Charli's finger. "I've never been so excited about something," he confessed. "Or felt so right about a decision."

Tears shone in his mom's eyes. "Then I'm sure it will all work out," she said.

Jack smiled, staring at the ring in the palm of his hand, wishing his flight was even sooner.

## nineteen
# THEN

**Jack** had the proposal all planned by the time he arrived in Charleston. First, he was going to take Charli to dinner at Poogan's Porch. It was an old historic home converted into a restaurant that served famous Southern cuisine. White lights were strung on the porch railings and on the roof, which he knew Charli would find romantic, and there was a fireside table inside, just like at Hayden's, which Jack had reserved. After their stomachs were full of fried green tomatoes, pan-seared jumbo scallops, and oysters, and they'd had a few glasses of red wine to wash it all down, he had a horse-drawn carriage scheduled to pick them up outside the restaurant. The carriage would drive them through the bustling city and down quaint cobblestone streets. And later, their driver would drop them at The Battery, a park surrounded by majestic antebellum homes and full of stately live oak trees, where Jack planned to pop the question. He couldn't wait to explain to Charli underneath the gazebo in the middle of the grove that he'd given baseball up and that he was ready to call off the pact and start that forever they'd always talked about, right then.

Before he could do any of that, though, he had to let Charli know he was in town.

From her letters, he knew her typical Saturday routine. In the mornings, she got up early, grabbed coffee at the two-story Starbucks on King Street and then usually spent time in the library, studying.

Around one, she took a break for lunch at one of three places—Colonial Lake, if she'd prepared food herself and it wasn't raining, Bull Street Gourmet, if she wanted a quick and easy sandwich, or Fleet Landing, a restaurant on the harbor she sometimes dined at with her friends.

Since it was twelve-thirty by the time Jack had woken up, showered, and stopped by the local Harris Teeter grocery store to buy champagne and roses for the fancy hotel room he'd rented for them that night, he decided lunch would be the best time to catch her and planned to hit all three of her usual spots.

He'd stayed at a cheap motel the night before near the lake and Bull Street Gourmet, so he took off on foot for those two spots first. Within minutes he was scanning the faces of people at the lake who were sitting on benches in the brilliant sunshine, eating and chatting. Charli didn't appear to be one of them, but he hung out under the shade of a sycamore tree for a few minutes just to make sure.

Every time he saw a twenty-something woman with brown hair join a group or walk past, his heart leapt. It hadn't fully hit him that he was going to see Charli so soon until now.

When there was no sign of her by one-fifteen, he pulled out the directions to Bull Street Gourmet that the front desk receptionist at his motel had written down, and jogged over there. It was a small grocery-type deli with only a couple of tables in the middle and a few barstool chairs along the windows. There was no sign of her inside, just a few college-aged students in line placing orders and a couple of businessmen dressed in suits, sitting at a table scarfing down sandwiches.

Feeling a little panicked, but still hopeful, Jack found a main street and caught a biker taxi to drive him across town to Fleet Landing, the last place she might be.

He was dropped off at one-forty in front of a historical white concrete building perched over the marsh with a wraparound deck and oversized windows aimed right at the Charleston harbor. Tall sea grass shot up from the river, and a couple of people were leaning on the side deck railings talking with glasses of beer in their hands.

Jack tipped his driver and headed inside first, but there were only a couple of people in the heavily air-conditioned room sitting at the high bar looking out through the windows at the harbor. After confirming that Charli was not one of them, he walked back out and started around the side of the restaurant toward the back deck, where he could hear boisterous laughter and a clamor of voices.

As he rounded the corner, he paused to keep himself hidden, surveyed the area, and within seconds spotted Charli. She was at the table furthest from him, right up against the railing, underneath an orange umbrella. Jack took in the sight of her, and that was enough to set his heart racing. She had on a dress, and her hair was tied back loosely, a couple of strands blowing across her forehead in the easy breeze. Damn, she looked beautiful in that natural way that made her stand out from the rest of the women dining alfresco that afternoon. She had what looked to be a taco in her hands and brought it up to her lips to take a bite. A moment later she stole a glance at a tugboat tooting its horn as it drove by, and then she reached for her glass of iced tea and fixed her attention across the table on . . . a guy. A curly haired guy. Jack couldn't see his face, but from the look on Charli's face, she was certainly enjoying his company.

Taking a few steps back, he hid behind the side of the building and leaned up against it, gathering his thoughts.

What had he just walked in on? Not a date, right? Just a friendly lunch between two friends? His mom's concern that Charli was seeing someone else couldn't possibly have been right, could it have?

He closed his eyes for a brief second and told himself not to jump to any conclusions. He had no idea the nature of the lunch Charli was having, and until he did, he shouldn't assume the worst.

Still, this was making him sweat. Thinking maybe he could get a better idea of what was really going on between the two of them if he spied for a moment longer, he peeked around the corner at their table again. For a second, as they continued to eat and talk, Jack convinced himself that it was just a casual lunch and that he had nothing to worry about. Probably just a study break, he told himself, before they regrouped to cram for a test together. But just as he was about to walk over toward them, the guy leaned across the table. And then, before Jack knew it, he'd tilted his head, and his lips were on Charli's and her lips were on his.

Jack's stomach dropped. *No! Why? Shit!* Tearing his attention away, he darted back around the side of the building.

He hadn't just seen that, had he?

He shut his eyes, and the image of Charli and the curly haired guy kissing played back like an instant replay in his head. Fuck, he had.

Turning toward the wall, Jack punched it, scaring away the few customers who were leaning on the railing nearby and sending a blond, teenage waitress running inside, probably to get her manager. His hand started to throb and bleed at his knuckles, but he punched the wall again, preferring to feel the pain there than in his chest, which was suddenly heavy, swelling.

"Damn it!" he cursed and leaned up against the wall, feeling sick. Either he was going to throw up or the manager was going to come out and ask him to leave. One way or the other he was going to make a scene for everyone, including Charli to see, if he didn't get out of there fast.

—

One minute Charli had been talking about how delicious her fish tacos were and the next minute Christopher's mouth was over hers, and his tongue was sliding along her front row of teeth.

Paralyzed with shock for a couple of seconds, she let him kiss her. But when she snapped out of it, she reached out, put her hand on his chest, and gave him a little shove. "What are you doing?" she asked him breathlessly. She brought her napkin up to her lips and blotted them with it.

"I was kissing you," Christopher said. He was grinning like a teenage boy who'd finally gotten the nerve to ask his crush to dance at a junior high mixer in the disco-ball-lit gymnasium. "You felt something there, didn't you?"

"What? No!" Charli reached for her glass of iced tea and finished it off, washing her mouth out.

Christopher's face suddenly turned a deep shade of red. "Really? Nothing?"

"Nothing, Christopher," she said, enunciating her words to drive her point home. It wasn't the worst kiss in the world. And under a different set of circumstances, maybe she could have felt something for him. But not with how she was still feeling about Jack. And definitely not considering Jack had mentioned in his letters that his future with baseball was up in the air. Charli didn't think he'd actually hang up his cleats for good, but there was no way she was going to get involved with someone else when she knew there was a chance Jack might be coming around soon.

Christopher's face reddened even more, and he stared down at his plate of shrimp swimming in grits. "Man . . . I thought maybe if I just went for it, you'd realize that you and I had something. Maybe I should have asked you first, but you know how you can ruminate about things, Charli. I figured I'd just bypass that step and take a leap." Then he laughed at himself slightly like he couldn't believe he'd thought that. "I like you so much," he confessed, looking up.

Charli softened, feeling sympathetic. She cared for Christopher and didn't like seeing him upset. "I'm just not ready for anything new," she explained, reaching across the table and resting her hand on his.

"What is it about your ex that's got you so hung up on him? From what Rebecca's told me, you two sound like such different people."

"We are," Charli said. Jack definitely didn't tick the same way she and Christopher did, but that didn't mean he didn't understand her. They connected on a deeper level than their interests, and there was something inside her that burned for him. He was the one person who made her feel like she had returned home anytime she stepped into his arms. "I can't help myself from loving him," she said, feeling no need to give Christopher any more of an explanation.

Christopher just nodded, slipped his hand out from under hers and then squinted up at her in the sliver of sunlight that had slipped in under the umbrella.

"Thank you," she said. "For understanding."

"I'm trying my best," Christopher said. He took a long drink of his iced tea and then apologized for making her uncomfortable.

"Don't worry about it," Charli assured him.

"So, can we just forget that ever happened? This won't ruin our friendship?" Christopher asked.

Charli pretended to seal her lips and toss the key away. "I won't tell anyone if you won't."

Christopher's shoulders relaxed. "Thank you." He cleared his throat and stirred his shrimp around a bit. Then, sitting up straighter in his chair, he said: "So, before that whole thing that didn't just happen, happened . . . what was it you were saying?"

—

Jack paced back and forth in his motel room staring at the phone cradled on the receiver on top of the coffee table. *Maybe I should just call Charli. Tell her I'm here and what I saw. Ask for an explanation.*

He'd been debating it for the last fifteen minutes. Part of him wanted to. But part of him was afraid of what she might say. "Yes, I've moved on. I'm sorry, I didn't know how to tell you."

*Fuck it. I've got to. I've come all this way.*

Taking a seat on the edge of the bed, he picked the phone up. After a deep breath, he punched in Charli's number.

Ring.

Ring.

"Hello?" A man answered.

Had he dialed the wrong number? He must have. Jack was about to apologize when he heard Charli's laugh in the background.

"Christopher, give me my phone!" she squealed.

Christopher . . . So the curly haired guy had a name.

Charli giggled again. "Christopher, come on. Hand it over! Who is it?"

"I don't know—random number. Try to reach it." Jack pictured Christopher dangling the phone above Charli's head. His heart ached at the sound of their flirtatious banter. It was almost more painful than seeing the kiss.

"Christopher," Charli laughed again.

"All right, all right," Christopher said. "Here you go." He must have passed the phone to Charli because the next thing Jack knew she was on the line.

"Hello?" she said. "Hello. I'm sorry. Who is this?"

Charli . . . Jack wanted to say something. It killed him not to. But what was there *to* say? Charli had clearly moved on. If the kiss hadn't completely convinced him of that, this phone call had.

"Hello?" Charli said again. "Hello? Is anyone there?"

Jack pinched the bridge of his nose. Their timing was off again. Just like when they made the pact.

As the realization set in, he slammed the phone down.

"Damn it!" he screamed. Standing up he grabbed a pillow from the bed and pitched it across the room into the blinds. Then he reached into his pocket and took out the engagement ring. He sunk down onto the floor and stared at the diamond until the room started to grow dark. He'd fucking lost her . . .

# twenty
# THEN

"**And** then what happened?" Jack's mom looked across the canoe at him as they took a break from paddling along the Tualatin River.

It was Jack's first time out of the house since he'd returned home three days earlier. When he landed in Portland, he texted his mom to pick him up at the airport, and once she arrived, he climbed into her car and didn't say a word the whole ride back to their house.

Although his mom knew something terrible had happened, she had been smart enough not to pester Jack with questions and allowed him the time he needed to make sense of what went wrong. That was the rhythm they usually settled into when Jack had to work things out. Over the years he had made her learn the hard way that there was no warming him up for the heart-to-heart chat that waited at the end of each of his crises. Jack was either ready to talk or not, and when he was, he always let her know.

Until then, she knocked on his bedroom door twice a day to tell him she was setting down plates of food for him. She'd left all of his old favorites—her extra-cheesy macaroni, spaghetti and meatballs, lasagna, fish tacos—but Jack hadn't been able to stomach most of it.

Now, after days spent tormenting himself, he finally felt ready to open up.

"Then I gathered my things and caught the first flight out of there."

His mom brought out the lunch she had packed for them. Although Jack had told her he still didn't have an appetite, she said she wanted to be prepared just in case he changed his mind.

"I can't imagine what that was like to see," she said, a pained expression crossing her face. "And then to hear them on the phone interacting like that."

"Yeah." Jack lifted the oar off his lap, set it down and sat back on his hands. "You were right, Mom. The surprise attack was not the best move."

Jack had lost count of the times in his life when he wished his mom hadn't been right. Like the time she warned him about going dirt bike riding with his older cousins and had ended up in the emergency room with a busted jaw. Or in junior high when she suggested he take a break from pitching during the summer to give his arm a rest, and he ended up with Little League Shoulder at the end of the summer season, which left him benched for part of fall ball. The look on his mom's face told Jack that she got little pleasure out of being right. She handed him a plate loaded with a turkey sandwich and his favorite barbecued chips.

"I know I wasn't a big fan of your plan, Jack, but I still find it so strange to think that she moved on. It just doesn't seem like Charli."

"It completely blindsided me."

"Are you sure you don't want to try calling her again? Get the whole story? I feel like if she knew that you wanted to be with her, then she'd dump the guy she was with."

"You didn't see the kiss for starters," Jack said, the image popping into his head again, his stomach getting queasy. "There are categories of kissing, Mom. This wasn't a drunken bar make out. It was a mid-day, I've-got-my-wits-about-me kiss. It was long, and it said, 'There's more where this came from.' And then the tone of her voice when I heard her talking to that Christopher guy over the phone . . . it was just like when she used to flirt with me. It's not meant to be with us . . . right now at least."

A warm wind picked up and pushed their canoe so that it started to drift diagonally toward a thicket of trees with broken branches dipping into the water. Jack set down his lunch, lifted his oar back up and tried to maneuver them back to the other side.

"It sounds like there's more than heartbreak in your voice," his mom said.

Despite his best efforts to control how much of his feelings he showed to his mom and when, she always managed to sense what he wasn't saying.

"I'll admit I'm mad too," he told her. "All that time when Charli was telling me in her letters to stick with baseball and give it more time, I thought she had my back, trying to make sure that I gave my dream my best shot before walking away. Now I'm thinking she was just trying to keep me from flying out to Charleston and ruining the good thing she had going with this other guy."

He saw his mom's eyes start to well up with tears as he set down his oar again.

"I'm so sorry, Jack. I know how disappointing it can be when someone you love doesn't live up to your expectations."

Jack knew this whole conversation had to be reopening wounds she was still nursing after separating from his dad, and realizing they were both dealing with such a letdown made him feel closer to his mom than ever before.

"This also must feel like such a big hole—Charli took up a lot of space in your heart for such a long time."

"Yeah, I know," Jack said. "And the part that Charli didn't fill, baseball did. Now I've lost them both."

"Well, have you?" his mom asked. "Can you go back to baseball?"

Technically it was an option. He could try and get picked up by another team next season as a free agent, but he didn't want that.

"Baseball wasn't doing it for me anymore," he said. "Charli may have fallen out of love with me, but I fell out of love with baseball, and I don't think knowing I can't be with Charli now will change that. Honestly, for the first time in my life, I have absolutely no clue what I want." He shook his head and stared out over the river, watching as a goose flapped its wings, rippling the water, and took flight.

"Well, okay, let's regroup here," his mom said, switching into problem-solving mode. "I don't think it's healthy for you to just sit around. Why don't you take off and try and start over somewhere fresh? There are so many memories around Portland of you and Charli, and California would probably remind you of baseball. Pick a new city. Move. Try and find something else there that will make you happy. It might be a job, a new girlfriend, a hobby. I'm sure your dad will support you until you get on your feet. He's all about trying to make things right with you now."

Different cities popped into Jack's head—Chicago, LA, Seattle, Houston, Denver, New York. He could even go abroad. Although the idea of starting over completely was the first suggestion that hadn't lodged a pit in his stomach in days, he wasn't sure.

"I don't know. It sounds a little bit like running away."

"I think it depends on which way you're facing when you leave," his mom said. "There's a new dream out there somewhere waiting for you, and you just need to have your eyes wide open to see it. I'm afraid if you stay here, you'll be so busy looking back at what you've lost, that the next best thing could be right in front of you, and you wouldn't see it."

She was right. Being here, Jack constantly felt reminded of what he'd lost. Even sitting out on this canoe triggered thoughts of Charli. How many rides had they gone on together over the years? Jack couldn't begin to count. If he got some distance from Portland and his memories of her, it might help.

"Okay, maybe you're right," he said.

His mom smiled across the canoe at him and took a bite of her turkey on wheat. To please her, he put a chip in his mouth and chewed on it slowly.

"But what do I do about the pact Charli and I made? Do I just forget about it now?" he asked.

He'd been carting the to-go box from Hayden's with the date and time of their reunion on it everywhere he went since he and Charli split. When he got home, he threw it in the back of his closet in a fit of rage and cursed Charli for ruining things.

"That's up to you," his mom said. "I doubt she's given up on the two of you completely, but it sounds like she has put you out of her mind for right now at least. You might need to put her out of your mind for a while, too, to allow yourself to get through this. If, down the road, you decide that you're still curious about a future with her, well . . . you can deal with that then." She set her sandwich down and reached across the canoe, resting her hand on Jack's knee. "In theory, what you and Charli were trying to do with the reunion was great, Jack. But things got messed up a bit here. You need to look out for yourself right now."

Jack stuck another barbecue chip in his mouth and looked back out over the water.

"So, I shouldn't keep writing her letters anymore either then." He said it as more of a statement than a question, but his mom still came through with her opinion.

"I wouldn't. Knowing what you know . . . it would be too hard for you to pretend you're doing okay."

"Yeah," Jack said. He definitely wasn't okay. And he had never been one to hide his feelings when he talked to Charli. If he kept in touch with her, he'd eventually give away the fact that he'd gone out there and that he'd seen what he saw. Then she'd be forced to write a letter confirming that she was seeing someone else, which would only make Jack feel worse. He'd already taken one dagger to the heart. He didn't need another.

His mom rubbed his knee. "You're going to get through this, Jack," she assured him. "I promise."

Jack sighed skeptically. Despite her track record, this was one time Jack thought she might be wrong.

—

Charli jogged out to her mailbox as she did every morning when there was a chance Jack might be responding to a letter she had last sent. Excited to find one resting there, she tore it open right away.

September 21, 2013

*Dear Charli,*

*I'd appreciate it if we stopped communicating. Our plan to stay in touch by writing letters isn't working for me anymore.*

*Sincerely, Jack*

She read it once. Then a second time. And then, in the middle of her driveway, she collapsed onto her knees and cried.

Visit sincerelyriley.com/scene-6 to see scenes from these chapters unfold and to Shop the Book™.

# twenty-one
# THEN

**Charli** had dropped five pounds in the past five days since she'd received Jack's two line letter telling her he wanted to cut off communication between them completely. The only thing she'd managed to stomach was a bowl of soup, which Rebecca had brought over and spoon-fed to her, a pint of Ben and Jerry's Cookie Dough ice cream, which Rebecca had insisted would make her feel better (it didn't), and a couple bites of pizza at a study session last night.

*Why?* she asked herself, rolling to the other side of her bed and pulling the covers up underneath her chin. *Why? Why? Why?* She'd been living in her bed unless she absolutely had to get out of it—for class, lab, or a study session—and ruminating about that very question.

It was a question Jack hadn't given her an answer to in his letter and that he wouldn't answer for her no matter how many times she tried calling him and no matter how many voicemails she left.

"Please explain this to me," she had said desperately the day she got the letter. "You can't just write me something like that. It's unfair."

No response.

"Jack, I need you to tell me what's going on," she tried another time. "At least let me know that you're okay."

She got a simple text message response:

*I'm fine. But please stop calling.*

She tried reaching out to his mom after that, hoping maybe she could give her an answer for why Jack didn't want to hear from her anymore. But Grace must have been under instructions not to communicate with her because she hadn't called Charli back.

Charli had been left to devise all sorts of different theories as to what his explanation for the letter could have been.

Sometimes she convinced herself that Jack had written it because it had simply gotten too hard for him to hear about her life knowing that he couldn't be a part of it. Other times she let herself believe he'd sent it because staying in touch with her was distracting him too much from focusing on baseball. She knew that those theories didn't make much sense. If they were the real reasons, it seemed Jack would have just explained them to her in his letter. He had to have known that she would understand both. But they hurt less than believing the most likely one—that Jack had met someone else.

Charli had made it clear when she and Jack made the pact that they shouldn't kiss and tell. His letter could very likely have been his way of telling her, without breaking that rule, that he was seeing another girl. She hadn't really considered how difficult it would be for whichever one of them moved on first to keep communicating with the other one. There was a chance writing to her was making Jack feel unfaithful to his new girlfriend. Or that his new girlfriend found out he was staying in touch with her and was uncomfortable with it.

Charli knew she had given Jack her permission to date other people during their break, but it killed her to think about him seeing someone else given how strongly she still felt for him.

Pushing the image of Jack with another woman out of her mind for the umpteenth time, she tried to think of even more explanations for his letter to ease her anxiety. Sitting up, she reached over on her nightstand for his most recent note to search it again for clues.

*The game's still not getting much better, Charli, he'd written. I'm trying to hang in here but it's tough. It just feels so different. If I do quit though, I'm worried I'll feel like I failed.*

Maybe he had gone ahead and actually quit, she considered.

Quitting could have had a weird effect on him and prompted him to write her the letter. Perhaps he felt the need to cut off communication with everyone and take off somewhere, find himself again. She could see herself feeling the urge to do something similar if she had given up her PhD program midstream.

Realizing she could look up Jack's baseball status on the Internet, Charli pushed her covers off and climbed out of bed. If he quit, there would probably be an article about it online or his name would be missing from the Giants' roster.

She sat down on the wicker chair at her desk and opened her laptop. Why hadn't she thought of this before? Setting her fingers on the keyboard, she typed his name into Google, and then took a deep breath as she clicked Return.

Sure enough, the first thing to pop up was an article titled, "Jack Logan of the San Jose Giants Gives the Game Up."

What? Her heart leapt, and she moved her mouse over to the link and clicked on it, opening the full article on MLB.com.

*"Jack Logan of the San Jose Giants, has left the game for good. The Giants' General Manager, Carl Duton, made the announcement Friday afternoon in a press conference. Logan, who played at Oregon State, was selected in the fourteenth round of the draft by the Giants in 2012. The twenty-four-year-old pitcher claims to have 'fallen out of love' with the game."*

In disbelief, Charli fell back against her chair. This was crazy. Reaching for her phone, she tried calling him one more time.

It went straight to voicemail.

"Jack, I just read the news about your decision to quit online." Her tone was different this time than in her last few messages. She was no longer speaking to him as a devastated ex-girlfriend, but as a worried friend, and she hoped Jack could hear that in her voice. "I'm so sorry. I can't imagine how difficult that choice was for you, and I want you to know that I'm here if you need anything. Please, Jack, call me so we can talk about this." She wanted to say more, but there was nothing else she really could say without him on the other end. After hesitating for a few more seconds, she hung up.

And then she stared at her phone hoping Jack would call her back.

Ten minutes passed.

Nothing.

Another ten.

Her phone didn't ring.

Charli folded her arms on her desk and laid her head down on top of them. She wished she had been able to see into the future back when she suggested they make the pact and that she'd known Jack was going to quit when he did. They could have made it a year and then some doing long-distance.

Now Jack was done with baseball, and she had no idea where he was. Although in reality, he could have been off soul searching like she'd originally thought, he had mentioned in a letter a year earlier that if he quit, he wanted to move out to Charleston and be with her. If he still felt strongly for her, wouldn't he have flown to Charleston instead of cutting her out of his life?

"Oh no," she moaned. She couldn't help but think again of her least favorite theory—that Jack had met someone else and that he had decided, even with his new freedom to move anywhere in the country, that he wanted to stay and keep pursuing the other woman. At least for a while.

She almost couldn't accept this. Her and Jack's relationship had been so great, and honestly, she thought it was indestructible. But she realized that one of the ingredients to their winning formula was their shared history. For the past year and a half, they'd been building new histories with new people, and considering that Jack had been going through such a difficult time, it was possible that someone on his end had been listening to and empathizing with his struggles on a day-in and day-out basis. Charli could see how that might have grown into something more, and how her periodic pep talks through snail mail might have seemed like a poor substitute for the TLC he really needed.

She suddenly felt nauseous and rushed to the bathroom. Kneeling down in front of the toilet, she threw up what little she had in her stomach and then propped herself up against the wall and started to cry into her hands. This wasn't how things were supposed to work out. There was supposed to be a happily ever after at the end of this story—her with her PhD, Jack with his successful baseball career, reuniting at Hayden's and picking up where they left off five years earlier. Why had they neglected to write a contingency plan for if one of them wasn't happy with the way things were?

"What was I thinking coming up with that pact in the first place?" Charli sobbed. She rewound her thoughts to that night at Hayden's when she heard a knock on her front door. Maybe it was Jack, she thought, coming to tell her the letter had just been a joke. "A terrible joke," she imagined herself saying as she took his face into her hands and kissed him for the first time in too long.

But her fantasy vanished when she heard Rebecca's voice on the other side of the door telling her to open up. Climbing to her feet, Charli flushed the toilet and ran some cold water over her face. She hadn't looked in the mirror in days and saw now how gaunt and pale her cheeks were. A couple of zits had also popped up on her chin. Brownie points to Rebecca for being such a good friend that she didn't comment on her appearance once during any of her visits.

"Charli!" Rebecca knocked again.

Charli shut off the light and came out of the bathroom to unlock the door.

"Oh, good, you're alive." Rebecca walked in with a bag full of groceries from Harris Teeter. "Come with me into the kitchen. I'm making you food. And I brought wine. We're getting over this Jack-doesn't-want-to-talk-to-me-anymore pity-party."

Charli closed the door behind her. "Rebecca, he quit," she said, still in shock over the news she had just read.

"What?" Rebecca paused in the entryway, resting the bag of groceries on her hip.

"Jack quit baseball," Charli said. "I read it online."

"Wow."

"Yeah." Charli's throat was dry. "At first I thought maybe this meant that he had written me the note because he'd decided to take off and go soul searching."

"But then you realized if he was still in love with you he probably would have just come here, to Charleston?" Rebecca said.

"Exactly," Charli sighed. So, her conclusion was logical. Rebecca had come to the same one.

"I'm so sorry, Charli." Rebecca pulled her into a hug.

With her chin on Rebecca's shoulder, Charli couldn't help but lose it again. For a few minutes, Rebecca smoothed down her hair, soothing her as Charli blamed herself for this whole disaster.

Then, Rebecca pulled back and said, "You know what you should do?"

"What?" Fly out to where she thought he might be? Try to win his heart back? Keep calling until he answered?

"Move on to someone new yourself," Rebecca said. "That's the fastest way to get over a broken heart. At least according to *Cosmo*." Rebecca reached into her grocery bag and handed the latest issue to Charli with a barely clothed picture of Cameron Diaz gracing the cover.

"You brought me *Cosmo*?" Charli said, crying and laughing at the same time. "What are we, sorority sisters?"

"Yeah, I know, it's no *Science Daily* or *Discovery* magazine, but it's got some good information. Maybe you should start reading it. I bookmarked the page titled, 'Top Ten Ways to Move on and Get Over Your Ex.' Number one on the list is to date someone new."

Charli flipped through the magazine and skimmed the article.

"Listen, Charli," Rebecca said, pulling her into the living room and sitting her down on the couch. "Not to be rude, but Jack obviously doesn't feel the same way you do right now. I can't imagine how much that must hurt to think about, but it's the truth."

Charli shook her head, not wanting to accept it.

"Now, I know you thought that you and Jack were perfect for each other, but you need to adjust your thinking a little bit."

"It's just such unfortunate timing," Charli said. "If Jack wasn't into someone else, he could have probably found a job in Charleston, and we could have been together again."

"But that's not the way it played out," Rebecca told her. "And as painful as that is, you need to go on with your life. You don't want to be the psycho ex-girlfriend who keeps calling him forever. That's not going to do you any good."

Ouch. That was harsh. Leave it to Rebecca to dish out the truth serum.

"What about our future?" she asked, her mind suddenly jumping ahead. "Am I supposed to forget about the pact we made? Or do I keep that date in the back of my head?"

She really wanted to hang onto the hope of a someday with Jack. The thought that this was it was unbearable.

Rebecca sat down beside her. "Honestly, Charli, that letter he wrote kind of sounds like him calling the pact off."

"Really?" Her stomach sunk.

"Well, it certainly doesn't make your future with him sound promising."

"I wish he would have added something to the bottom of the note like, *P.S. Pact is still on.* Or, *P.S. Pact is off.*"

"Yeah, but he didn't, so for now, I honestly think you need to give something else a chance."

"You mean someone else?" Charli interpreted. "You mean Christopher?"

"I would highly recommend him as a good place to start," Rebecca said. "He's here. He's available. And we both know he's interested."

Charli took her head in her hands. If Jack wasn't staying sidelined in the dating department, she knew that she shouldn't either. And she couldn't go on feeling this sorry for herself much longer. But she couldn't imagine pulling herself together. She didn't want to move on. She wanted Jack.

"I don't know if I can realistically do it," she admitted.

"Charli, you got into a top PhD program. You just came up with a blow-your-socks-off dissertation topic. You can surely get back up on your feet after this. Think of it as a challenge. You rise to challenges."

"Intellectual challenges, yeah. But this is an emotional one."

Rebecca dismissed her argument with a wave of her hand. "I've seen how you are when you put your mind to something. You'll get through this."

"You really think so?"

"I know so." She patted Charli's leg. "Come on. Why don't you hop in the shower? Wash up? I'll cook us dinner. And we'll start this road to recovery."

"I'm not sure."

Rebecca stood up. "I'm not taking no for an answer." She started toward the kitchen and then paused in the doorway and looked over her shoulder. "By the way, I also may have invited Christopher over for dessert."

"No. You didn't."

Rebecca flashed a guilty smile. "Oops."

"Rebecca, I look like hell."

"Oh? You're suddenly worried about impressing him?" She raised an eyebrow.

"No, I'm just not exactly up for entertaining."

"*I'm* the one entertaining," Rebecca said. "Just at your house. Come on. He's seen you after you pulled two all-nighters before our last set of final exams. He won't care. Having him come over will help you get your mind off Jack."

It would definitely do that. Christopher was always so talkative and so into her that he didn't give Charli a chance to think about much else.

"Allow yourself to have a little fun. Don't think so much," Rebecca said.

"Do you know who you're talking to?"

"Take a shower. If you really don't want him to come over when you get out, I'll call and cancel."

Grunting, Charli stood up. Then she went into the bathroom and locked herself inside. As she turned the shower on she willed herself not to think about Jack and to focus her energy instead on Christopher.

—

Dessert with Christopher went better than Charli had anticipated. He made her laugh most of the time by doing impersonations of their professor, Dr. Rhodes, who lectured in different accents to keep the class engaged. And while Rebecca did the dishes, he took the time to check in with her about Jack.

"Rebecca told you about the letter?" Charli asked.

He nodded and then said, "You know, in college I had a serious girlfriend. Her name was Amy. She was everything to me—The

One, I was sure of it. But right before graduation, she broke up with me for my roommate. I was crushed, and for the longest time I thought I'd never meet someone I'd feel the same way about ever again. I mean I was convinced of it. But lately, I'm not so sure."

Charli felt herself blush.

"Don't give up, okay?" he said.

She nodded, feeling better—feeling desirable too—which was a far cry from how she'd been feeling hours earlier.

At the end of the night, she walked Christopher out to his motorcycle, a Harley Davidson that he'd been dying to get her on for months.

"You want to go for a ride?" he asked as he tossed the keys up and then caught them. "Have a little fun?"

"I've already told you that's not exactly my definition of fun."

"It will help take your mind off things."

Charli eyed the dangerous red bike with its chrome tires. She guessed it beat going back in her house and moping around.

"Fine. I'll give it a try," she said.

Christopher smiled and helped her onto the bike. He showed her how to fasten her helmet, pointed out the passenger foot pegs, and told her to hold onto his waist the whole time.

"You better not go too fast," she warned.

"What'd you say?" he replied as he revved up the engine.

"I said not too—"

He took off before she could finish and rounded the corner onto Murray Boulevard, a street of impressive mansions. Christopher whizzed past them, slowing down just a couple of times to point out his favorites, and then he turned onto East Battery, where late-night walkers were strolling along the sidewalk that lined the Cooper River.

"What do you think?" he yelled over the roaring engine and the buzz of the wind.

Charli took a deep breath of the fresh air. For the first time since getting Jack's letter, she felt alive. "Not bad!"

Christopher gave her a thumbs-up and leaned into the turn as he sped onto East Bay Street. He maneuvered in and out of slow-moving cars until he got to the foot of the Cooper River Bridge.

"We're not seriously going up there, are we?" Charli asked. She was terrified of heights and didn't even like going over the bridge in her car.

Christopher answered by accelerating up it. Charli screamed and gripped his waist tighter as they worked their way to the top. She was tempted to close her eyes, but the view was too beautiful. Over the side she could see the twinkling city lights and the water sparkling below them in the glow from the illuminated cables.

"It sure is something, isn't it?" Christopher said.

"Breathtaking," Charli replied.

They cruised into Mount Pleasant, puttered around, and then pulled a U-turn and drove back toward her place. Instead of taking the route they'd come on, Christopher wove through side streets with hanging lanterns and gardens lit up by soft white lights. The peacefulness of it soothed her and left her feeling refreshed.

"That was just what I needed," she told Christopher when he dropped her off.

"I'm glad," he said.

Out of gratitude, she planted a tiny kiss on his cheek.

"Guess I should take you on motorcycle rides more often," he said, reaching up and resting his hand on the spot her lips had touched.

Charli thanked him for the ride and walked up her front porch steps. She was just about to open the door when Christopher called after her.

"What do you say to dinner tomorrow night at Joe's Crab Shack on the pier at Folly Beach? We can take the Harley now that you're a pro."

"You mean a date?" Charli said.

"We don't have to call it that. Although if you want to I'm not opposed."

Charli gave him a slight smile. *Jack has moved on*, she reminded herself. *You need to get on with your life too.* She decided that it couldn't hurt. That it might be fun. And it would get Rebecca off her back.

"Pick me up at six?" she said.

Grinning, Christopher started his engine.

—

Charli was in the midst of finishing off her second bottle of Samuel Adams and thinking to herself how well her date with Christopher was going when he shifted his attention from the sunset to her and said, "So . . . tell me about your childhood."

"My childhood?" Jack immediately popped into her head.

"Yeah. I know all the details about your dissertation topic. I know that you need at least one cappuccino a day to survive, and that if you die, you want all your organs to be donated for research, but I know nothing about your life back in Oregon growing up."

"What do you want to know?" Charli asked.

"What did you do, who did you hang out with, that sort of thing."

She felt her cheeks flush. What was she supposed to say? Her relationship with Jack pretty much defined her childhood. And yet she didn't want to bring him into the conversation. Christopher seemed to sense that he'd made her uncomfortable.

Fortunately, instead of asking why, he leaned back in his chair and said, "Do you want to ask me some questions first?"

Charli nodded, relieved.

"All right. Fire away!"

Unlike her he seemed thrilled about the opportunity to open up. Charli learned that his parents were not just a little wealthy as he'd hinted; they were *extremely* wealthy. "Family money," he explained, from his dad's late father who owned an oil company. Christopher had been to forty-eight countries and had stayed in some of the most exclusive resorts in the world—the types with butlers, warm cookies waiting on your bedside table every night, and infinity pool bath tubs. Growing up, he was a total Star Wars nerd, and at one point, during high school, he thought he might want to be an actor instead of a scientist.

Charli grinned. "So that's where your ability to do impersonations comes from."

"Luke, I am your father," he said in a perfect Darth Vader voice.

"You may have actually made it in Hollywood," she said. "With that talent. And that hair."

"Did you just give me a compliment?" he asked.

"Possibly," Charli said and flagged over their waiter for another beer.

As the dinner went on, she ended up sharing a *bit* her of past with Christopher. She told him her favorite memory growing up—a daylong water balloon fight in her backyard with all the neighbor kids. Although Jack had been a big part of why that day was fun, she left him out of it and instead shared stories about the other people who were there. Sean Jones, who got hit so hard with a balloon he got a black eye. Sandy Rogers, who barricaded herself inside a canoe and who everyone thought was lost for hours. Nate Owen, who brought out his older brother's Water Blaster 2000 and hosed everyone down with it. The ice cream man who eventually showed up and put an end to the fight by causing everyone to run home to get money for Creamsicles.

She also told him about her favorite restaurant in Portland—Montage (which was actually a close second to Hayden's, but he didn't need to know that).

"I used to go there all the time with my parents," she explained. "It's this great restaurant tucked underneath the Morrison Bridge. They have the best macaroni and cheese you'll ever taste, and they wrap your leftovers in tin foil that they mold into different shapes like balloon animals."

"So, you leave with your food looking like a giraffe or something?" Christopher said.

"It's an experience," Charli told him.

"Sounds like something I'll have to check out one day."

"Definitely," she said, wondering if she and Christopher would ever go there together down the road.

After dinner, their conversation switched back to talk of school and their friends, and Charli really started to enjoy herself again. Christopher took her to get ice cream down the street at a local creamery called Sugartime, and they ate mint chip cones while walking along the beach and listening to the waves crash down. At one point, Christopher picked her up and ran her over to the water, threatening to throw her in.

"Put me down!" she squealed. Although they were enjoying a warm October, it was too cold to swim.

"No way!" he said.

"Christopher!"

"You have to promise to give me something good first."

"Like what?" she asked.

"How about a kiss?"

Charli decided that maybe it was time. Jack was off locking lips with someone else. There was nothing wrong with her doing the same. "Okay," she said.

"Really?" He set her down on a wet patch of sand that the water had just touched.

"Sure," she said.

"You're certain that you're okay with it?"

"If you ask me again, I might change my mind."

Christopher smiled, wrapped his hands around her waist, and then touched his lips to hers. The kiss was soft. Sweet. Nice. Charli didn't let herself analyze it any more than that.

She grinned at him afterwards. "Where to next?"

Christopher drove her to Frankie's Fun Park for a game of miniature golf.

"You ever played before?" he asked as they waited in line for their clubs.

"No," she said, relieved that Jack had never taken her putt-putting.

"This should be interesting then. Neither have I. Do you want to bet on the outcome?"

"All right," Charli said. "If I win, you give me a back massage."

"Okay. And if I win," Christopher said, "I get to kiss you again."

"Deal."

On the very first hole, it was apparent that Christopher was *not* going to be the victor. It took him fifteen putts to knock his ball in. He didn't have one athletic bone in his body.

"Winner is the guy with the most points, right?" he said, making a joke to hide his obvious embarrassment.

Charli put her arm around him. "We can play that way."

She thought maybe, with a little practice, he would get better, but that wasn't the case. They were constantly letting people go around them, and by the eighth hole, they decided to call it quits.

Christopher dragged her inside the arcade for a game of Pacman.

"I have to redeem myself somehow," he said. "This is more my thing." He smoked her, even beating the arcade record.

"Wow," Charli said. "I'm impressed!"

"So impressed that you might consider giving me that second kiss even though you won at putt-putt?"

"Only if I get my massage," she said.

"Fair enough." Christopher led her outside and sat her down on a bench. She had tons of knots in her back from the stress of the past few weeks, and it felt nice to have Christopher knead them out one by one. He worked on her for a good five minutes or so and then she reached behind her and grabbed his hand.

"All right," she said. "A deal's a deal."

It took Christopher less than a second to sit down beside her. He smoothed her hair out of her face and gave her a grin that hinted this was the highlight of his month. Maybe even his year. She couldn't help feeling flattered as she closed her eyes, blocking out the flashing lights coming from the arcade, trying to be in the moment. This kiss was similar to the first one—gentle, not too long or too short—and Charli decided that it was a nice end to a wonderful evening.

Christopher drove her home and after parking his bike, he walked her up to her front door in true gentleman form.

"I had a great time tonight," Charli told him, relieved that she actually meant it. Perhaps this was the start of something promising.

"Me too," Christopher said. "Maybe we could do it again sometime."

"I'd like that." She gave him a kiss on the cheek, wished him a safe drive home, and then let herself inside and leaned against her door, listening as he started up his engine. When she could no longer hear the Harley, she walked down the hall to get ready for bed. Rebecca had insisted that Charli call her once the date was over, but she was too tired. She would wait until the morning. Sleep was calling to her, and she couldn't wait to climb in bed and curl up underneath her covers. She brushed her teeth and then changed out of her dress into a t-shirt and shorts and flipped off her lamp, flooding her bedroom with darkness. Once her head hit the pillow, she sighed deeply.

Christopher was all she wanted to think about while she drifted off—his curly hair, his deep brown eyes, how much he seemed to care that she was enjoying herself. She replayed the date in her head and smiled to herself, imagining that she'd have sweet dreams about the two of them together. But once she started to drift off, her mind drifted too, back to a familiar place.

*That was so different from a date with Jack—not in terms of what we did, but in terms of how I felt doing it all!*

It was so strange to not be able to fully explain her history to someone she could end up being intimate with. And those kisses . . . they were not even close to the type of kisses Jack used to give her. Where were the butterflies? Where was that crazy head-over-heels feeling?

*Damn it.* She rolled onto her back. What was that all about? Her subconscious must have been taking notes all evening, and the darkness and the silence had given it a voice. Frustrated, she picked up her phone from her bedside table and called Rebecca.

"Tell me everything!" Rebecca said.

Charli switched on her lamp and propped herself up with a pillow. "It went great," she said.

"But?" Rebecca must have picked up on the frustrated tone of her voice.

"But just as I was falling asleep, all these thoughts about Jack popped into my head."

"So?" Rebecca surprised her. "That's normal."

"You think?" She said, feeling immediate relief.

"Hell yeah. You've just had your heart broken. It will take time for you to stop thinking about Jack and for you to only think about Christopher. You have to give yourself that time."

Maybe Rebecca was right. Perhaps she'd overreacted.

"So, you don't think it's wrong for me to keep seeing Christopher?"

"Are you kidding? Of course, I don't think it's wrong. If you had fun tonight, then you should keep giving the relationship a shot."

"I just don't want to ever hurt him the same way Jack hurt me."

"Hurting people and getting hurt is part of the dating game. Just take things slow. You two have a lot in common. There's a chance this could work out, and you'll live happily ever after."

*Happily ever after.* That was how things were supposed to turn out with Jack. But he'd thrown her a curveball with that letter. Maybe happily ever afters couldn't be planned. Maybe they just happened, unexpectedly.

"I'm going to try and get some rest," she said. She was too tired to keep analyzing.

"Dream about the genius babies you and Christopher will have if you get hitched," Rebecca said.

Charli smiled into the phone, relieved for the lighthearted moment. "I'll try my best." She hung up and turned off her lamp again. Then she lay back down and pulled her covers up underneath her chin.

Despite how badly she wanted to fall right to sleep, she tossed and turned for the next hour or so. Was it possible for her to feel the same way about Christopher that she once had about Jack? Or was trying to move on pointless? Had she loved Jack so much that every other relationship would pale in comparison? Charli realized that most people did not end up with their first loves. First loves generally served the purpose of teaching people about themselves, helping them grow, enabling them to open up and be completely vulnerable with another human being for the first time. Maybe those were Jack's only roles in her life, and she needed to accept that. Was it possible? Had the last time she'd seen him been it?

Charli understood that time was the only variable that would shed some light on the answers to her questions. But the scientist in her hated the fact that time was a variable she couldn't control.

## twenty-two
# THEN

"**Where**'s your head at?" Christopher asked.

Charli blinked, snapping out of a reverie. "Nowhere," she lied.

"Yeah right," he said, scooting closer to her on their picnic blanket. "You haven't said a word since we finished eating ten minutes ago, and I think the seagulls are full." He took what was left of their French baguette out of her hands. "Talk to me."

It was a sunny Saturday in late March, and they'd come to the beach to bask in the sunshine and take a break from schoolwork. She and Christopher had been dating for five months now, and it felt like he was always getting on her for being distant—not that she could blame him; a lot of the time she was.

Rebecca had been wrong when she said that time would make her think of Jack less. He still crossed her mind often. Sometimes, out of nowhere, an intense longing for him would come over her. Other times, she'd see or hear something that would remind her of him, and she couldn't help but think of their past. Just a few minutes ago, she'd seen a couple down the beach throwing a baseball around, and that had made her nostalgic.

Thinking about Jack while dating Christopher filled Charli with the worst guilt, and she'd considered breaking things off with him multiple times since they got together. But Rebecca stopped her whenever she got close.

"If I had a Christopher in my life, there's no way I'd let him go," she'd told Charli just the other day. "Since you have feelings developing for him, why not hang in there?"

Charli *did* have feelings developing for Christopher. How could she not? He was just like her in so many ways. And everything with him was easy. They agreed on how to spend a free evening and what to talk about, and he understood her need to work on her dissertation as much as she did because he was equally as busy with his.

Physically things had progressed since their first kiss too. She hadn't slept with him yet, but they'd fooled around quite a bit, and it was safe to say there was chemistry between them. It wasn't out-of-this-world chemistry. When Christopher touched her, she didn't get lost in the sensation the way she used to when Jack put his hands well . . . anywhere—through her hair, up and down her arms, along her stomach, between her slightly parted legs. But she reminded herself that no two relationships were alike and also that Jack had been the first guy she'd been intimate with. Maybe that was part of what had made everything with him feel so much more exciting.

She believed that logic some days. Other days she wasn't quite as convinced it was the truth, afraid that it was just something she told herself to keep her guilt at bay.

She watched Christopher now, watching her, and she tried to decide what to tell him. Did she come out and say that Jack was on her mind, fess up, get it out in the open? Or did she lie like she had in the past when he caught her daydreaming and tell him that she was preoccupied with her dissertation. Or that she was lost in a memory. Or that she was just having a moment.

"It's him, isn't it?" Christopher said, catching her off guard. "It's Jack. He's who your mind drifts to. Am I right?"

Charli felt her face turn bright red. "What?" She couldn't believe he'd nailed it.

"You know," he went on, "part of me has thought this whole time that you weren't in this relationship one hundred percent. I just wanted to believe that one day you would be."

Tears welled up in her eyes. "I wanted that too," she said, fighting them back. "That's why I've hung in here as long as I have. You don't know how much I enjoy the time we spend together. I kept thinking that in time I'd forget about Jack. Or at least not think of him as often. But for some reason, he's still on my mind . . . a lot."

"And in your heart?" Christopher said. "Is he still there too?"

As much as Charli wished she could tell him no, the truth was Jack still had a big part of her heart. Maybe all of it.

"I'm so sorry," she said.

Christopher picked up a handful of sand and watched it slide through his fingers. "Me too. But mostly, for you."

Charli squinted at him in the sunlight, confused, waiting for an explanation.

"To not be able to let go of someone, to hang onto the past, that's a terrible way to have to live," he said.

She wiped her eyes. Falling for Christopher would have made her life a whole lot easier. But she realized now that she couldn't force something she wasn't ready for. As much as she'd wanted to.

"I hope one day I can let go completely," she told him.

Christopher shifted his gaze from the sand to the brilliant blue water. "I guess I swooped in too early. Bad timing, huh?" he laughed slightly at his misfortune.

*Bad timing*, Charli thought as she leaned back on her hands. Now where had she heard that before?

—

After ending things with Christopher, Charli poured herself into her studies, rising early and leaving her house for the lab by six a.m. and often not returning until as late as one o'clock in the morning.

Rebecca worried about her. For weeks she left care packages on Charli's doorstep filled with magazines, flowers, chocolates, and notes, and whenever she saw her in the lab, she let her know that she was around if Charli needed to talk.

Charli thanked her but explained that working in the lab was the only thing that made her feel better at the moment. By staying busy she was able to forget about how much she missed Jack. She needed that. She was hurting, and being in the lab took the pain away. Rebecca seemed to understand and left her alone for a while. But after about a month, she surprised Charli on a Friday night and pulled up a stool beside her at her work station.

"I know we've always joked that the lab is our second home," she said, "but you've taken that to a whole new level. I'm afraid the university's going to start asking you to pay rent."

Charli wasn't feeling chummy. She simply shrugged her shoulders and continued to look through her microscope.

"Do you want to come and have a beer downtown with me?" Rebecca asked. "A change of scenery might do you good."

"I'm okay," Charli said. Although she wasn't *really*. Both of them knew that.

"What about doing something together tomorrow?" Rebecca suggested. "Maybe in the morning we could go out to Cypress Gardens like we've always talked about. I bet the flowers are beautiful this time of year."

"I appreciate the offer, but I have too much work to do."

Charli felt Rebecca's hand come down on top of her shoulder.

"I'm seeing someone," Rebecca said.

"What?" That got Charli to look up. She couldn't believe she'd been so wrapped up in her own problems that this was the first she was hearing about this. For the first time in weeks, she felt herself smile. "Rebecca, this is exciting!"

"Is it?" Rebecca asked, tearing up. "Seeing you like this . . . it makes me afraid to fall in love."

"Oh, no, don't say that," Charli reached over and draped an arm around her shoulder. "You didn't get to see the good parts. I wouldn't trade the years I had with Jack for anything—not even to get rid of how I'm feeling right now. Falling in love . . . it's magical. Really, it's the greatest feeling in the world—scary and exciting and intoxicating—all at once. I want you to experience that."

"I don't know," Rebecca said, dropping her eyes to the floor. "You're so miserable."

"Only because what I had was so great. Rebecca, I hope you fall so hard for this guy that if the relationship does end, you're as broken up as me. Friends of mine from high school and college recovered from breakups after a day or two and moved on to new guys the following week. I don't think they experienced the real thing. The real thing is worth all this, trust me."

Rebecca looked up, her eyes a little more hopeful.

"Did I convince you?" Charli asked, praying that she had, knowing that she'd feel responsible if Rebecca decided to end things with this guy before it got serious.

When Rebecca nodded, Charli breathed a sigh of relief. "Good! Now tell me, who is it? What's he like? I want all the details." She remembered how excited she had been to share the news about her and Jack's budding romance with her best friend, Patti. After Jack kissed her for the first time, she'd called Patti at her college in Arizona, and they'd talked on the phone for three hours. Reliving the moment with Patti had almost been more thrilling than the actual kiss itself.

"That's the other thing," Rebecca said with a sniffle. "The guy . . . well he's actually . . . you see, the funny thing is . . ."

Rebecca gave her a look, and Charli immediately knew what she was going to say. *Of course,* she thought. *How did I not see this coming?*

"It's Christopher," Rebecca said, confirming her suspicion and then rushing to explain. "It just sort of happened. I was there for him when things ended with you, and we spent so many late nights together drinking wine at his place and talking. Then one night he kissed me . . . and I felt something . . . I mean, really felt something. Of course, I'm sure you don't want to hear all of this but—"

"No, I do," Charli said, half surprising herself, completely surprising Rebecca. "I want to hear everything."

"You do? You don't hate me?" Rebecca said.

"It's a little weird," Charli admitted. "But, of course, I don't hate you. I'm excited for you. For both of you."

It wasn't like she'd loved Christopher. If she had, that would be a different story. She imagined things would probably be awkward between the three of them for a while, but it would pass.

"Oh, thank you," Rebecca said giving her a hug. "I was so nervous to tell you!"

"I'm glad you did. Now fill me in. And don't leave anything out!"

Rebecca brightened as she got ready to explain how it all started, and Charli smiled, excited to see her friend falling for the first time.

—

In the months that followed, Charli remained focused on her work, breaking concentration only when Rebecca came to her with a new Christopher update. She knew that when she was ready, she would date again, but for the time being, she was fine vicariously living through Rebecca's love life as she poured herself into her dissertation.

Her topic interested her so much that even on her bad days, when she missed Jack like crazy, she still managed to feel happy some of the time. She reminded herself that she was the type of girl who needed this kind of personal fulfillment, and as much as it pained her to think that she might have lost Jack because she chose to pursue her passion, she knew that she would have never been content living a life with him if she hadn't.

Slowly, she forgave herself for coming up with the pact. And she forgave Jack for writing her the letter. She didn't know the whole story behind it, and she realized she might never get it, so she had no choice but to be at peace with his decision.

More and more time passed and Charli remained single. Though she could have jumped into a few relationships with other guys she met at school who expressed interest, she didn't want to get involved with someone just to ease her heartache the way she had with Christopher. As much as she missed having a companion in her life to share the day-to-day with, there was something about learning to be okay with being alone that made her feel strong and more confident than ever before. She was proud of her independence and was content being alone until the last year of her PhD program when she met Tim Willis.

Tim was a twenty-seven-year-old philosophy graduate student at College of Charleston who had gotten a job that September working at the Starbucks on King Street, where Charli often studied. He always chatted Charli up while he steamed the milk for her cappuccino, and she came to enjoy their brief exchanges.

She didn't realize how *much* though until she showed up one afternoon, and a young tattooed girl with a nose ring was behind the bar instead of him.

"What happened to Tim?" she asked, disappointed. She'd been dying to share with him the news that she'd finished a particularly difficult section of her dissertation.

His replacement explained that his class schedule changed, so now he worked evenings.

Charli decided that it would be a two-cup-of-coffee day and returned later to tell Tim of her accomplishment.

"That's great!" he said, lifting her already high spirits. "We should grab a drink when I'm off to celebrate!"

"Yeah?" Charli said. She hadn't expected that.

"It'd be fun," he replied.

She felt her heart pounding a little faster than usual as they chose a spot to meet—Kaminski's, a dessert restaurant and bar that she and Rebecca liked to frequent. It was a cozy setting with dim lights and candles on the tables, great for good conversation.

She wasn't sure if it was a date or just a casual drink between friends, but as she got ready later that night, she realized that she was hoping it was a date. She put much more effort into her appearance than usual, trying on three dresses before settling on an off-the-shoulder floral one. And right before she left, she even added a touch of mascara, laughing at herself as she applied it, remembering that the last time she'd put it on was for orientation.

When she arrived, she spotted Tim at a table near the bar. He, too, was dressed up, which secretly thrilled her. He wouldn't have worn a button down and slacks if he didn't think this was a date, would he have?

"I almost didn't recognize you without your Starbucks' apron on," she told him as he stood to give her a hug. "You certainly clean up nice."

"You don't look so bad yourself," he said looking blown away, looking like Jack used to whenever she walked into a room.

She felt herself blush as she smoothed out her dress and took a seat.

Tim had already ordered them wine, and he raised his glass in the air right away. "To you and your dissertation."

"And to a great night with my favorite barista," she added, clinking her glass against his.

"Your favorite barista, huh?" Tim raised an eyebrow as they both took a long drink. "You probably say that to all the Starbucks' employees you meet up with."

"You're right," she said, enjoying the sweet taste of the wine as it went down. "But you're the first to receive the compliment this month."

"Well, that makes me feel good. And it should make *you* feel good to know that you're *a contender* for my favorite customer."

"Just a contender?" Charli feigned disappointment as she took another quick sip, wanting the confidence that a little buzz would give her. "Who's my competition?"

"Well, there's Regina."

Charli wrinkled her nose. Regina was a woman in her mid-forties who came into Starbucks around the same time she did and always hit on Tim, despite the gigantic diamond ring on her finger.

A few weeks ago, she had taken the lid off her latte, stuck her finger into the foam on top, and sucked it off seductively right in front of him. Another time, she'd told him that he made the best coffee in the entire city and asked if he would come over to her house sometime to "teach her a few things."

"Hey, she fills up the tip jar," Tim said. "Yesterday she left me twenty bucks."

"Wow, really?"

"I couldn't believe it."

"I guess that makes her valid competition. Who else am I up against?"

"Betty," he said. Betty was an older woman who came in to get coffee for her and her husband every single morning. She always told the sweetest stories about the two of them while she waited for their drinks. Charli knew they'd met on a blind date forty years ago, that their parents had thought they were too young to get married so they eloped, and that every Friday night they went out to dinner at a new restaurant they'd never tried before.

"I can't compete with Betty," Charli said.

"You're doing a pretty good job right now," Tim told her.

"I am?"

"I'd say so. I'm enjoying myself."

He sat back in his chair, and Charli felt herself relax a bit, her pre-date jitters fading.

Then, eyeing him curiously she said, "So, why'd you pick philosophy?" It was something she'd always wondered but had never gotten around to asking him.

"Because it makes the big bucks."

She giggled, deciding that Tim's sense of humor was her favorite thing about him.

"No," he went on, "I took a philosophy class as an elective my freshman year, and my professor got me hooked. I remember her saying our first day of class, 'You'll never get rich from pursuing this, but by pursuing this you'll be the richest men and women.' That really spoke to me. It turned out to be the first class in my academic career that I was ever excited to show up for. It still does excite me. I love that questions lead to more questions. That it's a never-ending pursuit of knowledge."

"See, I'm different." She ran her finger around the brim of her wineglass. "I like when questions lead to answers and can be put to rest."

"Well, you know what they say," Tim grinned. "Opposites attract." His knee brushed up against hers underneath the table, and for the first time since dating Jack, her stomach did a full flip.

Things continued to go well the rest of the evening. Charli got so lost in their conversation that she didn't even notice the place clear out. If Tim hadn't pulled out his wallet and said, "I guess we should get out of here," she would have never looked around at all the empty tables. She finished off the final sip of her third (or was it her fourth?) glass of wine and stood up, staggering slightly.

"Whoa," Tim said, reaching out for her arm.

"I'm sorry," she laughed. "I haven't had this much to drink in a while."

"Did you drive?" he asked.

"No, I walked." Her house was just a little over a mile away.

"Me too," he said. "Let me take you home." His offer excited her not only because it meant she'd get to spend extra time with him, but also because it spoke to his character. She liked that he was the type to escort a woman home. Then again maybe *he* just wanted to spend more time with *her*. Both scenarios were a win.

Although the day had been warm, the night had cooled off, and as they walked down the deserted sidewalk, Charli rubbed her hands together to warm them up.

Tim offered her his jacket.

"That's okay," she replied. He took it off anyway and draped it around her shoulders. It smelled like coffee. "Does your whole wardrobe reek of Starbucks?" she asked with a smile.

"Most of it," he admitted. "Does that bother you?"

"No, I actually like it."

"Really? Because I'll gladly take my jacket back. I'm freezing now!" He blew into his hands for dramatic effect.

"Here," she laughed, "take my arm." He looped his through hers, and they walked side by side onto East Bay Street. The river came into view, and Charli looked out at the boat lights shining in the distance.

"This is my favorite spot in the city," Tim said. "I do my best thinking here." They climbed a couple of stairs onto the promenade and leaned against the railing, admiring the view.

"What are you thinking right now?" Charli asked him. She wasn't fishing for anything in particular, just curious.

"I'm thinking . . . that I had a great time tonight," Tim said.

Flattered but unsure how to accept the compliment, Charli made a joke, something about how it probably wasn't too hard to beat a late night studying or brewing coffee, but he shook his head.

"No, I'm serious. I haven't had that much fun with someone in a while."

She couldn't help a smile from creeping onto her lips.

"And you know what else I'm thinking?" he asked.

"What?" Nothing could top that. To know that the person she was crushing on was feeling the same way—there was no greater feeling.

"I'm thinking . . . that I might like to kiss you."

Except for that . . .

Their eyes met in the dim light from the streetlamps.

"Would that be okay?" Tim asked.

Charli hadn't felt the urge to be kissed by someone in a while. But she wanted this man to kiss her. Badly.

"I won't put up a fight," she said.

Smiling, Tim scooted toward her so that their noses were practically touching, and then his lips met hers. The first kiss was short. The second was longer. By the third, his tongue was in her mouth, rolling around, and Charli was completely lost in the moment.

After it was over, she realized that Jack hadn't crossed her mind once—not during the kiss or during drinks—and she was filled with a sense of relief. Maybe it *was* possible for her to move on. Maybe she'd just needed to meet Tim, the right guy, someone else who was capable of making her heart race. She knew that just like with Christopher, only time would tell, but at least for the moment she had hope.

# twenty-three
# THEN

"I think I'm in love," Charli said in between deep breaths.

Rebecca, who was jogging beside her, came to an immediate stop. "I must really be out of shape," she said. "I think I just hallucinated."

"I know, I almost can't believe it myself," Charli said. She'd only been dating Tim for five months. "I realized it last night when Tim was walking me out to my car. As I was giving him a hug goodbye, I felt this urge to tell him."

"Wow. We should be getting drinks right now to celebrate, not going for a run."

Charli put her hands against the trunk of a tree and walked her feet back behind her to get a stretch. She was wearing a new workout outfit by Year of Ours that she'd fallen in love with online and decided to buy, in her excited state. During the long period where she'd been single before meeting Tim, she'd learned the importance of treating *herself* to nice things, the same way a boyfriend might—whether that was a new outfit or an experience that lit her up inside.

"I have an update too," Rebecca said.

"Oh yeah?" Charli looked over at her. "What's that?"

"Christopher brought up marriage the other night."

"No way. What did he say?" The awkwardness between the three of them had passed a long time ago. Charli was completely comfortable with this line of chit-chat.

"He asked me where I wanted to live after we graduate. And I said I didn't know, where did he want to live? And he said, wherever you end up. So, I said, does that mean you think this is pretty serious? And he took my hand, looked me right in the eye, and said, 'Rebecca, I think you're The One.'"

"That is so exciting!" Charli gushed.

"Yeah, it amazes me how it all played out." They both stood up and started to jog again, settling into a comfortable pace.

"So," Rebecca said, "are you going to tell Tim how you feel?"

"No. I'm too nervous to put myself out there and be that vulnerable."

"I hate to break it to you, friend, but the fact that you're feeling the way you're feeling means you're already vulnerable."

Charli chuckled, knowing that she was right. It had been so long since she'd felt this way that she'd forgotten.

Fortunately, it only took three more weeks for Tim to tell her that he was on the same page. He waited until they got to the lookout at the peak of Table Rock Mountain and then whispered it.

For a split second, Charli worried that she'd heard him wrong. The wind was blowing so hard she wondered if maybe he'd actually said, "I love this view." It *was* spectacular—a forest full of green trees with the Johnson River winding its way in and out of them. But she took a leap of faith and confessed her own feelings, relieved when Tim took her into his arms and said how happy it made him to know that she had also fallen.

Later that evening, when Tim left for work, she went over to Rebecca's to share the news.

"That's fantastic!" Rebecca said. She poured them each a flute of champagne to celebrate. "To both of us being in love!"

"I'll drink to that!" Charli said, raising her glass.

They went out on Rebecca's small balcony and took a seat on her white wicker chairs. As they sipped their champagne and watched bicyclists and cars cruise by on the street below, Charli filled her in on all the details. She told her about the way Tim's face had lit up when she'd confessed her feelings, about how close she'd felt to him when he wrapped his arms around her, and even about the envious gazes she'd received from a group of women who were standing a couple yards away.

"It sounds like a perfect moment," Rebecca said.

"It was," Charli replied as she tipped her flute back and finished off her champagne, surprised at how quickly she'd downed it.

Rebecca stood. "Looks like someone needs a refill."

"I can get it," Charli offered. She could already feel the champagne settling in, and the buzz made her feel even giddier.

"No. You stay put and rack your brain for anything you might have left out," Rebecca said.

Charli was pretty sure that she'd covered it all, but she sat back and closed her eyes, reliving the magical moment yet again. Her phone buzzed, and she looked down and saw that it was a text message from Tim, as if he had sensed that he was on her mind. She picked up her phone from the arm of her chair, and her lips curled up as she read what he had written.

*I love you. So nice to be able say that whenever I want to now :)*

She shot him a quick text back: *I love you too. Call me after you're done with work?*

*Definitely*, he replied.

She had just started to fantasize about sleeping with him later that night and about how much better sex would feel now that they were this emotionally committed, when she heard Rebecca's footsteps. Snapping out of it, she turned in her chair to face her.

"You won't believe the sweet text Tim just sent me," she said. As she held up her phone to show it to her, Rebecca glared back at her, holding something up in her hands.

"So, I knocked your purse over in the kitchen and this fell out . . . I would have thought you'd have chucked this a long time ago, Charli. What are you doing still carrying this around?"

Without even seeing what Rebecca was holding, Charli realized what she must have found: her receipt from Hayden's with the date and time of her and Jack's reunion on it, which was just a month away.

"I've had that in there since Jack and I made our pact," she said, trying to play it cool. "It's no big deal." She stood up, took the receipt from Rebecca, and went into the kitchen to put it back, hoping that would end the conversation. She did not want to be talking about Jack right now on the heels of her great morning with Tim.

Unfortunately, in true form, Rebecca felt the need to dig deeper.

"Seriously," she said, following her, "why hold onto it? Just throw it away."

When Charli didn't make a move for the trash, Rebecca continued, "Come on. It's not like you're planning on showing up for the reunion."

Charli was silent for one beat too long.

"Oh my gosh," Rebecca said, pointing her finger at her. "You are!"

Hurrying to defend herself, Charli explained that she didn't know yet, that she needed more time to decide.

"More time?" Rebecca narrowed her eyes. "What's that going to do? Your feelings for Tim are as strong as they're ever going to be, am I right?"

Charli considered that for a minute. "Give or take a little."

"Okay, so if you can't say without a doubt that you'd pick Tim over Jack, then I'd say Jack wins. He's who your heart truly wants."

"Oh please," Charli said with a shake of her head, dismissing the accusation as preposterous. "You're jumping to conclusions."

"Am I?" Rebecca folded her arms over her chest. "Let's pretend tomorrow's the day of the reunion. Can you honestly picture yourself sharing a meal with Tim at a restaurant in Charleston?"

Charli thought about it and then happily told the truth. "Yeah. Actually, I can."

"Fine," Rebecca said. "Now tell me this. Can you picture yourself *not* showing up at Hayden's? Because that's the bigger question and one that I think both of us know the answer to."

Charli could feel herself losing her cool. "This is ridiculous," she said. "Why are you getting all upset? You're the one who has encouraged me all along to pursue other relationships despite my feelings for Jack."

"Because I thought if you put yourself out there, you'd fall so in love with another guy that the thought of going back for Jack wouldn't even cross your mind. But that's obviously not what happened. So now I feel like you're just stringing Tim along."

"I am not!" Charli said. "I love Tim! Where have you been?"

"I don't think this is about Tim," Rebecca said. "I think it has to do with you and Jack and with the fact that in *your* eyes, the two of you have unfinished business."

"I can't believe we're having this conversation," Charli muttered.

"I'm sorry. I'm the last person who wants to encourage you to go back for him. I saw you after he broke your heart the first time. I don't want to see that again. But based on the fact that you're still hanging onto that receipt and based on your answers to my questions, I think you need to be honest with Tim. Heck, he may be so in love with you, he'll be willing to take his chances while you play out this pact."

"No way. I know Tim. He'd tell me it's either him or the *chance* of Jack. By being honest, I run the risk of losing both of them, don't you see? This is easy for you to say because you have nothing to lose. I'm the one who'd have to give up a great guy, maybe for nothing."

"I'd hardly call taking a shot at true love nothing," Rebecca said.

Charli went over to the window and pushed it open, needing some fresh air.

Rebecca gave her a minute and then said, "Have you ever thought that you and Jack are . . . I dunno . . . soul mates?"

"Soul mates?" Charli turned toward her, wrinkling her forehead.

"Yeah . . . you know . . . meant for each other."

"No, I know what it means," she said. "I just didn't know you believed in such a thing. I know I did once, but I'm not sure if I still do."

Rebecca took a few steps toward her, then paused and said, "I've never seen someone love another person the way I think you love Jack. I mean seriously, it's almost been five years and a part of you is *still* hung up on him. If soul mates do exist, I think that's what you two are."

Charli felt the wave of emotions that she'd been suppressing ever since she got Jack's letter begin to rise to the surface. She did her best to fight them back as Rebecca went on.

"Soul mates are drawn together against all odds, and the odds have been against you and Jack this whole time. Think about it. Your careers pulled you to opposite ends of the country, which would have made most couples call it quits right then, but you two got creative. You made this interesting pact. Then Jack wrote you a letter that should have made you hate his guts or at least not trust him, but you never really changed your opinion of him. And on top of all that, you're in love with someone else, and you're still curious about a future with Jack. To me that means something. Like . . . like . . . there's some powerful force that keeps saying you two should be together. A force that you keep trying to ignore but that won't let you."

Charli was really fighting back tears now because what Rebecca was saying was resonating.

"Jack's probably not going to show up," she said. "You said it yourself when I got his letter."

"I know, but on some level *you* must obviously think he *might.* Otherwise you would have told me that you weren't thinking about going back at all. And you would have gotten rid of that receipt a long time ago. I know it's scary. But as your friend, I have to encourage you to follow your heart. That's what you made me do, and look how happy I am."

"Tim makes me happy," Charli said, desperate to keep the option of staying with him on the table.

"But think long term here. Who would make you *the happiest* for the rest of your life?"

"I don't know."

"You *do*," Rebecca said. "You just don't want to admit it to yourself. I know breaking up with Tim will hurt, but I'm sure you'll recover from it. What I'm afraid you won't recover from is the regret you'll feel if you don't show up for that reunion."

Rebecca reached out and took Charli's hands in hers. "Charli, you're too young to start living with 'what if's.'"

Although it killed Charli to have this thought, the idea of finding another man she loved as much as Tim *did* seem possible. She wasn't quite as sure she'd ever find someone who made her feel the way Jack once had. Still, she couldn't just recklessly follow her heart.

"You're asking me to just throw all logic out the window," she said, feeling the tears start to well up in her eyes, knowing that Rebecca was right, realizing what this meant, what she'd have to do.

"I know." Rebecca put her hands on Charli's shoulders. "For once in your life, I think you should let all logic go."

## twenty-four
## NOW

**Peter** was standing beside the butcher-block table when Gianna tentatively opened the kitchen door and stepped inside. He had on a blue button-down shirt, the checkered tie she got him last Christmas, and a heavy dose of his Calvin Klein cologne.

"Gianna." He said her name with a smile in his voice.

"Hi Peter," she said, her voice cracking.

Her kitchen staff had stopped what they were doing and were all watching them. Gianna felt like she might faint. Actually . . . maybe fainting wasn't such a bad idea . . . Passing out would postpone this whole thing.

Peter took a few steps toward her so that he was standing in front of her.

"Gianna," he said again.

*Oh God . . .*

She tried to give him an I've-waited-for-this-moment-for-so-long grin but couldn't manage one when inside she was screaming, "Shit! Shit! Shit!"

He drew in a deep breath and then dropped down to one knee and took her cold, shaky, hand in his.

"*Wait!*" she wanted to yell. "*Stop! Give me another week or two to come up with an answer.*"

But no words came out of her mouth.

Only Peter managed to find something to say. "From the moment I saw you—" he started, launching into what was clearly a well-rehearsed proposal speech.

Gianna listened, wide-eyed, to him put into words how he felt about her, and as wonderful as it was to hear how much he adored her, the whole time she couldn't shake the terrible feeling that she didn't care for him *as much* as he cared for her. That she didn't love him *as deeply* as she should have.

But God she wanted that not to be the case!

Was it possible that the spark she felt was missing would still materialize? She could try to crank up the romance in their relationship by renting a cabin at the coast and buying some sexy lingerie. Or by taking him wine tasting in Napa for a weekend, just the two of them. Maybe there was still a chance to make this work. Did she have to throw in the towel right this second?

Peter let go of her hand then and reached into his pocket to fish out the ring. When he popped open the box she gasped, pretending as if she hadn't seen it before.

"Wow, Pete."

"You like it?" he asked.

Gianna nodded. "Stunning."

"Well, you deserve the best, sweetheart. I just wanted to give it to you."

Oh, he was wonderful! How could she say no to him? She should have been counting her blessings that a man this terrific was even in her life, let alone down on a bended knee in front of her.

Peter cleared his throat. Gianna's heart felt like it was going to burst out of her chest as the words to that question she didn't know the answer to formed on the tip of his tongue. But just as he was about to get them out, Barbara burst into the room, her bouncy red curls coming in behind her. "Gianna, Gianna!" she called.

Gianna had never been so happy to hear her own name or see one of her servers in her life.

Everyone in the room looked over.

It didn't take Barbara long to realize what she'd just interrupted. "Oh no! I'm so sorry."

"So am I," said Peter with a slight laugh as he wiped a bead of sweat off of his forehead with the back of his hand. "Could you walk out and come back in two minutes, hon?"

"No! Wait. What is it?" Gianna practically yelled, surprising everyone, especially Peter, who looked up at her.

"Gianna," Peter said, "we're sort of in the middle of something."

"Look, she obviously has something really important to say."

"So do I!" Peter remarked, the veins in his forehead popping.

"Just give me one minute." She bent down and kissed the top of Peter's head, feeling terribly guilty. But Barbara had just bought her that extra time that she desperately needed, and Gianna couldn't let her get away.

All of her staff started to talk among themselves, gossiping about Gianna's decision to speak with Barbara.

"What is it?" Gianna asked. She prayed that whatever it was, it would require her to leave the kitchen immediately and keep this proposal on pause.

"Really, I can come back," Barbara said.

"No. Just tell me what's going on."

Nodding, Barbara said, "Charli's here!"

"What?" Gianna went to peek out the window, but Barbara grabbed her arm. "There's something else . . ."

"What?" From the tone of her voice, she knew it wasn't good.

"I found this." She pulled a crumpled piece of paper out of her back pocket and handed it to Gianna. "I'm sorry. I saw it and thought I needed to show it to you." She handed over the slip of paper. "You know that His and Hers cake that looks like a tuxedo and wedding gown in the fridge?"

"Yes," Gianna said. She'd gotten a glimpse of it earlier when she was grabbing a bottle of Chardonnay but had thought nothing of it. Private party cake orders were filled early in the morning by two of her pastry chefs, Jill and Kaylan, and then taken to the venues throughout the day and evening by Bob, her delivery guy. Gianna hardly dealt with them.

"Okay, well that cake is about to be delivered to this person," Barbara said, pointing to the name on the order form. "I saw it sitting on the dessert counter waiting for Bob to come in and pick it up."

Gianna read it. Blinked. Read it again.

"That's his name, right?" Barbara asked.

Gianna nodded, at a loss for words.

"That's what I thought," Barbara said, her shoulders sinking. "It might be a coincidence, right? Someone else in this city could have the same name as him?"

"I guess," Gianna said. "But that would be a *big* coincidence considering the cake has a mint torte base, and that's the cake he always used to order."

"So that would mean he's . . ."

"Yes," Gianna said, equally disappointed. She stared at it for another minute regretting that she'd prayed for an excuse to leave the room. She would have almost rather stood before Peter again and been forced to make a decision about marrying him than to deal with this. "Thank you for letting me know," she finally said.

The room started to quiet down. Everyone was growing curious about what it was that Barbara had shown Gianna. Gianna turned toward them to fill them in.

"I'm sorry everyone—Peter especially—but I need all of you to excuse me for a minute. Charli has just arrived, and I need to speak with her as soon as possible." She held up the rehearsal dinner order form Barbara had given her for everyone to see. "Jack will not be showing up tonight. He is marrying someone else."

—

The minute Gianna stepped out of the kitchen, Valerie jumped on her. "Where's the ring?" she exclaimed, reaching for her left hand.

"I don't have it."

"What do you mean you don't have it?"

"Barbara came in and told me Charli just showed up and then informed me that she'd found this." She handed over the order form with Jack's name on it. It hadn't occurred to Gianna until that moment just how invested she was in both Charli and Jack's return. It was as if some part of her—deep down—had been thinking all evening that if Charli and Jack *did* come back, then nothing was impossible when it came to love—even meeting someone better suited for her than Peter. But now it was hard to feel that way, and although that made her decision tonight easier, it also made her sad.

Valerie scoffed when she handed the paper back. "You want to tell me why you think her relationship is more important right now than your own?"

"I don't think it's *more* important," Gianna stressed, deciding that now was not the time to get into her insecurities about marrying Peter. "It's just that I'm at work, and Charli's my customer. I can't let her get stood up while I'm in the kitchen celebrating my engagement with Peter."

"Actually, you *can.*"

"Valerie, come on." Couldn't she sympathize with her situation a little?

Valerie sighed deeply. "Peter was so nervous about tonight, Gianna. He called me like six times this morning, freaking out."

"Look, I know it wasn't the best way to handle it." Gianna did feel bad for Peter, and she realized what she'd done wasn't going to win her the best girlfriend of the year award. "But if you'd just let me go now, I can tell Charli the bad news and then get back in there."

Valerie tapped her foot impatiently on the floor.

"Why don't you go keep Peter company?" Gianna suggested. "Put someone else on your tables for a bit."

Valerie didn't look crazy about the idea, but finally she extended her arm like she was a gatekeeper who, after interrogation, was going to let Gianna pass. Gianna started to walk but Valerie reached out and put her hand on her shoulder.

"Gianna," she said.

"Yes?"

"Peter was *so* nervous about tonight."

"I get it," Gianna said, swallowing the giant lump in her throat.

—

As Gianna walked toward Charli's table, Charli caught her eye, smiled, and waved.

*Wow, she certainly looks glamorous,* Gianna thought.

Her brown hair was curled and draped her shoulders, and her makeup was subtle but purposeful—a hint of blush, a touch of mascara, and what looked like rose-colored lipstick. She wore a fitted white dress that didn't scream, "I tried too hard," but that would have definitely made Jack's jaw drop if he had been planning on showing, and she had on a pearl necklace to top the ensemble off. As Gianna got closer, she could see that Charli was fingering the pearls one at a time as if her necklace were a rosary and she imagined her silently praying, "Let Jack come back, let Jack come back."

Suddenly Gianna thought she might chicken out. She didn't want to bear this bad news, but if she didn't, who would? *Maybe Jack.* What if he was planning on showing up at seven, right before his rehearsal dinner, and telling Charli he was getting married, himself? Should she wait and see if that happened before she went ahead and showed Charli this order form?

She stuffed it into her pocket when she got to Charli's table, deciding it was best to hide it until she'd made up her mind.

"Gianna," Charli said, standing. "It's good to see you." She stood and wrapped her in a tight hug.

"How are you?" Gianna asked.

"I'm a mess," Charli laughed. "Look, I'm shaking." She held one of her trembling hands for Gianna to see.

Gianna slid into the chair across from her.

"I'm sorry we never connected on the phone," Charli went on. "I was so anxious I could hardly sit still. I wanted to get in touch with you and find out if you'd heard from Jack. But then I realized that I couldn't let whether or not you had spoken with him influence my decision to come or not. I had to just take a leap of faith. So, here I am."

Another option, Gianna realized, as Charli continued to babble, was to never show Charli the order form. If Jack didn't come, Gianna could sit with Charli, hold her hand, and fill her head with less painful truths about why he hadn't shown up. "Maybe he was busy," she would say to her. Or, "Maybe he just forgot what day the reunion was." That was definitely a possibility . . .

"Oh my gosh," Charli suddenly said. "You have heard from him, haven't you?"

Gianna must not have been doing the best job at covering her feelings up.

"Is he not coming?" Charli asked. "Oh please, just tell me now."

This was her one chance to get out of sharing what she knew. She could tell Charli that she had no idea what Jack's plans were for this evening. But if she were in Charli's shoes, she'd want to know the truth. Wouldn't she? Before she knew it, she was retrieving the form from her pocket.

"He didn't call. But I did just find out about this." She reached into her pocket for the slip of paper and handed it over.

"It's an order form for a Chocolate Mint Cloud Cake—a His and Hers tuxedo and wedding dress cake for a rehearsal dinner that's being delivered within the hour. And as you can see, the groom's name is—"

Charli brought her hand up to her mouth.

"I'm so sorry, Charli," Gianna said, though she doubted anything anyone said could help soften a blow this big. "I was conflicted about showing this to you, but one of my servers saw it and showed it to me, and I felt I had to share it with you. Do you want me to call someone? A friend or family member to come get you and be with you?"

Charli just shook her head. Tears started to roll down her cheeks, and then she bowed her head and her back and shoulders began to shake.

"Oh sweetie," Gianna said, rushing around the table to Charli's side. For some reason, she felt like she might cry too. "You're going to be okay," she assured her, running a hand up and down Charli's back and willing her own tears not to fall.

The funeral party looked over then and so did a couple of other nearby groups. Gianna couldn't imagine what people must have been thinking about her restaurant tonight with all these meltdowns.

She reached for Charli's napkin on the table and unraveled the silverware from it. When she stuck it in Charli's lap, Charli picked it up and blew into it.

"I'm sorry," Charli said. "I was prepared for Jack not showing up . . . but not for this."

"I know," Gianna replied. "It's terrible."

It really was. And there was nothing Gianna could do about it. Talk about a useless feeling.

"I don't know what I was expecting," Charli sniffled. "I mean, it's been five years since I've seen him. And then he wrote me a letter a few years ago saying he didn't want to communicate with me anymore. I guess I just figured that if I was feeling this way about him after all this time, there was a chance he still felt something for me too."

"You were brave to come. And you would have always wondered 'what if?' if you didn't show," Gianna said. She felt weird giving relationship advice when she was so in over her head in her own relationship with Peter, but she didn't really have a choice here.

Charli shook her head. "Now I just feel stupid. And completely brokenhearted." She picked up the order form again and then reached for a crumpled receipt that was in front of her and held them side-by-side. The receipt was from Hayden's for a single slice of the Chocolate Mint Cloud Cake bought on June 14, 2012, and the date and time for her and Jack's reunion looked like it was written in blue pen on the bottom. It must have been her reminder for showing up tonight.

"I wonder who she is," Charli said. "If she's someone I know? If she makes him happy?"

"Do you want me to find out?" Gianna offered, tucking a loose strand of Charli's hair back behind her ear. "I could have Bob, my delivery guy, snap a photo of the bride and groom when he drops the cake off. He could say we like collecting shots of the happy couples we bake cakes for or something."

"No. I don't want that. I mean I do want to know, but I don't at the same time."

They were both silent for a moment, and then Charli asked, "Where do I go from here?" It seemed more like a question she was posing to herself than to Gianna, so Gianna just kept quiet. "I guess I go back to my hotel," Charli said. "Pull myself together. Try and forget about Jack. Move on."

"You *will* move on, you know," Gianna said. "People recover from heartbreak every day." She stared over at the funeral party's table. "Just look at them," she wanted to say. Collectively, they'd had their hearts broken so many times they had a whole ritual to accompany it.

Gianna suddenly wondered if losing Peter would be so painful that she'd feel the need to turn to some ritual to help with her grieving process. Somehow, she doubted that she would look as devastated as Charli if things didn't work out with him. Then again, was it good to be invested in a love affair that was capable of ungluing a person as much as Jack had just unglued Charli?

"I know," Charli said. "I don't really have a choice. Jack obviously has moved on. I can't pine after him any longer. But I'm just worried about not ever finding what the two of us had. I've been in other serious relationships, and although both of them were great—and the guys were great—it always felt like there was something missing. And I'm afraid that something was Jack." She closed her eyes like she was trying not to lose it again. "I just wish we'd never made this stupid pact. That we'd never broken up in the first place."

"You did what you thought was right at the time," Gianna told her. "You can't look back."

"I guess." Charli looked over at the door, wistfully, one more time, like she was hoping that maybe this had all just been a big misunderstanding and that Jack would be there, right in front of the hostess stand, smiling back at her and waving. But he wasn't. Gianna knew this without even checking the door because Charli's bottom lip started to quiver and then she stood up. "I've got to get out of here."

Gianna rose to her feet too. She looked over her shoulder and saw Peter staring out the kitchen window, watching her. She had to get back in there.

"I'm sorry for holding up a table all night," Charli said. She put on her coat and took some cash out of her purse.

Gianna closed Charli's hand around the money. "No need to apologize."

Charli offered up a faint smile. "I'm just going to use the bathroom then and head out."

"You be in touch if you need anything."

Tears welled once again in Charli's eyes, and Gianna put her hand on her shoulder. "I'm serious," she said.

Charli hugged her and then hurried to the bathroom.

It was time for Gianna to return to Peter. She started back toward the kitchen.

"Hey, over here." It was Ellie, from the funeral party.

She was flagging Gianna over.

## twenty-five
## NOW

**Gianna** knew that she should have told Ellie she would be back out in one minute and then sent Valerie to help them so Peter could finish proposing. She was pretty sure she had an answer for him now, so there wasn't a point in delaying it any longer. But she made the detour to the ladies in black, reasoning that it was best if she sat with her decision for a moment longer.

"What can I get for you?" she asked.

Ellie leaned toward her. "Some information, actually. We couldn't help but notice what just happened with that woman you were waiting on behind us. Is everything okay?"

Gianna looked back at the empty table. A few minutes ago, Charli had been glowing with hope in the flickering candlelight, and now the table was as dark and dismal as the pouring rain, splattering on the sidewalk out the window.

"She was stood up."

"That's what we assumed," Ellie cringed. "Was it a blind date?"

"Not exactly." Gianna checked to make sure Charli was still in the bathroom and then briefly filled them in. She told them about the pact Charli had made five years earlier. About Charli's decision to show up tonight, even though her Ex stopped communicating with her years ago. And about the rehearsal dinner cake order form they'd just found with his name on top.

Kendall folded her arms over her chest and sunk back into her chair. "Seems she and I are in similar boats. Is she all right?"

"She's crushed. But hopefully soon she will be."

Kendall nodded. "That makes two of us."

"You know what she should do," Ellie said.

"What?" Get really drunk with her girlfriends? Plan a long trip to Hawaii and try to forget all of this? Show up at his wedding in a smoking hot dress and make him wish he had showed up for the reunion? Those were all things Gianna would have considered.

"Bury him," Ellie said.

Both Tina and Kendall's faces turned red with embarrassment.

"Ellie, that's our little embarrassing ritual, not something other people would do," Tina said.

"Come on, you guys," Ellie replied. "Think about it. This woman's been living under the impression that she and her Ex might get back together for *five years*. Don't you think it would be freeing for her to bury her reminders of him, so she can put this guy to rest and move on? He's clearly not coming back." She gestured to his empty chair. "Does she have anything with her right now that reminds her of him?" Ellie looked up at Gianna.

Gianna didn't want to get Charli dragged into this. She sided with Tina and Kendall—Ellie was a little bit off her rocker here—but she didn't want to be rude either, so she ended up confessing, "She *does* have a receipt from our restaurant with the date and time of the reunion on it."

"That's great!" Ellie exclaimed. "Why don't you take her out back right now and put it under the ground?"

Fortunately, Tina came to her rescue. "Ellie, it's pouring out there. Just drop this. Our waitress doesn't want to do it."

"So?" Ellie said. "They can bring an umbrella."

"No," Tina continued to fight her. "This isn't the time and place for this."

"There's never a good time or place for this," Ellie said, ignoring her friends' and Gianna's obvious discomfort. "If she doesn't bury him now, she probably never will."

"Exactly," Tina laughed. "Ellie, everyone in here already thinks we're crazy showing up in these ridiculous dresses. Can we please just drop this, so no one thinks we're even crazier with all this talk of burying ex-boyfriends?"

Ellie shrugged her shoulders and then picked up her spoon and moved what was left of her Triple Chocolate Oblivion around in the puddles of chocolate sauce that had been drizzled on the side. "It was just a suggestion. I was only trying to help."

"It was very thoughtful," Gianna replied. *Crazy, but thoughtful.*

Charli emerged from the bathroom then. Gianna spied her first and then the funeral party realized she'd come out too, so they turned in their chairs to look. She had cleaned up the smeared mascara from under her eyes, but her face was still pale, and she seemed drained from the emotional toll this night had taken on her.

Gianna waited for her to walk over toward the back door, but Charli just kept staring at the front one like she was *still* hoping Jack would come back.

Watching her, Ellie's idea to bury Jack and put this whole thing to rest (literally) didn't seem that out there. Maybe crazy was just what Charli needed tonight . . .

Gianna considered this for a moment.

Then another.

And another.

Then, surprising herself, she blurted out, "Let's actually do this funeral thing."

The ladies all looked up at her and said, in unison, "What?"

"It can only help her, right?" Gianna *really* wanted to help Charli. And selfishly, she wanted some more time to decide what she wanted to say to Peter.

She looked over at the kitchen door and caught Valerie's eye this time. She was peering out of the kitchen, eyeing Gianna with obvious disapproval. Although Gianna felt guilty, she squatted down so that she was eye-level with the group.

"Will one of you come with me? I don't think I can lead this . . . ritual on my own."

"Oh, I definitely will," Ellie said. She turned to her party. "Ladies, do you mind? I'll be quick."

The other two exchanged confused glances, like they couldn't believe Gianna was up for this, but eventually they both shrugged their shoulders.

"Thank you." Ellie smiled, scooted her chair out a little bit, and turned to Gianna. "So where do you want to do this?"

Gianna tapped her foot. "There's an awning out back in the parking lot that we can take shelter under so that we don't get soaked, and there's a potted plant under the awning too. Will that work?"

"A perfect burial spot."

"You think?"

"A potted plant? For a small receipt?" Ellie made an A-OK sign with her fingers.

Gianna visualized the three of them out there burying Charli's receipt in the pot, and she second-guessed her decision. But the excited look on Ellie's face told her that she was too late to change her mind. Continuing along with the craziness she asked, "What do we need?"

"Let's see . . . just a spoon or two to dig up some dirt."

"I have some spoons right here." Gianna nodded to the silverware she was carrying to the kitchen from Charli's table. She set the silverware and napkins down on the funeral party's table and picked the spoons out. "Anything else?"

"That should do it." Ellie stood up, strategically keeping her legs close together so that her tight dress wouldn't tear. "This is going to be so therapeutic for her," she said. "You'll see."

"I hope so." Gianna looked down at the spoons and took a deep, nervous breath.

"You ready?" Ellie asked.

"Yeah," she said, exhaling. "Let's do this."

# twenty-six
# NOW

**Jack** stared out the window of his hotel room watching pedestrians trudge through the rain without umbrellas in true Oregonian style while he contemplated the decision before him and everything that had led him to this moment.

When he and Charli had said goodbye to one another five years ago, there had only been one way he imagined this night playing out. He saw himself flying into Portland from San Francisco the night before The Reservation. (He assumed he'd be living there, playing for the Giants, and thought he might even be the starting pitcher.) He had planned to book a luxury suite at the Marriott hotel overlooking the Willamette River, where he and Charli could celebrate their reunion after meeting up at Hayden's. And he had figured he would arrive at the restaurant a few hours before The Reservation because he wouldn't be able to contain his excitement about potentially seeing Charli again.

This night couldn't be any more different than that.

He'd driven here instead of flying in, for starters, because he didn't live very far away. After he had returned from Charleston brokenhearted he'd moved away, just like his mom had suggested, but he had remained close enough that he could visit her often, since she seemed to need his company more than ever after her divorce from his dad. He was also staying at Hotel Lucia, in the heart of downtown, instead of at the Marriott, because he'd booked his stay just that afternoon and the Marriott had been full. To top it off, there was only a half hour left until The Reservation, and he still didn't know whether or not he was going to show up for it.

A lot had changed since he and Charli had split. He'd created a new life for himself and to his surprise, he liked that new life. It wasn't at all like the life he'd imagined he would be leading when he was growing up (he was working in marketing for Christ's sake instead of playing baseball, and he wasn't with Charli), but maybe no one was supposed to lead the life he had dreamed of living as a kid. Perhaps the path he was on now was the right one, and he should keep moving forward and trusting it. But if that were true, then how did he explain the undeniable pull he was feeling to go to Hayden's and see if Charli was there?

A knock on the door startled him. *Who could that be?* He hadn't told anyone where he had gone. He knew he needed to be alone to make this decision, and he didn't have time for distractions. Maybe someone just had the wrong room. He gave it a moment, but the knocking persisted.

Leaving the window, he walked over to the door and opened it. It was his mom. Though typically the person he went to for advice, he really didn't want to talk to her right now. She'd once loved Charli like a daughter, but she had also seen how badly he'd been hurt by her after he got back from that trip to Charleston. He didn't want her swaying his decision. "How did you find me?" he asked, looking down at the floor, afraid to make eye contact with her.

"The Find My Friends app," she said. "And then the front desk agent let me know what room you were in."

Right. She was the one person he let follow him on there. He thought the app was creepy, but she'd insisted, for her own peace of mind.

"Meet me in the hotel bar in five minutes," she said. "You and I need to talk."

—

Jack changed out of his sweatpants and t-shirt into a black button-down shirt and dark-washed jeans before going down to the lobby. It was what he had brought to wear to Hayden's if he decided to show up and he would need to leave right from the bar if that was the decision he ended up making.

He spotted his mom at a booth in the restaurant near the crowded bar. She was running her finger around the stem of her half-empty wine glass. Nervously he slid into the booth across from her. "Jack," she said sternly when their eyes finally met, and the guilt he'd been trying to suppress all day rose to the surface. "How could you have done this?" she asked. "How could you have broken up with Kendall the day before your wedding?"

He bowed his head and closed his eyes. It was a horrible thing that he'd done. Unforgivable, really. And he felt sick about it. "Have you talked with her?" he mumbled.

"Not much," his mom said. "Tina and Ellie picked her up from the house. She's been with them all day. But she looked absolutely devastated when she left, Jack."

He didn't doubt it. He hadn't given her a reason for calling the wedding off. And everything with them had been going so well. She must have felt completely blindsided.

"This is about Charli, isn't it?" his mom asked.

He looked back up at her, faintly relieved to talk about it. "Yes," he admitted. "Today is the day of our reunion."

"I thought you had let that go," his mom said.

"I *had*," Jack stressed. "I'd mentally blocked out the date. I didn't even know it was this weekend."

"Until you found this?" his mom guessed, reaching into her purse and pulling out the to-go box from Hayden's with the date and time of his and Charli's reunion written on it. She must have gone rummaging through his room, looking for a clue to explain his behavior.

"Yes," he admitted. "I'd thrown that in the back of my closet after I returned home from Charleston and left it there when I moved to Seattle."

That was where he had gone. And where he had met Kendall. He didn't meet her right away. His first year in the city he remained pretty brokenhearted, and the thought of dating someone else didn't even cross his mind. All he could think about was Charli and the fact that she was dating someone else. It didn't help his state of affairs that the job he landed in sales at Brooks Running Company was unfulfilling and left him questioning his decision to leave baseball. But he knew he couldn't go back to Charli or to baseball, so he had no choice but to keep moving forward.

After a year of moping, he decided to mix things up and apply for a new job. He figured if he could find a job that he loved, his situation might improve and his spirits might lift, so he was relieved when he ended up landing a marketing position at Amazon.

It was there that he bumped into Kendall on his very first day. They rode the elevator up to their fifth floor offices together, and when their eyes locked, Jack's numbness lifted for the first time since he'd gotten back from Charleston.

He struck up a conversation with her, eager to keep that good feeling going, and when Kendall learned he was the new guy in the building, she went out of her way to make the rounds and introduce him to everyone. He was impressed with how approachable she seemed, despite being a knockout and by the end of the day, he mustered up the courage to ask for her number.

He was so relieved to discover that maybe, just maybe, he could feel something again for someone, and over a late dinner at Figaro Café and Wine Bar that Friday night, his feelings for her only intensified. As they ate their way through crostini and a smoked prosciutto pizza, their conversation flowed endlessly like the wine they kept having their waiter pour, and by the end of the evening,

Jack was sitting only inches away from Kendall in the wraparound corner booth. Intoxicated by the scent of her citrusy perfume and the four glasses of wine he'd had, he ended up confessing, "I'm not sure I want to be *just* your friend, Kendall."

To his great relief, she had let her pinky finger graze the rough fabric of his dark-washed jeans and replied in a quiet, sexy voice, "Good, because I'm not sure I want to be *just* your friend either."

They were exclusive a month later. It had felt a bit weird at first to be dating someone who wasn't Charli, but it also felt nice to put his heartache in the rear-view mirror for a while and eventually, he grew to develop intense feelings for Kendall. Her quick wit, kind-hearted nature, and model good-looks made her a guy's dream girl and he felt lucky that she seemed to be head-over-heels for him.

Looking back now, he couldn't help but wonder if the intensity of their relationship was more a reflection of his desire to reassure himself that a life without Charli was possible rather than a sign of his compatibility with Kendall. Regardless of the why, after just a couple of months, he and Kendall had built somewhat of a nice, comfortable life together and their life remained nice and comfortable for the next two and a half years.

Charli eventually stopped crossing his mind, which he took as a good sign that he'd moved on. Although looking back now, he wondered if she stopped crossing his mind because he'd shut down emotionally on some level to protect himself from ever having to feel such an intense heartache again.

Clearly he was afraid of heartache because the reason he proposed to Kendall had less to do with the fact that he couldn't picture a life without her and more to do with the fact that he didn't want to lose her the way he'd lost Charli. A new guy had started working at Amazon a few months before he popped the question and Jack noticed him flirting with Kendall all the time. He couldn't blame him, given how striking she was, but it made him feel insecure, tapping into that vulnerability he thought he'd left behind. So eventually, he proposed and Kendall accepted. He had every intention of going through with the wedding, until he saw that to-go box from Hayden's that afternoon. Now he ran the risk of being a real jerk.

"Seeing the box triggered hundreds of memories of Charli," he told his mom. "Memories that I'd blocked out. Memories that I tried to replace with new ones of Kendall and me." He hadn't planned on opening the box. If just seeing it made him care about Charli that much again, he couldn't imagine what opening it would do. But he couldn't help himself. And that was when he saw the date—that evening's date—written at the top. *What were the odds that his wedding weekend was the same weekend that his reunion with Charli was supposed to be?* It gave him chills, and for a long time he sat on the floor just staring at it. So long that tears ended up on his cheeks.

*But Charli probably wasn't even going to show up for the reunion,* he kept telling himself. And he had a wonderful woman downstairs who he knew loved him.

Maybe it was just nostalgia that he was experiencing, he considered. But it *felt* like more than that. A big part of him wanted to show up for that reunion. So badly in fact that it felt like an actual need. It was as if something inside of him had been lying dormant since he got back from Charleston and that something had suddenly been reignited within him. For the first time in five years he felt like his true self. *What did that mean? Had he been acting this whole time he'd been with Kendall?* It hadn't felt like that. But perhaps in an effort to protect his heart, he'd tricked himself into believing that Charli wasn't the love of his life and that he could be just as happy with someone else.

He hadn't really had a plan when he called off the wedding. He just knew he had to, in order to sit with his thoughts and his feelings longer. He couldn't keep playing the part of the happy fiancé, even if ultimately being with Kendall was what he really wanted.

"So, are you planning to show up for the reunion?" his mom asked. "Is that why you called the wedding off?"

"I don't know," Jack answered honestly. "I've been thinking about it."

She nodded and took a moment, as if processing this. When she finally opened her mouth, he was prepared for her to advise him to go back to Kendall. He knew that she, too, was afraid of him getting hurt again by Charli. Plus, she had grown to care for Kendall during the years they'd been together. Whenever Jack brought Kendall into town, she and his mom would go out to long lunches or get their nails done together and talk for hours. They had even taken a girls' trip to New York City to shop that past holiday season.

But she surprised him by saying, "The decision is obviously up to you, Jack. I won't think less of you either way. I'm dressed for the rehearsal dinner if you decide to try and get Kendall back, but I will also wait by the phone all night to hear from you if you decide to go to that reunion. You are my son, and I just want you to be happy. But there is something I think you should know before you make your decision."

From the tone of her voice, Jack knew that whatever it was, it couldn't be good. "What is it?" he said, bracing himself.

"I ran into Charli's parents a few months back," she said.

Jack stiffened. "How's her mom?" he asked instinctively, hoping she was still in remission from the breast cancer she'd gotten when he and Charli were in college.

"She's fine, health-wise."

Jack nodded, then held his breath, preparing himself for the rest.

"They came back to visit their old house and see the old neighborhood," his mom went on. "They told me that Charli is doing great. And apparently . . . she's seeing somebody."

His heart sank.

"Wendy didn't mention anything about the reunion or about Charli wavering on her feelings for the guy she was seeing. In fact, she said that Charli seems pretty serious about him." His mom looked up and reached across the table for Jack's hand. "I just think that's important information for you to have, honey, because it seems highly unlikely to me that Charli's going to be there tonight. And I really don't want to see you get your heart broken again."

His mom was right. The odds were stacked heavily against Charli showing up for the reunion. And yet, surprisingly, it didn't totally deter him from wanting to go to Hayden's anyway.

He knew he couldn't do both—show up to Hayden's and see if Charli was there, and then go back to Kendall if she wasn't. That would make Kendall his second choice, and he couldn't marry someone he'd pegged as his backup. It wasn't fair to him or to her.

No, he had to choose: go to Hayden's for Charli or fight to get Kendall back. And he had to make his decision soon. It was six forty-five. If he was planning on going to the reunion, he had to leave for Hayden's within the next five minutes to get there by the time he and Charli had agreed upon. And if he was planning on trying to get Kendall back, he had to find her and start apologizing as quickly as possible so that they could still hopefully make their rehearsal dinner at eight.

"What would you do?" he asked his mom. Never in his life had he wanted her guidance more.

"I wish I could tell you, honey. I wish I could point you in the right direction. But we both know this is your decision to make."

He pictured himself fighting to get Kendall back and saying goodbye to any hope of a future with Charli. Then he imagined himself walking into Hayden's to see if Charli was there and giving up all hope of a future with Kendall. The choice seemed impossible. "I'm not sure I'm going to be able to figure this out," he said. "At least not in time."

His mom slid the Hayden's to-go box across the table to him. "You will. The right choice will come to you."

She stood up and collected her purse from the seat. "You let me know if you need me to call everyone and tell them the rehearsal dinner is still on. I haven't cancelled our reservation at Genoa yet." She bent down and kissed the top of his head before walking out.

Frustrated and more confused than ever, Jack flagged over a waiter to order a drink to sip as he waited for an answer to come.

# twenty-seven
# NOW

It had taken some coaxing to get Charli to agree to come outside, but eventually Gianna had succeeded in convincing her. Charli still didn't know exactly what she was in for—Gianna had just explained that Ellie was a therapist with a creative way to deal with heartbreak.

"I guess it beats going back to my hotel and being alone with my thoughts," Charli had finally said and then followed them out.

The rain was so loud that Gianna could barely make herself heard over the sound of it. "The potted plant is this way," she yelled, pointing up ahead.

They hugged the side of the restaurant, trying to get as much shelter as they could from the awning. There were five or six parked cars back here, and Gianna prayed that no one dashed out while the three of them were performing this ritual. She didn't want people thinking that the owner of Hayden's was some kind of loony.

As soon as they got to the plant, Ellie took charge. "Hand me the spoons," she instructed, holding out her hand. "I'll get started with the digging."

"The digging?" Charli wrinkled her eyebrows. "What are we digging?"

*Oh boy*, Gianna thought, *here goes the explanation*. Either Charli was going to buy into this thing, or think Gianna was absolutely crazy for dragging her out here. Judging from the look on Charli's face as Ellie explained the ritual of burying reminders of ex-boyfriend's, it wasn't hard to guess that she was thinking the latter.

Gianna jumped in once Ellie had finished in an attempt to change Charli's mindset. "I thought this was crazy when she first explained it to me, Charli. But then I thought about it a little more and realized as out there as it was, it kind of made sense in a quirky way."

"It really does help," Ellie said. "Before my friends and I got here this evening, we buried one of my friend's wedding dresses under the ground at a park down the street from Hayden's because her fiancé jilted her today, the day before her wedding."

Charli just stared at them straight-faced as the wind howled, and then finally she broke into an unexpected smile. "You two can't be serious. You're just trying to get me to laugh and lighten up, right?"

"No. This is a real thing we do," Ellie said.

Charli was smiling wider now. "I don't believe it."

"You see, if you can part with the reminders of your Ex, it's a start to parting with him," Ellie said, sounding like Gianna's own shrink. "If you hold onto the reminders, then every time you look at them, you'll continue to miss him. That significantly drags out the grieving process. It might help you to get the closure you need if you bury a reminder of your fella in this pot right now. I was told you have a receipt with the date and time for tonight's reunion on it. That would work."

"Come on, Gianna," Charli said, turning to her, the smirk still on her face. "This a joke, isn't it? How much did you pay this woman?"

Although Gianna had been eager to tell Charli that yes—this was a joke—just a few seconds ago, now, after listening to Ellie, she was back to thinking the burial ritual was a good idea. How did the woman do that?

"You don't have to do anything you don't want to," Gianna told Charli. "But I *do* think it might help."

"Come on," Ellie encouraged her. "Why don't you just bury it and see how it feels?"

"What? No. This is crazy."

"So crazy it just might work?" Ellie challenged.

Charli laughed. "Look, I appreciate this injection of humor into my night, but really, I don't need to do this."

"I think you're just not ready to let go," Ellie said, refusing to let her off the hook. Gosh she was tough. Weren't therapists supposed to be easygoing and not pushy?

"My Ex is marrying another woman," Charli said. "Whether I want to or not, I have to let go. I know it's over."

"So why won't you bury the receipt?" Ellie asked.

Gianna wasn't sure if she should let this play out or interject and get Charli off the hook since she clearly wasn't a fan of this whole burial idea. When Charli's eyes turned glossy, Gianna opened her mouth to intervene, but Charli spoke up before she could.

"It's just . . . I think I need a little more time to process all of this. I'm not ready to let go of the few reminders I have of my Ex quite yet."

"You know the Jews bury their dead within twenty-four hours of the death," Ellie told her.

"Yeah, well, I don't have a decaying body on my hands here," Charli said, smiling tiredly. "Ladies, I appreciate this. I really do. But I think I'm going to just go back to my hotel, take a warm shower, pop an Ambien, and put this night behind me."

Gianna stepped in before Ellie could push her anymore. "We were only trying to help."

"I'm incredibly grateful," Charli said. "To both of you. For everything."

Gianna wanted to offer to walk Charli to her car, but she had to get back inside for Peter. She had made him wait long enough. It was time for her to accept his proposal.

Charli pulled her hood up over her head, and Gianna reached out and hugged her, wishing that she were her Fairy Godmother in this moment instead of her waitress and that she could swirl her wand around and made Jack appear in thin air.

"Well, here goes nothing," Charli said, looking out at the rain. She sucked in a deep breath, met Gianna's eyes one more time and then darted out into it.

# twenty-eight
# NOW

Jack knew what he had to do about halfway through his whiskey and Coke. When he realized it, he couldn't believe that he'd considered the alternative. His heart had been certain what he should do all along; he'd just been too afraid to listen to it.

And he was still afraid, he realized as he stood up from the booth and laid down a twenty-dollar bill to pay for the drink he'd ordered after his mom left. His server, Otis, was serving someone else, and Jack didn't have time to wait for change, so he waved a quick goodbye and bolted out of the bar and through the hotel lobby, past its ridiculous orange couches and over-the-top chandelier.

Out on the curb he found the valet standing behind a platform desk holding an umbrella.

"Can you get me a cab?" he asked. He didn't want to have to wait for someone to pull his car around or worry about parking once he got to Hayden's.

He was headed back for Charli.

Was he out of his mind? Probably. Was this a shot in the dark? Yes. But damn, it felt right.

Imagining walking through the glass doors at the restaurant and seeing Charli back there waiting at their old table by the fireplace filled him with more excitement than he'd felt in years.

Kendall had been wonderful. Kendall would have made a great wife. But Kendall wasn't his true love. He had finally admitted that to himself after years of denying it. And now that he had, he couldn't believe that he'd gotten so close to standing at the altar with her and exchanging vows.

Jack knew he should have been mentally preparing himself for Charli not showing up, but he couldn't force himself to think of that yet. He didn't know what was waiting for him at Hayden's, and until he did, he'd hope for the best.

The cab rolled up, and Jack tipped the valet and climbed in.

"Where to?" his scruffy-faced driver asked.

"Northwest 23rd Street," Jack said, tapping his hands on the dashboard. "Hayden's."

The car sped off into the rainy night. He stared out the window through the rain trickling down the glass at the blurred building lights on the other side of it and took a deep breath. *Please let her be there. Please.*

The cab arrived at Hayden's just minutes later.

Jack checked his watch. Seven o'clock on the dot. He'd made it.

He thought about asking the driver to do a loop around the block so he could peer into Hayden's out of the cab window and see if Charli was already seated, but he was so antsy that he decided against it. After handing the driver a sweaty ten dollars for the six dollar ride, he opened the door and darted through the rain into the restaurant.

There was a crowd of soaked pedestrians in the stuffy entryway waiting behind the hostess stand to put their names in. Jack pushed his way through them, looking over the tops of their heads, trying to get a peek at the table.

"Sir, are you meeting someone?" the hostess asked him.

"Well, I—"

"Jack?" The sound of his name coming from the back of the restaurant excited him until he realized it wasn't Charli's voice. It was Kendall's. A second later he saw her, in the most ridiculous black dress, stand up from her seat at the table right next to the one where Charli would have been waiting for him.

The table was empty.

Jack stuck his hand out and grabbed onto the hostess stand, his knees going weak.

"Are you okay?" the hostess asked, helping him stabilize himself.

*No,* he wanted to shout, *I'm not.* He scanned the room, hoping maybe Charli was somewhere else, but there was no sign of her.

"Sir?" the hostess said again. "Can I get you some water?"

*Fuck water*, Jack thought. "I'm fine," he said, trying to keep it together. Kendall was flagging him toward her. Jack had no choice but to go back there.

As he walked, he kept checking over his shoulder and looking at the front door. Maybe Charli was still planning on showing up. Women were always late, weren't they? Although Charli was a planner. And he'd never known her to be late for anything. He had always been the one who ran behind. Was it possible that she'd changed in the years they'd been apart though? Maybe. Hopefully.

"Jack, what are you doing here?" Kendall stared at him with a hopeful glint in her eyes, and he suddenly realized he'd probably gotten her spirits up. A phone call would have sufficed to reiterate an apology, and since he'd shown up at the restaurant, she must have assumed he'd tracked her down to see about getting her back.

It was hard for him to think with Tina glaring at him from her chair like she was ready to punch him in the nuts, which, to be honest, he wouldn't have blamed her for.

"I just—I felt weird how we left things," he said. "I wanted to see if you were okay."

"Well, now you've seen me," Kendall said, throwing her arms up and letting them fall to her sides. "Do I look okay?"

He should have gone with something else. She looked like hell—in that dress, with her red-rimmed eyes, and her hair all messed up—and he felt terrible—he was responsible.

"Let me explain myself better," he said.

Jack looked at the empty table where Charli was supposed to meet him, and his stomach sank again. He considered launching into the full story right then so that Kendall would know everything. He'd told her about Charli when they first got together during that obligatory past-relationships talk, but he'd never mentioned how serious they were or their pact. It wouldn't have taken long to explain, but what was the point? It wasn't like he was going to end up with Charli. And if he started talking about her, he honestly thought he might break down. He was already struggling not to.

"I just had a change of heart about spending the rest of our lives together," he said. "I don't know what came over me, and I honestly wish I didn't feel the way I was feeling, but I do."

Kendall folded her arms over her chest, and Jack watched the expression on her face change from one of hope and confusion, to anger and frustration. Her eyes burned into him.

"So sometime between this morning," she said, raising her voice, "when you were fucking me," she practically screamed it, "and this afternoon, you just had a change of heart?"

The room started to fall quiet. Curious heads turned. Whispering began. There were a few chuckles. Jack's ears began to ring. He wanted to crawl into a hole in the ground.

"You're better off without me," he said.

"No shit." Tina tossed her napkin on the table.

She stood up, and Jack took a step backwards. He needed to get out of the restaurant.

"I'll be staying at my mom's place for a few days," he told Kendall. "Feel free to go to my place in Seattle and get all the stuff you have there while I'm gone. If it's still there when I get back, I'll box it up and send it to you. I'll get my stuff whenever is convenient for you." He took a deep breath. "You truly are wonderful Kendall and again I'm so sor—"

Tina cut him off. "Did you hear that, Kendall? You're wonderful. Now get the hell out of here, Jack."

Kendall crumbled into her chair, covering her face with her hands.

Jack dropped his head, turned around, and with everyone's eyes on him, started to walk out of the restaurant.

## twenty-nine
# NOW

**Gianna** and Ellie had turned to head back inside when Charli shrieked. "My clutch!"

Gianna spun around and saw her running back toward them.

"I must have left it inside," she said, as she ducked under the awning.

Gianna wrapped her arm around her. "I'm sure it's still there. We've only been gone a few minutes. Let's go in and look. Or I can just go . . . if you're not comfortable going back inside."

"No. I'll come," Charli said. "Let's just make it quick."

Gianna led the women back to the door and pushed it open.

The second she stepped into the restaurant, she noticed that Kendall, from the funeral party, was in tears again. Ellie rushed over to her before even taking off her jacket. Charli darted into the bathroom to look for her clutch.

At the exact same moment that Charli bolted, a man in the front of the restaurant bumped into the hostess stand. Gianna heard it first and then looked up and saw him and Rosie stabilizing it. He didn't waste much time apologizing for the incident, which Gianna found odd. He just made sure the stand was upright and then scooted around it in a flash, shooting a look back toward Charli.

When Gianna saw his face, she thought her eyes were playing tricks on her at first. They had to be, right? Because Jack was getting married to someone else, and it was already past seven o'clock—the reunion had come and gone. But, God, he looked just like him—a little older and with shorter hair—but almost identical to the Jack Gianna had last seen five years earlier. She reached into the back pocket of her slacks for her glasses and shoved them on. When he came into full focus, Gianna's mouth dropped. Brown hair, green eyes, broad shoulders. It *was* Jack. He had come back after all.

*But why?* Gianna wondered as he wove around the tables toward her. She might have thought that he had come to tell Charli about the wedding himself if he had had a different look in his eyes, but he seemed mesmerized by the glimpse he must have gotten of her before she bolted to the bathroom. The only conclusion Gianna could logically draw was that he was here for the same reason that Charli was—because he wanted to give their relationship another shot.

The moment she realized this, she felt a pit in her stomach for assuming that the wedding cake order form had been his and for sharing this assumption with Charli. She and Barbara must have been mistaken and caused Charli all of this heartbreak for no reason.

Of course, there was a chance that it *was* his wedding cake order form and that he had simply had a change of heart at the last minute, just like Kendall's fiancé had. But what were the odds that two men in the same city both decided to stand up their fiancés the day before their weddings? That would have been too coincidental!

Jack continued to make his way toward the back of the room. As he wound his way through tables, customers turned in their chairs to watch him. She found it strange that they were doing this, because only her staff knew about Jack and Charli's reunion plans and none of them had been around five years earlier to know what he looked like. What could have been their curiosity with him then?

Jack was almost to Gianna now. She looked over her shoulder to see if Charli had come out of the restroom yet, but she was still in there. Gianna wanted her to see what was happening. If she thought it would have sped things up at all, she would have run into the bathroom and gotten her, but Charli would be out in a second regardless. There were only three stalls in the bathroom and a sink. The clutch could only be in so many places.

Gianna turned back around. Her expectation was to be face to face with Jack at this point, but it seemed he had encountered a roadblock a few feet from her. And to Gianna's surprise, that roadblock was none other than . . . Ellie.

"Tina told me she asked you to leave," she said, placing her hands on her hips. "What are you still doing here?"

The funeral party knew him?

Jack looked longingly over the top of Ellie's head toward the bathroom. She could tell it was killing him not to push Ellie aside and keep on toward Charli. It was killing Gianna as well! What was Ellie doing? *Move aside, move aside!*

But Jack seemed to understand the holdup and resisted the urge to plow through it. He wearily addressed the whole funeral party.

"I'm sorry. I haven't been completely honest with all of you." His eyes closed for a brief moment as if he was searching for the words to say, and when he opened them, he drew in a deep breath and looked at Kendall. "Five years ago, I made a pact with my first love, Charli."

That was as far as he got before Kendall interrupted him. "Wait. Hold on. You mean the woman who was sitting here all night at that table was Charli," she pointed to the two-seater in the corner.

Jack looked blown away. "You know her?"

"You're the man that she was waiting for?"

"You know about the pact? I'm confused."

But Gianna wasn't anymore. It had all just clicked for her, and apparently for Kendall and the rest of the funeral party. Jack was Kendall's ex-fiancé. The wedding cake order form did belong to him. He had had a last-minute change of heart, realized he wanted to be with Charli, and that was why he stood Kendall up.

*Wow!*

Just then, Charli stepped out of the bathroom. "Gianna, I found it!" she called. "It somehow ended up in the trash! That shows you where my head was at. I can't believe that I . . ." She must have seen Jack because her voice trailed off, and her clutch dropped to the floor with a thud.

"Charli," Jack said, breathlessly.

Gianna pivoted around and saw Charli open and close her mouth a few times like she wanted to say something to him but couldn't get the words out.

"I—I don't believe this," she finally stammered.

"Neither do I," Jack said, his face brightening. "When I didn't see you at the table, I assumed you hadn't come back. I can't believe you're here."

Charli crossed her arms over her chest, defensively. "No, I mean I don't believe that you came back . . . considering you're about to get married."

She seemed to have caught Jack off guard because he looked like he was floundering for words.

"If you're here just to tell me that, please just leave now," she went on. "I already know. A few minutes before seven, Gianna found an order form with your name on it for a cake for your *rehearsal dinner*."

Jack shook his head and countered with a forcefulness he seemed to hope was convincing. "No, no. You've got it all wrong. I'm not getting married."

Charli narrowed her eyes at him. "Then how do you explain the order?"

"Well—I mean—I uh—I *was* getting married. To *her* actually." He pointed to Kendall who was still stuck in her chair looking like she was trying to come to terms with all that was happening. "But yesterday I stumbled upon the box with the date and time of our reunion on it in my mom's house. I had an overwhelming feeling when I saw it that I should come back here and that getting married was a mistake."

Jack wiped his hands on his jeans. He now had a room full of curious customers and servers looking over at him and listening as he explained himself. Gianna's kitchen staff, as well as Peter and Valerie, were peering out the window at him too. They must have noticed the eerie silence out here and realized something was up.

"I'm sorry, Kendall," Jack turned to her. "I loved you. I really did." Gianna could tell from the genuine look in his eyes that he was telling her the truth, and she thought Kendall sensed this too, although she wasn't sure it was much of a consolation. "I thought I had moved on. But deep down, I think I was just telling myself that because I figured Charli had moved on."

"You did, didn't you?" He looked over the top of Ellie's head back at Charli.

Charli unfolded her arms and let them drop to her sides, softening a bit now that she knew Jack wasn't here to break her heart. "Only once you wrote me that last letter."

Jack tilted his head to the side. "Are you sure about that? I wrote you that letter because I came to Charleston after I quit baseball and saw you out on the back deck at Fleet Landing kissing some curly haired guy."

Charli must have remembered that afternoon because she cocked her head back and rolled her eyes like she couldn't believe her bad luck. "It wasn't what you thought," she sighed. "He wasn't—we weren't . . ."

"You mean . . ." Jack said, pausing for a moment as he processed this. He looked deeply pained by what was obviously a big misunderstanding. Gianna could sense that he wanted to ask for more clarification, but he seemed aware that this wasn't the right time or place. "It's a moot point now," he said instead, giving Charli what was clearly a forced smile. "Anyway, I knew the odds you'd be here would be slim-to-none, but I felt I had to come back just to see. I figured I would always wonder about you if I didn't. And seeing you now . . . well . . . I can't believe I ever considered *not* showing up."

He stared at Charli intensely for a long minute.

"What a mess I've made though, huh?" Jack looked from Charli to the funeral party. "This is certainly . . . awkward to say the least. I feel like a horrible person." He stuffed his hands in his pockets.

The room was silent for only a couple of seconds before Kendall rose from her chair. "Let me make it less awkward then," she said. "I'll get going."

Gianna wasn't sure if her standing up and giving Jack a full visual of her frumpy dress made things any *less* awkward, but Kendall was right. She needed to get out of here.

"Why don't *I* just leave?" Charli offered. "I've already got my coat on."

"No, *really*," Kendall insisted, turning pinker with embarrassment by the moment. "You two . . . obviously have a lot to catch up on."

Jack looked sick with guilt. "Can I at least walk you out?" he asked Kendall.

"No." Kendall's voice was firm. "I have *friends* who can do that."

Ellie and Tina were already at work gathering up their party's things. Ellie pulled out a wad of cash from her wallet and set it on the table, and Tina collected her and Kendall's purses and stuck them under one arm, then wrapped her other arm around Kendall.

"You ready?" Tina asked her softly.

"Yes," Kendall said. "Get me out of here."

Tina nodded and together the three of them walked past Jack through the room full of onlookers and out the front door.

Jack watched them as they rounded the corner and headed to their car. He pinched the bridge of his nose, clearly struggling with remorse. Charli gave him a moment alone with his thoughts and then she walked over to him and rested her hand on his shoulder.

"You okay?" she asked.

He noticeably relaxed with her touch. "Yeah," he said.

He reached up, felt her hand, and then set his on top. "I am now."

—

By the time Charli and Jack made it over to their table and sat down, the customers in the restaurant had turned back around in their chairs and picked up their conversations again, realizing the drama was over. Gianna's kitchen staff wasn't watching them anymore either, and her servers were back to waiting on their sections.

Gianna couldn't take her eyes off them though. They looked so happy to be together again. And so right for one another. It was like they were . . . soul mates. The phrase suddenly popped into Gianna's head. She had always desperately wanted to believe there was such a thing, and now . . . seeing Jack and Charli together . . . it was impossible not to.

Gianna blinked back tears, her decision about Peter's proposal obvious now. Mary Pat had been right—something would speak to her. And this just had, loud and clear. With her mind made up, she went back into the kitchen.

Peter and Valerie were sitting on the counter waiting for her. "Thank God. You're back," Valerie said, jumping down.

"I'm so sorry," Gianna apologized. "It was just such a crazy night, and I had customers to deal with and—"

"Is it yes or no, Gianna?" Peter cut right to the point.

Although he didn't get down on one knee again, he pulled the box back out of his pocket and snapped it open, holding the diamond up in front of her.

Gianna took a deep breath, considered her answer one more time, and then reached out and closed the box. "No," she said.

"What?" Peter and Valerie both gasped simultaneously.

Gianna looked at Valerie. "Will you give us a minute?"

"No." Valerie stuck her hands on her hips. "I want to hear this too."

"I just want a couple of minutes with Peter. Alone."

Valerie sighed deeply and then said, "Fine. But for the record, I think you're making a *big* mistake here."

Peter obviously did too. Once Valerie left he shook his head. "I don't understand. Everything with us was so great, Gianna."

"I know," she said, apologetically. How could she explain to him that although he was perfect on paper, she wasn't sure he was her soul mate? That although she loved him, she didn't feel a crazy spark toward him? "I'm not the one for you," she told him.

"I'm pretty sure you are," he objected.

"No. I'm not, Pete." She took his hands in hers. "You should be with someone who doesn't hesitate for a second when you ask her to marry you. *I* hesitated."

"I can give you more time, if that's what you need."

"I've taken enough of your time. I know this is the right thing, as much as it hurts." She had to honor her gut. She couldn't hang onto Peter out of fear that she wouldn't meet her Mr. Right. That wasn't fair to either of them.

"This is what you really want?"

"Yes," Gianna said.

Peter gripped her hands tighter. "There's nothing else I can say or do to get you to change your mind?"

"No," Gianna said, wishing that there was. That somehow Peter could say or do something to magically create the spark Gianna felt they were missing.

Peter closed his eyes for a split second, bowed his head, and muttered something like, "I don't believe this."

Gianna didn't either. She never thought she'd turn down a wonderful man's proposal at the age of thirty-seven in the hopes of meeting someone better for her. And yet, here she was.

Peter drew in a deep breath. Then in true gentleman form he leaned down and kissed her on the cheek. Keeping her close he whispered, "I hope you find whatever it is you're looking for."

His words were so kind that Gianna was momentarily tempted to take back everything she'd just said and accept his proposal. But then an image of Charli and Jack flashed into her mind and she bit her tongue. She *really* wanted a love like that. She deserved to find a love like that.

"Thank you, Pete," she said instead.

He stuck his hands in his pockets. "I guess this is goodbye."

Gianna just nodded and watched with tears in her eyes as Peter turned around and walked out of the kitchen.

# thirty
# NOW

**Despite** that evening's unexpected turn of events, Charli couldn't deny that she was thrilled to see Jack. She'd never believed that Jack "completed her," or that any man would, but being with him did feel completely right. And Jack seemed just as pleased with his decision to show up. He kept saying how surreal it was to see her, and he had just admitted that this was the first time in five years that he felt like he was exactly where he was meant to be.

But as much as her heart was racing forward, her head was telling her to slow down. Jack almost *hadn't* shown up. He'd been engaged to someone else. She couldn't just gloss over that.

"I realize I have a lot of explaining to do," Jack said, as if reading her mind.

"I know you're not a bad guy, Jack," Charli said. She'd been trying not to jump to any conclusions about him before she heard him out. "But what just happened here was hurtful to both your ex-fiancé and to me. I do have quite a few questions."

"I'll get them all answered," he assured her. "I promise. But can I ask you to clarify what happened in Charleston first? I saw you kiss another guy when I flew out there. You said it wasn't what I thought, but it certainly looked serious."

"*He* was into *me*," she explained. "That day he kissed me, I told him I wasn't ready for a relationship and that I just wanted to be friends. After I got your last letter, I decided to go out with him and try to move on, but the relationship didn't last."

"So, I just happened to show up in Charleston at the exact wrong moment," Jack said, shaking his head in disbelief. "Talk about bad timing. I was going to ask you to marry me that day, Charli."

"You were?" Her eyes teared up as she thought of all the heartbreak that could have been avoided and all the time she and Jack could have spent together instead of apart if Christopher had never kissed her that day or if Jack hadn't witnessed the kiss.

"Don't cry," he said, scooting in closer and reaching across the table to wipe away a tear that had fallen onto her cheek. "I didn't mean to tell you that to make you upset, but because I think it will help you better understand what happened next."

"What did happen next?" she asked.

Jack filled her in on how devastated he'd been when he flew home from Charleston and how his mom had encouraged him to start over in a new city where he wouldn't be reminded of Charli. He chose Seattle and spent a year fairly depressed thinking of Charli dating someone else while working an unfulfilling job in sales at Brooks Running Company. Following that year, he decided sales wasn't for him and got a job in marketing at Amazon. That was where he met Kendall.

"Being with her initially helped ease my heartache," he said. "The same way it sounds like dating that guy I saw you kiss in Charleston eased yours."

"Yes, but eventually I broke up with him," Charli said. "Because I couldn't stop thinking about you. It feels like you forgot about me completely when you met Kendall. Until today."

"That's because you're looking at *what* I did and not *why* I did it. I was *trying* to forget about you," he admitted. "And in that process I completely suppressed my true emotions. I mean, Charli,

I managed to forget the date of our reunion—something I thought I'd never be able to do. And I almost married someone I shouldn't have." He placed his hand over hers on top of the table. The gesture was both comforting and familiar and at the same time made her heart race wildly. "You've always been the girl for me, but because I love you so much, you are also the person most capable of hurting me. I was afraid to put my heart on the line again. Being with Kendall meant I didn't have to, so for a long time that option sounded better."

Charli's mind immediately went to Tim.

"My mom mentioned earlier this evening that she ran into your parents a while back and they told her you were seeing someone else. Did you ever think about staying with him and not showing up for a similar reason?"

"Yes," she admitted, softening toward Jack even more. She guessed she couldn't really fault him for something she had been somewhat guilty of herself. "I never blocked out the date of our reunion, but I did consider not showing up. Luckily, I have a friend who encouraged me to follow my heart. Which has always been with you."

Jack smiled softly. "My heart has always been with you too. It just took me a bit longer than you to get over the fear of potentially having my heart broken again. I hope you know that while I was happy with Kendall, it was a completely different level of happiness than I feel being with you, right now. I can't believe how close I came to jeopardize never feeling like this again just because I was afraid of getting hurt. I'm so glad I took a risk. That we both did."

"Me too," Charli said. "I guess the bright side is that we found our way back to each other even though we both tried to move on. I think that really speaks to what we once had."

"And to what's to come," Jack said, optimistically. "That is, if you can find a way to forgive me."

Charli could tell that Jack was still filled with guilt—both for breaking the heart of his ex-fiancé and for making Charli question the bond they had. These past twenty-four hours clearly hadn't been easy for him and she was reminded how much she cared for him by how much she didn't want to see him hurt, even when he was hurting because of something he'd done to her.

There was one thing she was still hung up on though. "What about the rehearsal dinner cake order?" she asked. "It seemed insensitive to me that you ordered your cake from here and that you got the Chocolate Mint Cloud. That was *our* cake."

"Kendall's parents were in charge of the cake for the rehearsal dinner and the wedding," Jack explained. "Our wedding was going to be very small and non-traditional so everyone was helping out where they could. I honestly didn't know they'd placed the order here till you mentioned it. They must have found Hayden's through its good reviews on Yelp or OpenTable. And they knew I liked mint desserts so they ordered the Chocolate Mint Cloud. I promise I had nothing to do with that."

Charli let out a deep sigh. "The idea behind this pact was so that we could come back to each other and pick up right where we left off with only good memories to return to."

They both chuckled at how far off that was from what had actually happened.

"The bigger point of it though was for us to pursue our dreams," Jack reminded her. "And I'm dying to hear how it's been for you to chase yours. You must be just months away from getting your PhD at this point."

"I'll be done in June, as I anticipated," Charli told him. "These past five years truly have been fulfilling intellectually. But I feel so terrible for you. I was devastated when I learned that your dream didn't pan out the way you'd expected."

"Being with you is my dream, Charli," Jack said, tracing his thumb back and forth over hers. "Your letters helped me realize

I was chasing after the wrong dream. I didn't feel the same way about baseball as you did about your research. Part of it was the less-than-glamorous lifestyle and being thrown together with guys who saw my success as the price for theirs. But most of it was because I came to realize that you were part of the formula that made baseball fun. Without you, the game wasn't the same," he admitted. "I wrestled with my decision to quit for a long time, but I knew it was the right call. And I don't regret my decision to move to San Jose and play for the Giants. If I'd just followed you to Charleston five years ago, I would have always wondered about that path. I'm sure I will have more career goals and new dreams in this lifetime, but I have every intention of living out these dreams *with you*, from here on out."

"So, what does that look like, in your eyes?" Charli asked. "Where do we go from here?"

"I currently work with Kendall," Jack said, "so regardless of whether or not you'd shown up tonight, I would have been looking for a new job. I would never want her to feel uncomfortable going to work and if she had to see me every day, she probably would. I do like marketing, and would like to continue working in that field, but for the time being I would love to move out and be with you until you finish your PhD. I could work a few side jobs and then depending on where you end up getting a job, I could search for a new marketing position there. Assuming that all sounds okay to you."

"That sounds like a dream come true," Charli admitted and Jack's face lit up.

"Do you remember when we made this pact, what the first thing you said you were going to do when you saw me again was?" she asked.

"Kiss you so hard," Jack said without missing a beat. "Believe me that is *all* I've been able to think about since the moment I saw you. You've somehow gotten even more beautiful, Charli," he said, eyeing her up and down. "And that dress," he whistled.

If only he knew how many different ones she'd tried on. She'd gone back and forth all evening in her hotel room, debating all the different options she and Rebecca had shopped for and packed. She felt so silly, knowing that Jack had never seemed to care what she wore. And she typically didn't put a lot of thought into it either. But she'd wanted to tonight. Because tonight was special. Not only because she was back with Jack, but because she had remained true to herself. Was there anything more wonderful than that?

"What do you say we split a slice of cake," she said, "for old time's sake. And then let's get out of here and make up for all that lost time."

"I think," Jack said, smiling, "that's the best idea I've heard in the last five years."

Visit sincerelyriley.com/scene-7 to see a scene unfold that wasn't in these chapters and to Shop the Book™.

# thirty-one
# NOW

It was a little after one o'clock in the morning and the last few customers had just finished up and headed out into the now-calm night. Gianna's closing manager, Kim, locked the front door, and Gianna and the rest of her servers got to work wiping down the tables and chairs in their sections.

Kim came up to her as she was blowing out the tea candles that were still lit.

"You know, you or I could assign someone else to clean up for you," she said. "You don't need to stay."

It hadn't taken long for word to get around that Gianna had turned down Peter's proposal. Everyone was feeling sorry for her.

"Two servers have already offered, but I want to keep busy," Gianna said.

Kim nodded and then went into the kitchen to count the day's receipts and send the credit card reports.

Gianna picked up some left-behind items—a black cotton sweater hanging on the back of a chair, a business card for Molly Neilson's Pet Grooming Services, a Blackberry cell phone. She crumpled up the business card, stuck it in her pocket, and put the lost-and-found items on the windowsill. Then she moved to the table where Charli and Jack had sat and ran a warm, damp rag over the dark wooden tabletop.

The long-lost lovers had been among the last to leave. After Peter walked out, Gianna had brought them a slice of the Chocolate Mint Cloud

Cake, which they shared just like they used to, and then they'd ordered a bottle of Cabernet and took their time drinking it as they caught up.

When they finally asked for their bill, it was around midnight. "It's on the house," Gianna told them.

"No, I insist," Jack had said, holding out his credit card.

Gianna shook her head. "You already paid me in full tonight. Seeing you two together after so many years . . . I couldn't be happier that you both showed up." She didn't get into the details—how they'd saved her from making, what could have been, one of the biggest mistakes of her life. How they'd given her something to believe in again. She was eternally indebted.

"I couldn't be happier either," Charli had smiled, and it was such a real and genuine smile that Gianna felt excited, for the first time in years, about going back out into the dating world. She wanted to find someone who could put that kind of an expression on her face. And she finally felt there was a chance of that.

She flipped their chairs up and then moved on to wipe down the funeral party's table. Years from now, even after hundreds of new customers had eaten at that table, Gianna would still think of it as the place the funeral party had once sat.

She chuckled to herself, picturing the ladies in their crazy black get-ups. It was too bad things hadn't turned out differently for Kendall. Gianna truly wished that Jack had not been her Ex, and that her fiancé had come into Hayden's with a change of heart at the last minute and told her that he'd just had temporary cold feet. As much as Charli deserved to find love, Kendall deserved to find it too.

But Gianna felt strongly that Kendall would get her very own happily ever after someday. She hadn't realized, until seeing Jack "rise up" in Charli's life after Kendall "buried" him, how cyclical relationships really were. And it was a reassuring realization.

Who knew? Maybe on this very night in Kendall's hometown there was an unhappy couple breaking up, and tomorrow (or the next day, or the day after that) the guy was going to appear in Kendall's life just like Jack had appeared in Charli's. She was hanging onto that same belief for her own personal life.

Looking across the room as she stacked all of the chairs on top of the table, she made fleeting eye contact with Valerie. Although Gianna had pulled her aside once Peter left and explained her reasoning for rejecting his proposal, Valerie still wasn't a fan of her decision.

"I want you to be happy," Valerie had said. "And I feel like you just took a huge step away from that."

"But I didn't," Gianna had tried to assure her. She hoped Valerie would see that in time. After watching Charli and Jack together, Gianna knew that true love had a look—an absolutely, positively, destined look—and she was banking on Valerie recognizing that look between Gianna and her future husband, whenever she met him. It was a look Valerie couldn't have possibly seen between Gianna and Peter because it had never been there, as much as Gianna had willed it to be.

"Gianna," Barbara called, looking up from the chair she was wiping off in the front of the room. "Someone's knocking on the door."

Gianna glanced up at the clock. It was one fifteen in the morning. Whoever it was had to be drunk. She walked over to shoo him away.

But as the figure came into focus, she realized it wasn't a drunk. She recognized the guy immediately—the dark features, the hipster style. It was that scumbag customer who made his girlfriend so upset she felt compelled to shatter a wine glass. What did *he* want?

"We're closed," she said through the glass.

"I left my phone," he said.

The Blackberry.

Gianna held up one finger and went to the windowsill to get it. He could wait in the cold. He deserved some punishment for what he'd done, didn't he?

When she opened the door and gave it to him, he thanked her.

*Yeah, yeah, whatever*, she thought. She started to close the door again, but he pushed it back open.

"Wait, I want to apologize for earlier."

*You shouldn't be apologizing to me*, Gianna wanted to say. Some poor woman was probably sitting on her bed with a pint of Ben and Jerry's right now bawling her eyes out because of him. *She* was who he needed to apologize to.

"I didn't mean to shatter the wineglass."

Gianna blinked. *He'd* shattered it? Hadn't his girlfriend?

"That was my girlfriend I was with, and she told me when we sat down that she's been sleeping with my best friend."

*She'd* slept with someone else. He hadn't been the one who messed up?

"I got so upset that I threw my napkin down on the table and it knocked the wine glass off. I'd like to pay for it. I would have offered earlier, but I wasn't thinking straight." He reached into his pocket for his wallet.

Gianna was so thrown off by her misconception that it took her a moment to find her voice.

"Don't worry about it," she finally said. "We drop plates and glasses all the time." She would have felt weird taking his money given that she'd judged him so hard. It just seemed like men were always the ones screwing relationships up—at least in her dating experience before she'd met Peter.

"Oh no. I wouldn't feel right if I didn't pay for it," he said. "Here, do you want ten? Twenty?" He extended some bills.

"Really. It's fine." She dismissed him with a wave of her hand. "Use the money to go buy a stiff drink. There's a great bar one block down called Neiman's that's open for another forty-five minutes."

He nodded, obviously realizing she wasn't going to budge. Putting the money back in his wallet, he closed it. "Thank you, Miss . . . ?"

"Gianna," she told him.

"Thank you, Gianna. For bringing out my phone. And for cleaning up the glass. And for not charging me for it. It's nice to know that not all women are complete bitches—excuse my language."

Gianna couldn't help but smile. *It's nice to know that not all men you peg as assholes actually are*, she thought but bit her tongue.

"Don't worry about it. And if it makes you feel any better, the little scene you two caused was far from the big drama of the evening."

"Really?" He raised a curious eyebrow.

Gianna leaned a little closer to him, hanging on the door. "It's a very long story. A good one, but too long to tell you while you're standing on my doorstep in the cold."

He took his keys from his pocket. "Maybe some other time then." Smiling, he turned to go, but then he spun back around. "Tell me this: does it have a happy ending or a bad ending like mine tonight?"

"A happy ending," Gianna said. "And I guess a bad ending too. It's a great love story though."

"Really?" He looked even more intrigued.

"Yes."

He folded his arms over his chest. "I know I may not look it, but I'm a total sap for a good love story. Like *The Notebook*—I completely bawled at the end."

"You're kidding?" Gianna said, feeling herself smile.

"Nope, I'm not," he said. "I used to be an editor for the 'Modern Love' column in *The New York Times*. Have you read it?"

Gianna grinned. "That's the first thing I read on Sunday mornings." This guy was getting more interesting by the minute.

"This love story stuff kind of pulls at my heartstrings. It's what I'm into."

Gianna was impressed. "Then you'll definitely have to come back in to get this one. But if you do turn it into a book or something and make millions, you better share half the profits with me."

"Deal," he said, turning his lips up slightly.

Although Gianna had noted his attractiveness when he first came in earlier, now, seeing him underneath the security light—and in a completely different light, one where he wasn't a jackass—it was even more noticeable. His long hair had a nice wave to it, his eyes were a mix of black and brown, and he radiated an intense energy that made Gianna, for some reason, fantasize about seeing him naked. She couldn't believe it, but she was picturing the tattoos she was sure he had on his chest or his shoulders—a peace sign and something meaningful—a poem he'd written or the lyrics to his favorite hard rock song. He definitely listened to hard rock.

"Well, I'm here almost every day. I'm the owner," she said, snapping out of her fantasy. "You should drop in sometime."

"The owner?" He looked impressed, not intimidated by the fact, which was a relief after dating Fred who'd felt the opposite. "I'd really like to," he said, offering her a slightly crooked, *definitely* flirtatious smile.

In all her time dating Peter—all of it, the beginning included—she had never felt even an inkling of what was going on here, and suddenly she was overcome with relief and reassurance that her decision had been the right one. Even if she never saw this guy again.

"What was your name?" She was desperate to know it. Desperate to know more about this stranger.

He extended his hand. "Luke."

He looked like a Luke. In fact, that was the name she would have probably given him if she hadn't asked, and she were, say, relaying the details of their encounter to Mary Pat, something she definitely planned to do tomorrow morning.

"Nice to meet you, Luke."

"You too, Gianna." He sounded sincere when he said it, like he really meant it, and when he finally let go of her hand, he looked as disappointed as she felt that it meant their conversation was coming to a close. "I look forward to seeing you soon then."

"Me too," Gianna said.

He smiled, nodded, and with nothing left to say, turned and started to walk across the street. Gianna stared after him in the doorway, mesmerized by the sight of him—his head bowed down, his easy gait, the way his jeans hugged his legs. She had just reached into her pocket for her phone to text Mary Pat that they *definitely* needed to talk in the morning, when she noticed that he'd turned around and was jogging back.

She opened the door a little wider.

"Okay, you know what, I'm just going to say it. Would you want to come and get a drink with me at that bar you mentioned? I'd love some company right now."

Gianna just stood there, shocked.

"You don't have to," he said backpedaling, like he realized maybe that was the last thing she wanted to do after a busy day at work and that it was entirely possible she hadn't been flirting with him; she'd just been trying to be nice because of what he'd been through.

"Sure," she finally said.

"Really?"

"Yeah, let me just go grab my jacket."

He broke into a grin. "All right then. I'll wait."

She gestured for him to come inside, thinking how crazy it was that just a few minutes earlier she'd wanted to keep him out in the cold.

He stepped in, his shoulder brushing hers as he walked past. She got a whiff of his scent when he was close—something spicy and rustic, and her stomach did a tiny flip.

When he sat down on the black bench in the foyer, a couple of Gianna's servers glanced over from their cleaning tasks and checked him out, speculating, Gianna assumed, about what he was doing in here after hours. Valerie, who knew that he wasn't a friend of Gianna's, looked especially confused.

Gianna hurried over to her. She wasn't sure how Valerie would respond to her taking up Luke's drink offer, but she still wanted her to know. Valerie was her closest friend after all, and she did need someone to take over cleaning up her section.

"That's the guy from your section earlier, isn't it?" Valerie said.

"Yeah," Gianna said. "Walk with me." She had Valerie follow her toward her section in the back, so they'd be out of Luke's earshot.

"I'm going to get a drink with him," Gianna said after a few steps.

"You're what?" Valerie eyed Luke on the bench. "You just met the guy."

"I know, but it just . . . feels like something I want to do."

Valerie folded her arms over her chest. Gianna watched her, watching him, hoping that she'd come around. "Well . . . he is cute," she finally said.

"Oh, Valerie, thank you for understanding." She drew her into a hug.

"Yeah, yeah," Valerie said.

"You won't mind finishing cleaning my section, will you?"

"Doesn't look like I have a choice, boss."

Gianna thanked her again.

"Go on now. Don't make him wait any longer. You've already blown one relationship tonight. Let's not ruin another."

"Right," Gianna said. She gave Valerie one last smile and then turned and hurried off into the kitchen to get her things.

As she pulled her jacket and purse off the peg on the wall, she took her phone out of her pocket to text Mary Pat. She typed up something, quick.

*Lots to tell you. Charli and Jack came back. Said no to Peter. Just met someone else.*

But her words didn't seem to do the night justice. So much more had happened than just that. She believed in something now. She was hopeful again.

Before she could press "Send," she ended up deleting the whole thing. She would fill Mary Pat in tomorrow over a cup of coffee in her kitchen. She could already see Mary Pat asking lots of questions, being her normal interested self, never admitting, even though it was probably the truth, that she knew from the start how the whole night would play out.

When Luke saw her walk out of the kitchen, his face brightened, and he stood up. "You ready?" he asked.

She smiled. "Let's go."

He opened the door for her and followed Gianna out. A warmer breeze had started to blow, and there were a couple of stars peering out from the clearing clouds.

"So," Luke said, falling into step beside her. "That story you mentioned? How does it start?"

Gianna looked up into his gleaming eyes for just a moment, wondering if this was how Charli felt the first time she ever realized she had feelings for Jack. "Well," she said, turning her attention back to the dark crosswalk in front of her, "it began about five years ago on an evening when I took down a very unusual reservation . . ."

# ACKNOWLEDGMENTS

The idea for *Waiting at Hayden's* was *very* loosely inspired by a pact I made with my first love, Josh. I want to thank him for all the wonderful memories we shared in high school and want to thank Papa Haydn's restaurant in Portland, Oregon for inspiring the setting.

I wrote the first draft of this novel in Charleston, South Carolina during a gap year in college. I found the college dating scene disheartening so I impulsively moved to the romantic setting of Nicholas Sparks' novels to write about it. Thank you, Nicholas Sparks, for instilling in me, at a very early age, my love for the South and for love stories.

Margaret Hayes, my Charleston roommate, and her wonderful family made my experience in South Carolina one of the best phases of my life. I can't thank them enough for all their kindness and support.

Christy Bittner was one of my very first readers of my very rough first draft and she told me she loved it. She has loved every draft since. Christy, I am so grateful for your encouragement since day one.

Other early readers who gave me feedback that was invaluable were: Jordyn Prince, Steve Duin, Sarah Duwelius, Linda Hundhammer, and Christina Wieselman. Audra Iness and Banu Gumusoglu answered all my questions about PhD programs and Ben Swinford and Jim Goethals helped me with my questions regarding minor league baseball. Thank you all, from the bottom of my heart.

I've always been much more interested in writing books than reading textbooks, so I almost didn't go back and finish school at Santa Clara University, but I am so grateful I did as my education broadened my mind and made me a better person and storyteller. I wish I could say that I had a feeling that would happen, and that it was that feeling which influenced my decision to re-enroll, but the truth is I went back solely because I saw a picture online of a law school student there who I had a sense I would really like. My sense was right. Corey, thank you for our wonderful relationship throughout our time at SCU. It will always hold such a special place in my heart.

In recent years, I have Ryan Selewicz to thank for enthusiastically jumping on board as my photographer when I told him I wanted to start Sincerelyriley.com. Ryan, none of this would be possible without your help.

The same can be said of Kelsey Jacobsen, who designed my website. Kelsey, you took a dream of mine and made it a beautiful reality. Thank you for your creativity and for your friendship all my life.

Kyle St. James and George Kovacevich provided me with legal advice this past year as I branded shopfiction™. Thank you both for your willingness to help. Thank you to Formatting Experts for their guidance as the interior of the book became a reality. Also a shout-out to Randy Huft for his PR expertise.

Chelsea Kovacevich, thank you for dreaming big with me every day on our morning walks. Francine Kovacevich, thank you for always believing in me and sending me encouraging text messages. And thank you Brittany Salemme and Robert Linggi for helping with blog shoots.

To all the actors and friends who played the parts of my characters and helped bring this story to life in video form—thank you! Thanks, Brooke Thompson, for your help and support the week of the shoot. Thank you, also, to acting coach Karen LaVoie for helping connect me with several of the actors.

Special thanks to my videographers at Define Motion, Francisca and Jason Andrus, for filming the video scenes in this book. They were absolutely wonderful to work with! And thank you, Olivia Ashton, for taking the beautiful photos of my characters for my lookbook.

Moana Dherlin and her songwriting class at Los Alamitos High School came up with a beautiful, original song for the video clips. Thanks to all. Lizzy Land and Schier, thank you for the permission to use your song, "Holding out for You," in one of the video clips as well.

Thanks Brittany Brown co-founder of Winston White, Andrea Van De Vort, founder of Van De Vort, Amy Armstrong, founder of Ash and Ky, Terry Leon, founder of SAVI STYLE, and all the other entrepreneurs in the fashion world who sent me pieces from their collections for my characters to wear and for my readers to shop.

To my editor, Kirsten Salyer, at Refine Editing, I can't thank you enough for carefully editing these pages and for your thoughtful suggestions for how to improve this manuscript. You were terrific to work with! I sent my cover designer, Danielle Christopher, an elaborate Pinterest board filled with inspiration and she took it all in and created the cover of my dreams. Thank you, Danielle!

I want to thank my seventh-grade language arts teacher, Suzanne Yost, for inspiring me to want to be a writer. Thank you, Amy Wang, for taking a chance and hiring me at *The Oregonian* in high school after I pitched the idea for an opinion column from the perspective of a teen. I loved writing for the paper and that job gave me confidence that I could one day be a published author.

Some people have been a part of this journey since day one.

Aunt Betsy, thank you for making me feel like anything is possible and for always reminding me that life is about love and following our hearts. My Aunt Gwen, who passed away, loved this story since I first dreamt it up. Aunt Gwen, I wish you were here for publication day but will be looking for a rainbow in your honor. Thanks Aunt Leslie, too, for always cheering me on and telling me to call you on days I doubted myself. And thank you Taylor Thompson, for listening to me read this story out loud during our travels through Europe and encouraging me to stick with it.

My siblings, Brady and Casey Costello, have not always understood the decisions I've made while pursuing this dream, but they have always supported me in making them. I'm so lucky to have you as my best friends (and I think publishing a book makes me Golden Child—at least for one day!).

And last but not least, Mom and Dad (I cried just writing your names). This book would not have been written nor would it have been published without your endless love and support. Never once, in all these years, did you question my dream. And when I questioned my *own* dream you continued to believe *for* me. This has not been an easy journey—you two know this more than anyone—but it has been such a rewarding one. And I'm so glad we found a way to share this love story with the world. I won the jackpot in the parent lottery. I love you both so much.

CPSIA information can be obtained
at www.ICGtesting.com
Printed in the USA
FFOW02n0557140618